Three Reasons

Elite Escorts MM 3

Lynn Burke

Three Reasons

When I go back to college to prove my worth to my pop, the hot, grumpy professor in my first class is a temptation I can't resist.

Matteo D'Angelo is also straight, in a position of authority, and a widower, but those three reasons he thinks he's unavailable are irrelevant.

He's my Prince Charming come to life.

I manage to weaken his stubborn defenses against the magnetic draw between us, giving him a taste of what could be.

But one of EEMM's past clients threatens to release damning photos, doubling my workload and stress. I've never been the best behaved or the brightest, and I quickly spiral to my breaking point.

Will Professor D'Angelo relent to the pull between us and be the oak I need to help me stay the course? Or will I have no choice but to once again show my family that I'm nothing but a failure?

Chapter 1

Sean

Mr. and Mr. Chesterfield welcomed me into their hotel suite in downtown Boston. The younger was giddy and smiling like sunshine, and the older had downturned, full lips I could envision wrapped around my cock.

But I was there to serve them. I loved being a willing hole or offering my dick in return for a client's night of debauchery. Being the head of Elite Escorts MM was a dream come true, the money simply an added perk of the job.

Only once before had a married couple booked with Elite's gay branch, and I'd jumped at another chance for a little triple M action. I'd yet to be in the middle of a beef sandwich and had high hopes for the night ahead.

There could never be enough tight holes and hard dicks to slake my hunger for sex. I'd been insatiable from the morning I'd woken to a mess in my underwear and realized what had happened due to a hazy dream where I'd kissed another boy.

From that day on? I'd taken care of my morning wood

without embarrassment. Made out with every gay in the school, closeted or otherwise. I'd sucked cum from countless cocks, swallowing my first load at age fourteen. Took a hole or gave mine over whenever time and location allowed after my first flip fuck at sixteen when I figured out I was vers.

I'd been called it all because of my openly sexual lifestyle too. Flirt. Immature fuck boy. Slut. I didn't give a shit how people saw me. I wasn't ashamed of loving sex or the fact my lucrative job included getting laid a few times a week. Acting as the top or bottom, I looked forward to blowing customers' minds in the bedroom and satisfying their every need.

The latest of which came as a seriously non-matching, major size-differenced pair.

The younger Mr. Chesterfield wore lace panties, and the sight of his small cock trapped in the feminine scrap of cloth made my mouth water. Bare of hair from the neck down, he proved to be a tempting treat I imagined sampling from throat to toes. He smelled like a delectable slice of strawberry pie I wanted to gorge myself on.

His stern husband?

A total bear with a dad bod I hoped to rub myself all over before night's end. Maybe even cuddle once we finished with the good stuff.

But they'd made other plans prior to my arrival, which first had me stripping to my skin for the smaller's viewing pleasure.

I'd always been a confident bastard—yet another name I'd been called and couldn't deny. More lithe than bodybuilder, I carried the perfect amount of muscle. A six-pack rippled my core along with the V men loved to lick down toward heaven. I waxed my groin to better showcase my more than ample dick size. My blond stubble I kept permanent to leave behind beard burn when eating out an ass. Hair in an artful freshly fucked look, I was ready to face the clients EEMM allowed me to enjoy.

"My present is pretty, Daddy," the younger stated with a sexy British accent that sent a shiver through me.

Fuck, did I love hearing praise. Made me preen like a goddamned peacock.

He circled around my back, not touching but close enough I felt the heat of his slight body. While some might consider me twink-ish due to my youthful appearance, the boy rounding my left ticked each and every box. Maybe five-foot-four. Baby face. Curly light brown hair, big innocent blue eyes that ate me up with a hunger I could appreciate. He was thin and pale like a spoiled little boy used to lounging on cushions all day long, and that goddamned lace with a darker wet spot...

I bit the inside of my lip and clenched my hands at my sides to keep from reaching for him. Sucking on his dick. Tasting his sweetness on my tongue. Swallowing down every pulsed shot of spunk I could coax from his smooth balls.

My dick already strained toward my belly button without the help of a little blue pill, and I was ready to go no matter how or where the couple wanted me.

The twink's daddy made a low rumbled noise in his thick chest at his boy's appraisal of the goods they'd purchased for the evening.

I turned my focus on the naked man looming a few feet in front of me, wanting his approval as well. Easily topping my five-ten height, he absently stroked his thick cock, studiously obsessed with his husband checking out his birthday gift.

A mat of hair expanded over the older guy's pecs and

belly, and a full, untamed patch covered his groin too. While that area could use some tidying up, I didn't find fault with his girth or the heavy balls hanging low. He would stretch me good, and his sac would make a nice slapping sound against my body while he railed my ass.

Or maybe I would get to nuzzle and tongue those balls. Nose over his taint and breathe in his musky scent while his boy attempted to swallow my dick.

My mouth watered again while I waited to be told what to do, excitement fluttering in my stomach and lust twitching my cock.

Twink boy once more stood behind me. Soft hands grasped my cheeks, pulling them apart.

My back arched on instinct.

"Can I have his hole, Daddy?" the boy asked, breathless with enough lust to cause pre-cum to ooze from my shaft.

"You may, sweet cakes," the man murmured his reply, adoration in his tone even though he continued to frown.

I got the feeling he wasn't keen on sharing his boy but had hired an escort out of love for his *sweet cakes*. Oh, to be spoiled like that.

If only.

While the whole daddy thing wasn't a kink of mine, I could appreciate their dynamic and the trust between them. They communicated openly, the younger taking charge and directing me onto the bed. The twink ended up the meat in our man sandwich, the lucky dog, rocking between me and his daddy to get the best of both worlds.

I could admit to being jealous. His hole filled by his daddy's thick cock, his own dick encased in the tight heat of my ass, being in control of the fucking in every way...

"Fuck yeah," I groaned, reaching back to hold onto the boy's hip as he shoved his little dick in and out of me. I'd come prepped as requested in their file, not caring that the misters didn't want anything more than a hole. Zero kissing. Zero foreplay. Zero intimacy.

The best type of connecting—nothing but lust, fucking, getting off, and a thank you before I strolled out the door.

I couldn't imagine trying for a relationship with one dude let alone two, but a threesome sure as fuck would be a fun fantasy to live out.

Maybe with the next couple I would be crammed in the middle.

It wasn't like I could go looking for an orgy outside work, or I would have. Elite Escorts, owned by my older brother Micah, didn't allow fucking on the side. Our bodies were contracted to please customers, and even though I'd managed the gay branch of the business for the previous two-plus years, the rules applied to me as well.

But hey...easy hookups and even better pay? I had no complaints.

The twink's daddy didn't lay a finger on me or even acknowledge the fact I shared the bed with them, which I was fine with as well. He was all about his boy, gifting him the fuck toy he'd wanted. My hole was being used, and I had my own hand to get me off. The night would go down as a win in my book.

I stroked my dick in time with the twink's thrusts, his mewling noises a softer music in my ears to his Daddy's grunts. I preferred a rougher tumble in the sack, but as long as cocks and spunk were involved, I was a happy boy.

"Oh..." the twink gasped, his hips starting to stutter. "I'm c-close, Daddy."

"My sweetest boy," his bear's voice murmured, and fucking hell, that low timbre, those words, sent a shudder through me. "Come for me. Squeeze my dick with your hot, little hole."

My balls seized.

I shot my load all over the sheets, cursing up a blue streak as my ass clenched around the twink's cock.

"Daddy!" the twink cried and shuddered, his dick pulsing in the condom while buried in my ass.

"Good boy." The deep, bear-like groan behind him in response to his husband's orgasm sent another spurt of cum up through my length.

"Oh shit," I moaned, still stroking myself while coming down, my ears ringing from the bigger man's praise even though it hadn't been meant for me.

Tonight's clients hadn't given me the climax of the century, but I'd emptied my balls, and my extremities tingled long after I'd been told I could dress and leave. I'd found release with hardly any effort on my part along with an extra tip in the form of a couple of crisp one-hundred dollar bills.

Easy fucking money, pun definitely intended.

Steps light and grin plastered on my face, I left Mr. and Mr. Chesterfield to their cuddle fest in a world of their own where no one else was welcome.

I wasn't bothered in the least.

Unlike the twink boy, I had no desire for a sugar daddy to own and spoil me rotten. I loved my freedom and the variety of dick EEMM allowed me to sample.

But I wouldn't mind hearing those words like the older Mr. Chesterfield had spoken.

Yeah, I had a praise kink, I'd recently learned, but I refused to be ashamed of that shit even though my insides wanted to cringe. It had taken a whole two minutes to recognize where it stemmed from.

Micah had gotten all the affirmation in our household growing up—for his good grades, amazing athletic ability, and even better behavior while I'd been a terror who couldn't focus worth a shit and always tripped over my own feet.

I would never measure up to my big brother, but goddamnit, I'd put in major dedication and hard work to help build the gay branch of Elite. While I'd yet to be recognized for my effort outside my big bro's occasional, "Good job," I'd planned my next step that would take me to his level of professionalism.

An MBA like the one hanging on his office wall. One sheet of paper declaring I'd finished a two-year college program and had accomplished something worthy of making our pop proud of his younger son, who'd only ever been compared to Micah and found lacking.

Sure, I'd secretly failed out at my first attempt at college while fresh out of high school, more focused on cock and beer than classes, but I'd grown up since. Back then, I'd claimed to my family and friends that I'd dropped out to save my parents' money. Some didn't see how I'd matured from lying my way through life, so I would be stubborn as fuck and prove myself capable.

I exited the hotel, taking note of the pink and purple streaks in the deep blue sky overhead as August's muggy heat prickled my skin with sweat. My ass didn't ache like I preferred after bottoming, but at least my balls had emptied.

An early Saturday night for a change.

Normally when off the clock at a decent hour, I would walk to the nearest bar and enjoy a few cold beers, but I could use a good night's sleep. It had been ten years since I'd last stepped foot into a classroom, but Monday morning would find me sitting at a desk attentive and ready to take notes.

It was time to prove I could stand apart. Be just as accomplished outside the bedroom as I was in. I dreamed of congratulations. Pop's eyes shining with a sense of pride like he did whenever he looked at Micah, his firstborn son.

Goal firmly fixed in my brain, I hopped in my car and headed home to my apartment. My future was so goddamned bright I was going to need another pair of Ray-Bans.

Chapter 2

Matteo

Sweat soaked my shirt and shorts. Hell, even my socks squished inside my running sneakers with every slap of rubber on pavement, but I pushed through the muggy air. Only one more mile lay ahead of me until I reached my destination.

Katie's grave.

I no longer choked up at the thought of my wife's name or how her strawberry blonde hair used to spread over our pillows while she lay lax beneath me. The memory of her gorgeous and sated green eyes peering up at me while we'd fought to catch our breath didn't knife my chest anymore.

Reminiscing of past happiness didn't make me ache.

It was the sense of emptiness and deep longing for what I would never have again that got the best of me.

My feet pounded the road, my breaths harsh and lungs oxygen-starved. Running had become the way I punished my body until I was too tired to function. It also blessedly numbed my brain into quietness. A better choice than alcohol or drugs, but at forty-two, my knees sometimes complained about all the action. The only kind I'd gotten since losing Katie.

The sun had begun to sink, but more than enough daylight hours remained for my weekly visit.

I turned into the cemetery's entrance, the black wrought iron fence open and as inviting as the meticulously groomed landscape. Towering oaks and maples lined the main road, the smaller branches curving off along either side dotted with shrubs.

The scent of nature bursting with life, a cloying, sweet perfume of flowers, lay heavy in the humid air. My sharp inhales attempting to fill my lungs broke the stillness around me. No chirping birds, chittering critters, or sounds of the main road behind me reached the cemetery's depths where my wife's body rested.

I slowed while rounding a bend, hoping for privacy. While I'd come into contact with her family a few times since her funeral, I preferred to keep my distance. Seeing my mother-in-law, a spitting image of my beautiful wife, and being reminded I hadn't done enough for her precious girl intensified my guilt tenfold.

Even though I panted for oxygen, my breath left in a thankful rush at finding no one near Katie's corner of the cemetery. A white granite headstone marked where she lay. The bouquet of wildflowers I'd left the week before had wilted, no longer vibrant as she had once been.

A vase of peach-colored roses sat atop the rectangular stone left by her parents. Fresh, so there was no chance they would show up while I visited, thank God.

I sprawled atop Katie's grave and attempted to catch my breath while staring into the cloudless sky overhead. Lush grass cradled my backside but would make my bare skin itch eventually. I didn't care. Hands atop my chest, I rested as my inhales and heartbeat slowed until I felt sure my body could melt into the ground and join my wife wherever she'd gone.

While I didn't believe her spirit was there in the cemetery with me, I hadn't yet been able to let go of the physical. Knowing her bones rested deep in the earth beneath me gave me a bit of comfort I hadn't been able to find anywhere else. But I hadn't been looking, much to my parents' and sister's disappointment.

Heaving a sigh, I rolled onto all fours then sat back onto my heels. Crouching in such a position would be a regrettable offense to my legs if I sat for too long, which I usually did.

Katherine Evelyn D'Angelo.

The sight of her etched name didn't move me as much as the truth of her too-short life in the dates below. Only thirty-six years of age. Taken from my side by bone cancer that had been diagnosed too late to save her. I'd had no choice but to hold her hand as she faded away, her final months nothing but pain and heartache for both of us.

But she'd left me for either peaceful darkness or light, and I was alone to grieve the loss of my sunshine.

I picked a blade of grass and tore it into tiny pieces, each bit of green fluttering quietly to the ground in front of me as I considered the afterlife she'd believed in and the comfort it had given her while she'd lain on her deathbed. No such assurances made my existence without her easier.

Grief counseling had gotten me through the worst, but I still couldn't find my footing.

Swallowing hard, I glanced around the cemetery, my aloneness intensified by the lack of others visiting the final resting places of their loved ones. How had *they* moved on?

Drawing breath came easily—instinctively. Choosing to get out of bed, to face another day did not.

Some mornings proved a hard struggle.

"Summer is finally over, and classes begin again tomorrow," I murmured to Katie even though she wouldn't hear me. "A new semester to fill the hours with the job I still enjoy and my mind with thoughts outside missing you."

Guilt rose inside me as it always did whenever I took comfort in knowing something would distract me from lingering sadness.

A part of me wanted to live again, but I didn't have the right to.

Katie's illness and passing hadn't been my fault—fuck cancer—but I should have done more, especially after her mother had outright spewed that exact accusation over my wife's casket. I should have noticed her sickness sooner or at least encouraged her to see a doctor long before she'd made the decision to do so on her own.

Katie had been my world, and I should have taken better care of the one I'd been lucky enough to have by my side.

"Wherever you are, love," I whispered as I always did, "I hope you find happiness. I hope you find peace. I hope you remember our love as I do."

What we'd enjoyed had been perfection. A true connection of like-minded souls with vulnerability and honesty. We'd learned how to be self-aware and open to growth.

We'd shared the type of love found only in fairytales.

A lone tear slid down my cheek, but I didn't bother swiping it away. The feel of it, a mere droplet's presence, was yet another reminder of my missing half I desperately clung to.

Near the end, I'd promised Katie that I would live,

squeeze out every bit of joy I could before I joined her in the afterlife she'd believed in.

But I'd done nothing to keep my word.

I merely existed, going to work, which gave my life purpose, and running myself to exhaustion every day. I attempted to meditate while doing the yoga poses I used to tease my wife about, but at night, I lay in bed, staring through the darkness that matched the vast solitude in my chest.

Heaviness settled over my shoulders, bowing my head as I emptied my lungs with a weighty sigh.

I'd been sitting and stewing for far too long. Pushing up to my feet, I grimaced at the ache in my knees I'd expected and hadn't done a damned thing to avoid.

"I'm getting too old for this shit," I told myself what I did every time I sat too long on the ground, wanting to experience a little bit of pain to help me remember her. "That yoga isn't doing jack for my bones."

Katie didn't reply, nor did a breeze sent by her cool the sweat clinging to my overheated skin.

Shower, food, and sleep, I told myself while readying to once more punish my body on the run home.

Then wake up and greet a new classroom full of college students interested in learning about financial accounting, something I was still passionate about.

Turning away from my wife's grave, I headed back the way I'd come, feeling no better than when I'd arrived. Not that I'd expected anything different. Reminiscing and thinking about the what-ifs rarely helped me rise from the ashes of grief.

I longed for a break in the clouds of my mind. A ray of light to caress my face while peacefulness from having my person at my side welled inside me. Katie used to sit at my feet, sweetly submitting in tender love.

Hands clenched, I focused on the next step, the next stride. My exhausted legs ate up the miles back to a house that was nothing more than a place to exist in my misery from every reminder of her in every room.

But my continued breaths meant that her memory lived on. As long as my heart beat, Katie would remain in the world and in my mind.

It would be enough, seeing as I had no other choice.

My lover was gone, my chance at happiness in my lifetime ripped away from me along with her last exhale.

Chapter 3

Sean

I gave a courtesy knock before letting myself into my parents' home. Micah had bought it for them a few years earlier, receiving a shit ton of accolades while I'd stood off to the side, ignored as usual. Their side entrance let me into the kitchen where Mom would be getting our Sunday night dinner ready, since it was her turn to host.

Once Micah and Jasmine had married, we'd started flip-flopping our monthly get-togethers between them and our parents. The condo I'd bought was "too far away" for Pop, so I hadn't been invited to host. Not that I wanted to cook or serve my father's negative ass anyway.

While the time mostly consisted of sports talk and not much else, I enjoyed picking on my sister-in-law and the fact she was older than me. A mere three months, but still. At least she knew how to relax and just have fun, regardless of my grumpy pop.

Since he'd given up hard liquor, he'd been a little more bearable, but enough damage had been inflicted when I'd been young for me to ever really like the guy. He and Micah got along well, but what else was new? Micah could do no wrong.

I didn't dislike my big bro for having a better relationship with our father, just envied the praise he got. I'd managed to gain attention, just never in the right way. But as a kid, having my parents' undivided focus felt good regardless of it bringing consequences.

I was probably ADHD. Definitely hyperactive. In my own little world, Mom had always stated.

But I'd made do. Barely managed to graduate from high school and worked odd jobs throughout my early twenties while still living at home. That failed year of college? I didn't discuss it except when bragging about being an out-and-proud frat boy. It'd been fun while it lasted.

It had taken me years to get Micah to open a gay branch of Elite to keep me busy and balls deep in either hot mouths or ass. By then, he'd already become successful as fuck with a mansion and a few cars.

Eventually, my nagging got under his skin. Being persistently annoying had gotten me what I'd wanted as a kid, and I'd been called spoiled too many times to count. Pop enjoyed shutting me up by giving in, so I'd manipulated the hell out of him.

Sure, I was a brat, but a kid had to do what a kid had to do in order to get ahead.

And I finally had. Financially, anyway.

Now, I just needed that degree, and Micah wouldn't have shit on me.

"Sean," Mom greeted me with a smile, and I leaned into her cheek to kiss her where she stood at the oven, mitts on her hands.

"Hey, Mom. What can I do to help?"

"Nothing." She pulled a covered pan from the oven

and set it atop the stove. It smelled like pot roast. "Everything is ready. We're just waiting for your brother and Jasmine."

"Are her parents coming today?" I asked and popped an olive from the small cheese tray Mom had placed on the island into my mouth. Salt burst on my tongue, and I hummed my approval.

"No, they had plans."

I nodded and snagged another olive. Jasmine's parents, while conservative to Mom and Pop's liberal outlook on life, had become close friends after their kid's wedding. The lack of alcohol in their home and their influence had helped Pop get sober.

Almost three years later, and Pop still avoided the hard stuff. While it was too late for his liver, he wasn't quite the bastard he used to be.

"Is the grump watching football?" I asked, already knowing the answer.

"He's in the den."

A quiet knock sounded from the front door—Micah, no doubt letting himself in a second later. Seeing as how he didn't have issue with Pop, he wouldn't mind greeting the old man first. I'd always preferred Mom, but that was because she tended toward kindness rather than negativity. Even when she would purse her lips and give me a disapproving look, I never doubted she at least loved me.

Pop?

Yeah. A whole other story.

I tossed two more olives onto my tongue as Micah rounded the corner into the kitchen. He glanced at the cheese tray.

"You little shit—save me some of those," he muttered, setting a boxed pie alongside the tray.

I grabbed the last two olives and chowed down, grinning and chewing with my mouth open just to get on his nerves.

Jasmine laughed, rounding the island to say hi to Mom. While my sister-in-law had healed a lot from her touch issues, I still took caution when approaching her. She kissed Mom, and I watched her, waiting to see how hesitant she would be.

Smiling, Jasmine gave me a little wave rather than getting too close.

"Hey, Sis." I didn't reach for her since she'd set her boundaries of no touching for the day.

"Hey, brat."

I stuck out my tongue, and she laughed.

Micah elbowed me, and I turned to give him a bro hug, slapping his back. "What's up, old man?"

"Shut up," he muttered, and my grin widened. He had twelve years on me but still didn't look a year over thirty-five-ish. Not one gray hair had made an appearance in the darker blond on his head or scruff. I could admit my brother was hot—but I'd gotten the best of our parents' genes. My chest puffed up a bit at the knowledge I'd done something better than him even if I had taken no part in it.

"So...college again," he said, picking up a piece of Monterey Jack cheese and a cracker as Jasmine went back to Mom's side to help her. "Are you ready this time?"

Unfortunately, he was one of the few who knew why I'd really dropped out—or had gotten kicked out, rather. Shitty grades and a shitty attitude. I'd quickly learned professors and the dean couldn't be manipulated like Pop.

"Yep." I folded my arms and leaned against the island.

"Nervous?"

"Nope," I lied.

"You shouldn't be," Micah said with an assured nod.

"The almost three years working for Elite will give you a leg up in the classes you're taking. There's nothing better than on-the-job training."

I snorted. On-the-job training—sucking cock and getting dicked down were my favorite aspects of my employment, but I understood what he'd meant.

Mom and Jasmine chatted quietly while finishing up with the dinner prep, but Micah continued to watch me rather than the woman he normally couldn't tear his focus from.

"Has Pop said anything to you about it?" my brother asked.

I shook my head. "Not a single word." And, he hadn't. Not when I'd announced I was going to college and not even when Mom prompted him to converse about it.

He'd grunted, not bothering to tear his attention off the TV rather than even offering me a good luck.

A muscle ticked in my jaw.

One day, I would prove I could be just as accomplished as his favorite son.

At least Micah always had my back. Because of him and Mom's affection, I'd managed to have a decent childhood regardless of Pop's assholery. Some love was better than none, but the kid inside me would mourn not having that pop/son relationship I'd wanted as a kid.

We sat down to a late dinner during halftime so Pop wouldn't grumble more than usual. Still, he focused on the TV through the archway leading into the den more than he paid attention to the chatter at the table.

He drank water, same as the rest of us since we'd agreed as a family to avoid my favorite beverage—beer—in their home. With him being sober, Mom's stress had lessened. Her features were more relaxed than pinched, and I'd wondered over her happiness in the past. Had she stayed with my asshole of a father out of love? Or for me and Micah? Somedays, I wished she had left his ass and taken us with her. Being away from Pop would have been for the best for all of us.

But she'd made her choice, and we lived with it.

"Tomorrow is the big day!" Jasmine stated loudly, jerking her head my way, eyes wide as though she'd just remembered.

"Yep." I shoveled a bite of gravy-covered beef into my mouth and grinned.

"Are you excited?" Jasmine appeared enough of that emotion for both of us. Fuck, did I love the woman. Yet another person who accepted me regardless of my wildness.

I shrugged.

"I think it's incredibly brave what you're doing," she went on, her cheeks a pretty pink, her blue eyes sparkling. "I couldn't imagine heading back to school after all this time. You're going to do amazing—I just know it."

Pop snorted, but I ignored him as my throat tightened.

"Thanks, Sis. I appreciate your vote of confidence."

She winked at me and turned toward Mom, jumping into the conversation they'd been having prior to her outburst.

Micah met my gaze across the table. "I'm proud of you, kid."

I swallowed hard and nodded, ignoring the man at the head of the table same as he did to me. Pop had helped spawn me into existence but could care less about what I'd tackled in life. While I recognized the fact he only hurt himself by not having a relationship with his second son, his lack of interest in who I was still stung. Always would.

"Thanks, Micah," I choked out, longing for more of that damn praise.

But I made myself content with what I had. Between the three loved ones at the dinner table and my handful of friends, I couldn't ask for more.

Even if my heart wanted it.

Chapter 4

Matteo

I used to love the summer months, all those long hours of extra time to spend with my love. We would travel for weeks around her birthday. We'd visited the corners of the US. One year, for our fifth anniversary, we'd jetted across the pond to visit Ireland, the land of Katie's ancestors.

But in the years since her death, summer on my own had proven the toughest to slog through.

For that reason, the first day of classes brought a breath of fresh air regardless of the continued humidity laying over New England like a heavy blanket. My chinos chafed, and my dress shoes pinched. The short-sleeve button-down I'd donned restricted my biceps and neck that had thickened up a bit due to extra hours spent in the gym over the previous couple of months.

Dress-up clothes were my least favorite part of my job.

The best?

Leaning against my desk and watching new students file into my classroom. I'd been a professor for twelve years, and the excitement of the first day hadn't faded. I offered greetings and smiles to those who glanced my way, attempting to figure out personalities by their body language and where they chose to sit. Some would prove my assumptions about them wrong, but I still got a thrill out of guessing.

A few studious kids—the ones who fulfilled my passion for teaching—went straight to the front row, readying laptops and notebooks. Most took to the center of the room, wanting to maybe hide a bit but needing to be close enough to avoid distraction. I eyed the three who ignored me entirely while slipping into the back row. Perhaps trouble, but definitely the ones I expected would visit my office toward the end of the semester looking for extra credit because they couldn't be bothered to pay attention during class.

I glanced at my watch, noting the time.

Who would be the student to come rushing in a minute after we got started? There was always one—

Someone hurried in just as I straightened to officially greet my class, pulling everyone's attention to my right.

The lopsided smirk caught my eye first, but blue eyes swung toward me and latched onto mine, so bright with life I blinked. His grin widened, a twinkle glinting in his orbs.

"Sorry I'm late, Teach."

"Professor D'Angelo," I corrected him, my voice low and firm compared to his flirty tone.

He two-finger saluted me with a wink, and I fought off a smile that caught me by surprise.

His late arrival, the playful...*sunshiny* attitude radiating from him, promised trouble like those in the back of the room.

I expected him to slink toward them and make himself comfortable, but he waltzed in front of everyone to sit directly opposite my desk. Like the others brave enough to claim that row, he rifled through his bag for his laptop, as though intent on acing whatever I threw his way.

Upon closer inspection, I realized the man wasn't as young as my other first-year students. While he still had a youthful appearance, he was more seasoned than the eighteen and nineteen-year-olds sitting around him. Mid-twenties, I expected, dressed nice in designer jeans and an ironed button-down. A Rolex was clasped around his left wrist and Ray-Bans tucked into his collar. Nicely trimmed blond scruff lined his strong jawline. Three earrings glinted in his left ear.

Our gazes caught, and I realized I stared, captured by the open...warmth he radiated.

Clearing my throat, I turned my focus off the conundrum of a young man who'd so quickly hopped out of the box I'd initially put him in. "Welcome to Financial Accounting," I stated my old-as-time spiel about the core course I taught while retrieving the stack of syllabi on the desk beside me. I offered them to the student in the front corner and repeated my name, glancing at the latecomer once more.

Rather than slouching like I'd expected, he sat forward, his attention flitting away from me only when the girl beside him handed over the stack of syllabi. He murmured a thanks, kept one, and turned toward his right to pass them on.

Something about the young man kept pulling my focus his way while I gave my credentials and I went over my expectations for the class. Once finished with discussing the topics we would cover, I asked the students to share a bit about themselves since our class was on the smaller side. Their names, preferred pronouns, where they were from, and their life's goals and how studying finance would help them achieve their dreams.

While most of my co-workers didn't do the whole meet-and-greet thing, I'd been encouraged to do so by my own freshman year. I hadn't known a soul, and finding a handful of close friends because one professor had us go around the room to introduce ourselves had influenced my actions whenever a new group entered my classroom.

We had two kids from Arkansas. A blonde girl from Georgia with a heavy southern twang drew more than one appreciative glance from the men in the room. Another girl hailed from Minnesota. And of course, a handful of students from Massachusetts littered the class, most with heavy Boston accents like mine.

I'd started with the back row, making the potential troublemakers go first, but my awareness lay on the sunshine in my periphery. He fidgeted even though he fought the need. Or perhaps my senses were attuned to his every move, and I didn't notice others weren't that interested in learning about their classmates either.

While the girl beside him gave her name and spoke about her hopes for the future, I struggled to keep my attention on her rather than glancing at the man on her right.

His knee bounced, a distracting-as-hell movement, his fingers tapping on his thigh.

"So...yeah?" The girl shrugged—I hadn't even caught her name. "I guess that's about it?"

I smiled and nodded, turning toward the one I'd been too damn aware of for the previous fifteen minutes.

His blue eyes ensnared mine again, and I swore the sun's rays broke through the clouds, caressing my face with heat. I wanted to stand taller to bask in his presence and breathe the life-giving force emanating off him deeper into my lungs.

The strange stirring inside me intensified as his lips quirked up in a knowing grin.

Shifting on my feet, I crossed my arms over my chest, my lips tight, and lifted an eyebrow.

"Sean Fox," he stated at my silent prompt. "He/him. Proud gay member of the LGBTQ+ community."

No big surprise there with how his focus slid down over me where I still leaned against my desk. His perusal made me feel like a piece of meat—and strangely, I didn't hate it.

I sure as hell didn't understand why that was though. Mr. Fox wasn't the first student, let alone male, to check me out with interest in his gaze. In all my years as a professor, I'd had more than one student offer sexual favors in exchange for grade changes, male and female alike.

I'd never been tempted, nor would I ever be. Integrity was something I prided myself in. So were loyalty and faithfulness even though my better half no longer waited for me at home.

"It took me ten years to figure out what I wanted to do with the rest of my life," Mr. Fox continued, his focus once more on my face, "but better late than never. I'm here to get my MBA. I'm looking forward to my first class, Professor D'Angelo."

At least the kid kept from outright flirting like I'd expected and addressed me properly, showing he could be taught.

I forced my gaze onto the person on Mr. Fox's right.

"Hi!" They waved around the room. "I'm Jazzie Jones, they/them, and I'm also a proud member of the LGBTQ+ community."

Mr. Fox gave them a fist bump, and the two shared a smile, one of understanding and acceptance.

The final student introduced themselves, and I stood to round my desk. Shuffling noises began as I turned my back. Students readied to take notes, and the introverted ones breathed a sigh of relief at having my focus off them. Those less interested in school itself settled in for what they would see as a boring last forty-five minutes of class.

I dove into the introduction to our first topic of the semester, watching my students to see how well I'd categorized them. Like always, some would show their true colors immediately, others after a couple of weeks. A few would prove me wrong like Mr. Fox had already somewhat done.

I... Hell, I didn't know what to think. His presence caused my skin to heat and stretch thin. His steady stare on my face, were I an inexperienced professor, would have proven too much to ignore. Even still, I fought to be attentive to the others in my classroom while my gaze strayed toward the student in front of my desk.

Part of me wanted to escape him.

Another piece wished to linger and soak in the happiness radiating off him with addictive allure.

Conflicting didn't begin to describe how Sean Fox made me feel.

Class ended sooner than I'd expected.

"Remember—my office hours are listed on the syllabus. Stop in if you need to, or if it's after hours and an emergency, I've listed my cell number as well. I want you all to succeed!" I raised my voice to be heard as my students rushed to pack up their things and leave. "Have a great rest of your day!"

Refusing to glance at Sean, I settled behind my desk, readying for the next class that would be making their way in soon enough. But the awareness of his presence, how he lingered in my periphery proved too potent to ignore.

Chapter 5

Sean

Hot for teacher took on a whole new meaning.

Professor D'Angelo...

I licked over my lower lip, checking him out for at least the hundredth time since walking through the door and finding him leaning casual-like against his big-assed desk. He'd owned the room from minute one with his steady presence, never mind his gorgeous appearance.

Muscular arms had crossed over his chest and stretched the cotton button-down he wore while he'd droned on about class expectations. Said shirt was tucked into dress pants and belted around his trim waist. Those thighs of his filled out his pants, and I'd wondered if his ass would do the same.

He had the perfect amount of scruff to leave delicious beard burn all over my body. Equally dark hair just long enough on top to grab hold of while he sucked my cock. And that mouth—fucking hell, the man had full lips with a perfect cupid's bow I wanted to lick and nibble on.

Being perched on a hard seat with an even harder cock trapped inside my jeans was uncomfortable as fuck—had been from the moment I'd sat down. My knee had bounced non-fucking-stop as I fought to keep from shifting every few seconds while he'd spoken. It was like the man had brought ants to existence inside my goddamned pants.

Could. Not. Sit. Still.

And his voice? Fucking swoon-ville-USA. Low and sultry. Rumbly with a hint of growl that would definitely come out when balls-deep inside my ass. My hole had twitched more than once with the need to be filled while he'd spoken. I'd imagined hearing curses panted against my ear as he blanketed my back. Whispered words of praise over how well I took his cock made my dick leak.

Finally, he'd given me those chocolate eyes of his when it had been my turn to introduce myself to the class. His gaze hadn't flickered when I announced I was gay, and my eyes told him exactly what I wouldn't mind him doing to me.

Professor D'Angelo was a rock of indifference—feigned or otherwise, I couldn't tell.

And I'd never crushed so damn hard or so damn quickly in all my life. I loved everything about him. His swarthy, Italian looks. His perfectly lean yet muscular build. His unwavering stare that promised confidence—a man who knew his mind. I expected his way around a bed too.

But did he like dick?

And even more, would he be interested in becoming acquainted with mine?

I hadn't been able to get a read on the man throughout class, but he'd reminded me of the Prince Charming I'd dreamed about when I was a kid. That was before I'd been introduced to the joy of sexual freedom and a plethora of dick. I wanted Professor D'Angelo in any way shape or form. Under me. On top of me. Sideways, upside down—fucking hell, I lusted like I'd never done before.

And when he'd finally turned his back on us after class introductions?

God*damn.*

I'd had no choice but to shift to ease the ache in my groin. The man's backside was even finer than the front, more than I could have imagined or hoped for. A perfect bubble butt I lusted to grasp and squeeze. Bury my face in. Bite and suck on.

I was going to fail his class if I couldn't get my mind off sex. But the man was so damned delicious. I salivated. Couldn't stop myself from staring as his mouth moved, forming words I hadn't heard. I'd drooled, desperate for a little taste.

Okay, who the fuck was I kidding? I wanted more than a sample. An all-you-can-eat D'Angelo buffet sounded more like it, and I wouldn't mind having my fill.

He didn't wear a ring, so he was probably unmarried. But was he straight? He'd given pronouns but no indication of his sexual orientation, and as the minutes had slipped past, I hadn't gotten a read on him.

His eyes didn't reveal a goddamned thing either.

Somehow, I'd managed to jot down a few notes, but when the class ended, I quickly exchanged numbers with Jazzie because I was going to need all the assistance I could get to pass the class.

But first, I needed some questions answered because patience was not one of my strong suits.

I took my time packing up my stuff, lingering long enough I was the last student in his classroom.

Quiet settled over us, and Professor D'Angelo eventually lifted his focus off whatever he'd been looking at on his desk. His eyebrow quirked, same as it had earlier when he'd silently told me to get on with it and introduce myself.

A yummy shiver pebbled my arms with goose bumps.

I grinned.

He didn't. "Can I help you with something, Mr. Fox?"

"Sean."

He didn't reply, simply waited, those dark eyes of his unmoved by the obvious vibes I was putting out like the desperate little cock whore I was. Even if the man was straight, he *had* to know I was interested in getting my freak on with every inch of him.

To hell with it.

I leaned forward, my gaze flicking down his neck to the opened top button of his shirt that didn't reveal a damned thing to my inquisitive mind. Smooth or hairy? Either way, he would be perfect beneath, no fucking doubt. "So, Teach —you're kinda hot. Make my day and tell me you like dick."

Professor D'Angelo blinked. "C-come again?" he sputtered.

I chuckled, unable to help myself over cracking his shell with bluntness that usually turned people off or made them laugh. "You've had me on the verge of blowing my load since I walked through that door, but I promise I'm good for two if that's what you want. Three if you're lucky."

The gorgeous man cursed under his breath—a deeper fissure in his facade. But he didn't demand I get the hell out of his lecture hall. Lips pursing, he studied me until I shifted, still grinning like a damned dork, my balls throbbing.

"Mr. Fox—"

"Sean," I insisted.

"—I'm going to pretend the last few minutes didn't happen, and I suggest you do the same. There is a level of professionalism expected in my classroom, and if you can't comply, I will have you removed for the rest of the semester."

My fucking heart fell to my toes, but I sighed dramatically rather than showing my disappointment. It was too bad he hadn't said something along the lines of wanting to spank the brat out of me because the man's hands looked like they would easily put me in my place...

Since when did the idea of being over a man's lap—*not* fucking—make my cock buck in my jeans?

"I can be a good boy if that's what you really want," I stated with a wink while grabbing my bag off the floor. Standing, I slung the strap over my shoulder and blatantly adjusted my obvious bulge.

Sexy Professor's gaze flitted down to my groin but jerked back up just as quick.

Busted.

I grinned at the flush of pink rising over his cheek bones. "See ya around, Teach," I murmured.

A muscle ticked in his jaw, but I could feel his gaze follow me as I sauntered out the door. I might have added a little extra sway to my hips. Flexed my fine ass for his enjoyment while cursing myself for not wearing tighter jeans that properly showed off the goods. Still, I definitely had left behind an impression I hoped would haunt him, straight or otherwise.

I could honor his wishes to keep professional with what came out of my mouth just so I could remain in his class since I needed the credits to graduate. But my eyes? They had a mind of their own, same as my dick, and I wasn't about to police either.

As for the whole not fucking on the side while employed by Elite as one of their escorts?

That man was temptation enough I would kick my brother's rule to the curb given the chance to bend over a desk for Professor D'Angelo's enjoyment—and my own.

Chapter 6

Matteo

I'd never been so blatantly hit on in my entire life.

I'd also never been so off-balance and embarrassed by the absolute lack of filter on a person. Hell, I even felt angry although I wasn't sure exactly why.

Sean's eyes had flirted from the moment our gazes had met, but the words out of his mouth once alone with him? The boy was beyond trouble, and while I should have been turned off by him coming on to me, I found my ego... *boosted.*

I scrubbed a hand down over my face, my scruff scratching my palm.

What was I going to do with him?

My better sense told me to get him transferred out of my class immediately, but on what grounds? I refused to ruin a driven student's desire to further their education, so reporting his behavior was out of the question. He'd found the guts to return to school ten years after graduating high school, so the kid obviously meant business about getting his degree.

I got the feeling he took his latest step in life seriously, but what about the rest of how he'd acted? As the next generation, had he simply been dishing out compliments I wasn't familiar with, or was my gut instinct he'd wanted more than an exchange of words spot-on?

Either way, he'd made me uncomfortable in my own skin, and I was strangely moved and annoyed by that truth.

The door to my classroom opened, and adrenaline shot straight to my heart. It wasn't Sean returning for more banter but students for my next class.

How had time slipped by without me knowing?

I glanced at my watch, stunned at how long I'd been stewing over every minute of being in Sean Fox's presence. Never had a student—or another person for that matter— affected me so thoroughly or quickly upon meeting them.

Katie was a burst of sunshine.

The thought flitted through my mind, halting my brain's ambling. She'd stolen my breath and infiltrated my dreams from the moment we'd met. Instantaneous attraction had tightened every muscle in my body, and I hadn't been able to tear my eyes off her from across our college's cafeteria that first day our freshman year.

Sean had definitely woken...*something* inside me I hadn't experienced since Katie. I'd been aware of him throughout the class, distracted by the upbeat energy he radiated. My skin continued to tingle from his presence regardless of the fact he'd left.

Katie had been the same.

I scowled, wondering why I compared my wife's effect on me to that of a young man. There *was* no comparison since I was straight and not attracted to the same sex.

A throat cleared.

Blinking, I realized I had a room full of students who all stared at me in expectation. Warmth flooded my face, and I released a slow exhale, scrambling to remember what I was supposed to be doing.

Introductions.

Syllabus handouts.

The normal first-day things I couldn't wait to finish up so we could dive into the good stuff and I could challenge young minds that were as passionate about accounting as I was.

Somehow, I made it through the rest of my classes, thankful as hell that Sean didn't show up for any of the others I taught.

I headed to my office once finished and slumped in my chair, head tipped back. Never had a first day wrecked me in such a way. Usually, I rode a high from the beginning of a school year, but exhaustion pulled on my muscles and mind. My temples throbbed, and my eye sockets ached. Pinching the bridge of my nose, I closed my eyelids, plunging myself into darkness even though bright afternoon light flooded the room through the window overlooking the campus green.

Same as throughout the day, the instant I no longer had something to focus on, my memory kicked in, replaying Sean hurrying into class. Even more so, when he'd walked out. Why had I noticed how his jeans fit? That he obviously spent time in the gym doing squats?

What the hell is wrong with me?

My shared office door opened without a knock, and I cracked an eyelid to find my friend and fellow professor Hanson Martin shuffling in. Unlike me, he wore a tie, but he'd already ripped it loose to leave it hanging around his neck. Similar tiredness hugged his eyes, and his full head of gray hair looked like he'd been running his fingers through it.

"Long day?" I muttered.

"You could say that," he grumbled. "I'm getting too old for the level of stupidity from today's youngsters."

I snorted a laugh, thankful to have something other than Sean to think about, and pushed up to sit right in my chair as Hanson sank into his. We had shared the office for the previous five years, and even though he neared retirement age and we didn't have much in common outside teaching, we'd become good friends, often complaining about what we were *too old* for.

"What happened to respect?" he asked. "Common courtesy? I swear, kids don't understand that you reap what you sow."

I nodded in agreement.

"If this was the seventies, I would have taken a switch to some of those little bastards and set them straight since their parents obviously failed them."

Snickering, I rubbed my hand over my face again, thinking about a certain little blond with sparkling blue eyes and sly smirks who had more sass than anyone I'd ever met. The boy needed his ass reddened—

My groin tightened at the image of doing the honors, and I stopped breathing.

What. The. Fuck.

I glanced down, baffled by my dick that hadn't shown a hint of life in...I couldn't remember how long. Sure, I sometimes woke with morning wood a quick jerk took care of, but never...not since Katie had anything even remotely sexual stirred inside me.

First of all, I didn't do violence behind closed doors or in public for that matter. Some might consider me a Dom with how I'd experienced fulfillment when Katie had sweetly submitted at my feet, but the other aspects of the BDSM lifestyle hadn't been our thing.

Second, I was *straight*. I'd never crossed that line in deed let alone my mind. I'd never been turned on by a masculine body, had never looked at another guy and wondered what it would be like to touch, kiss, or make love to him.

So why did Sean stir strange...*weirdness* up inside me? Swallowing hard, I shoved the image of him from my mind.

"Dinner tonight?" I asked Hanson, assuming we would go out together like we did every first day of school to celebrate the start of a new semester.

"Albert suggested O'Malley's if that's okay with you," he replied about his husband, who had left the work force two years earlier.

"Sounds good to me. How's he enjoying the retirement from teaching?" I asked, needing to fill my mind with thoughts that didn't include a very confusing young man I had no business even thinking about let alone being confused over.

"He's pushing for me to join him early in old man bliss."

I smiled even though my chest ached for what Hanson and Albert shared and looked forward to. What I'd lost... love and companionship through my later years. "And what would you do with your time if you did?"

"Twiddle my thumbs." Hanson laughed, shaking his head. "Just kidding. Nothing about life with Albert is boring. He would force me to skydive or...try spelunking I believe he calls it? We would probably hike the Appalachian Trail again. Go deep sea diving even though I can't swim. He would make me watch him climb a rock face since these old hands wouldn't allow me to do the same—thank God."

Hanson waved his gnarled fingers at me. "One good positive about arthritis! Your partner can't force you to attempt some of the scary things he's stubbornly set on doing!"

We both chuckled, but my smile faded long before his did as I stared at the wood grain of my desk, my mind returning to Sean.

"How are you doing, Matteo?" Hanson asked after a bit, his eyes full of concern.

I considered my friend's quiet question. We'd had a lot of in-depth conversations over the years. He and Albert had been there for me when Katie had passed. They'd stuck beside me through my grief long after my parents and sister had gone home to South Carolina, and Katie's family turned their back on me. There wasn't much Hanson didn't know about my life—or lack thereof the previous three years since I'd lost the sweetest partner a man could ask for.

"Have you ever..." I filled my lungs and slowly let it leak out, my focus on my tidy desk where nothing lay out of place. If only my brain could be so organized. "You knew you were gay at an early age." I repeated what he'd told me long ago, but he nodded as though I'd asked a question. "Have you ever found a woman attractive? Been...strangely moved by the opposite sex when you never were before?"

"No." He didn't hesitate to answer, his chair squeaking as he shifted. "But I can appreciate beauty for what it is— sexual orientation not being an issue."

I caught his eye. "But you've never felt...a strange draw, almost like a...an instant infatuation you didn't understand?"

"Never," he replied, his gaze curious.

Nodding, I glanced out our lone window, expecting I was already too tired to get my nightly run in before collapsing onto my bed. My head hurt, and I wanted nothing more than to pass out and stop thinking.

"Who is he?"

Huffing an exhale, I turned back toward my friend. Hanson studied me with serious hazel eyes that didn't reveal a hint of judgment.

"A student?" he pushed when I didn't answer.

My stomach tightened, and I managed a stilted nod.

"Sexuality is fluid," he stated with assurance I wish I could feel. "You wouldn't be the first forty-something man to find out he's not as straight as he'd always believed. My own Albert never looked at a man twice until our eyes met across the faculty room."

I'd forgotten that story, and the reminder soothed me slightly.

"Perhaps you should talk to him," Hanson suggested. "Maybe he can help make sense of what you're experiencing."

I nodded, still unsure of what to say let alone think about how Sean had unsettled me.

"Take the time to figure this out, but please, for the love of God, don't do what Joe Barkley did."

A huff of laughter left me. That idiot had been married with four adult children, six grandkids—and he'd gotten a freshman pregnant three months after she'd first walked into his class.

"At least I don't have to worry about knocking him up," I muttered without meaning to.

Hanson chuckled, and fuck me, if an image didn't flash in my head of filling Sean with cum.

"Jesus," I hissed, rubbing my forehead.

"Matteo."

"Hmm?" I wearily met Hanson's steady gaze.

"It's okay—questioning your sexuality at any age is normal. Don't let anything or anyone from your past dictate otherwise. Search through what this young man stirs inside you. Put a name to it. Accept it without acting on the temptation to touch him. Then move on with the knowledge that you've grown in self-awareness, and maybe find a man who isn't off-limits."

I'd always been open to expanding my mind and who I was as a human being. Katie had helped me walk that path, for which I would always be grateful, but the situation with Sean was bigger than anything I'd faced before.

With consequences I couldn't begin to imagine.

Chapter 7

Sean

"**D**ude," I said into my cell when Drake answered. "What's up?" My best friend since middle school sounded distracted.

"You're working tonight?" I asked even though I already knew the answer while flopping onto my bed fully clothed after a long-assed day of classes. The pillow-top mattress cradled my body, and the soothing scent of clean sheets put on by the cleaning company I used filled my nose.

I snuggled in deeper with a sigh.

"Yeah. Returning client. Easy to please type. Tasty little morsel too."

"Lucky bastard," I muttered, my closed eyes bringing to mind the deliciousness of one hot stoic professor. I wanted to strip him down and hear him groan as he sank his cock into my more than needy, willing hole.

Drake chuckled. "How was it?"

"Long as hell. I'm tired and have a shit ton of home-work. Who hands out homework on the first day of classes?"

"That asshole our freshman year...what was his name?"

"Professor Boswell," I muttered, having forgotten about

the one class Drake and I had together at Boston College before I'd flunked out. We'd hated the fucker, but while Drake had aced that class, I'd failed because I'd been serious about partying while my friend had focused on graduating.

"Should I feel sorry for your ass or laugh?"

"Fuck off." I was jealous as hell he would be fucking for money while I buried my face in a goddamn textbook instead of an ass, headache already throbbing in my temples.

"I'll bring you a six-pack for breakfast tomorrow," Drake offered, and I grinned.

"I don't have class until ten, but I'm not fucking up college again, so no booze before dinner from here on out."

"You're going to kill it this time around. I have faith in you."

I grinned, getting the warm fuzzies inside. "Love you, boo."

"Fuck off."

Kissy noises left my lips, and he replied by fake gagging in my ear. "*You love me*," I sang.

"Damn right I do, but I gotta go. Elite's limo is picking me up in five."

"Don't forget your little black bag," I ordered, once more envious over the lube and sex toys he'd be using while I messed with notes and a laptop. "Bust a nut for me, will ya?"

"Definitely."

"Bastard," I muttered after hanging up. Blowing out a heavy exhale, I stayed put in my comfy heaven, allowing myself a few more minutes of rest before dragging my ass into the kitchen to scrounge up something to eat for dinner. Fuck knew I would need the energy to get started on my homework.

At least I didn't have a demanding job waiting on me once I finished for the day like some of the other students. I ended up having a second class with Jazzie, and they told me how they waited tables on weekends and ran the cash register at a twenty-four-hour pharmacy Monday through Wednesday nights. When they would find time to study baffled the fuck out of me.

Thoughts of work and the demands on me trickled away as I went back to my first class.

My Italian Prince Charming lived rent-free in my fantasies. And I'd had a fuck ton while struggling to pay attention to other professors drone on about stuff I needed to hear but hadn't.

In my twenty-eight years, I'd attempted every sexual position under the sun minus bending my cock backward to fuck my own ass. I'd even attempted to suck my dick when I was a bit more bendy, managing to lick at my slit but not much else, unfortunately.

But Professor D'Angelo?

I wanted him in all the ways—even ones beyond my imagination. Surely there were some means of getting dicked down I'd yet to hear about or see in porn.

My dick thickened, and I groaned over the ache once more rising in my balls. I'd been dealing with the fuckers all goddamned day.

Time to take care of that shit.

I ripped off my shirt and shoved at my jeans, kicking impatiently until they landed on the floor, satin sheets caressing my bare skin. My dick slit stared straight up at me, weepy around my piercing.

"Yeah, yeah," I muttered, grabbing hold of my shaft to give it a little loving squeeze. "Cry me a river."

A firm upward stroke released a stream of pre-cum that

had been simmering all day, the slickness coating my palm and fingers to ease my downward glide.

Hissing, I lay back again, closed my eyes, and gave over to the images in my mind while stroking my cock. I was so damn wet for him, and the sounds of a slick hand fucking made my balls tighten up against my groin in a matter of minutes.

I was going to come like a motherfucker. Soak my chest. Probably hit my goddamned chin.

My abs contracted, lifting my upper body from the mattress. Grunts and whimpers flooded my room, the sounds of sex a beautiful symphony in my ears. I was a one-man band, and I got off on the music I created.

"Oh fuck." I gulped and opened my eyes, head lifting to watch my swollen head fuck through my fist with hot-as-fuck schlicking noises. The muscles in my forearm corded, and I grabbed my balls, pulling them down.

There was no stopping my orgasm.

Groaning, I erupted, head tipping back, eyes rolling as euphoria crashed over me. Spunk splattered up my chest. Landed on my chin as expected. Even my fucking nose received a gift from my pulsing dick.

"Jesus—fuck." I spasmed, my entire body jerking with every jet of cum up my throbbing shaft. My heels dug into the mattress as I humped my fist with desperation. "Fuck!"

I grunted and fell back, milking every last drop from my slit. Moaning a litany of curses, I continued to stroke over my slick glans, still horny as fuck. My ass ached to be filled, so I splayed my legs wide and toyed with my second piercing before coating two fingers in my own cum and shoving them in my hole. I was so damn greedy for it I didn't even mind the slight burn while I reached deep for my prostate.

"Ah, fucking...right there," I whispered to myself and started stroking inside and out.

The head of my dick squished through my cum-soaked palm, and I took myself to the point of intense pleasure/pain, beyond sensitive from having already erupted once. Every rub over my sweet spot inside my ass ramped me back up until I writhed beneath self-torture.

Wide shoulders and olive skin. Dark alluring eyes. Sensual mouth parting...

Come again.

I heard the professor's words in my head—and I gave him what he hadn't meant to ask for. A second orgasm kicked me in the groin, shooting lesser spurts up over my lower abs.

Pathetic whining noises spilled past my lips, but I felt too fucking high on endorphins to care. One last twitch of my dick, a final pulse of my ring around my plunging fingers, and the rest of my body went limp.

Sated—completely drained—I lay spent as adrenaline continued to race through my pounding heart and to my extremities.

Best jerk off session ever.

Grinning, I slid my fingers from my ass and stretched over my soft bed. Luscious tingles skittered over my skin from the kick-ass orgasms that had been simmering in my nuts all day.

If my Prince Charming had been present, I'd have climbed aboard his dick and ridden him until I came a third time.

I rubbed my cum up over my abs and chest, imagining it was his hands, his spunk soaking into my skin. Never had I ever wanted a man's scent to bury deep inside me. Stick around until dry...mark me with some Neanderthal-like show of ownership.

My dick twitched at the image in my mind, and I lifted my head once more to eye the damn thing.

"Seriously?" The fucker attempted to move again. "Jesus fucking Christ." I laughed and rolled off the bed onto jelly-like legs. My dick swung and wetly smacked against my thigh. "Stay that way, will you? I've got work to do."

But shower first.

I ended up with three fingers up my ass and another weak orgasm's spunk disappearing down the drain before I finished beneath the spray.

Even though I wanted to pass the fuck out afterward, I sat at my kitchen table and ate a dinner of leftover cold pizza loaded with black olives, a textbook open in front of me. My eyes crossed a few times, and I guzzled an energy drink loaded with caffeine rather than the beer I thirsted for.

Who knew school at almost thirty was so damn tiring? And how the hell was a man supposed to focus on words when fantasies were so much more exciting and rewarding?

That thought gave me pause.

I had something to prove and a father to make proud. Attaining both would be the greatest reward of all.

But fuck, did I struggle to finish my assignments before crashing face-first onto my bed.

Winning, I told myself, giving over to dreams that would have me aching come morning.

Chapter 8

———————

Matteo

O'Malley's wasn't busy seeing as it was a Monday night, so the lack of chatter would make talking to Hanson's husband about what had happened earlier that morning in class easier and a bit more private. My mind still wasn't sure about the affair or the consequences it could potentially have.

Leaning over the table between us, dinner finished and a New Hampshire IPA in hand, I slowly released an exhale, preparing myself.

Albert eyed me, waiting patiently since Hanson had told him earlier I had something to share with him and needed advice.

"For the first time in my life, I felt drawn to a man," I admitted, my voice low. "And I don't just mean that I thought he was a good-looking guy in passing. The interest stemmed deep inside me, a feeling I haven't experienced since I first saw Katie."

Albert smiled, his eyes twinkling. "That sounds familiar."

"That's why Hanson suggested I speak with you.

Albert settled back in his chair, glancing around the quiet bar as though gathering his thoughts. "As we grow, experience the world around us, and learn more about ourselves, things begin to change. Our views, beliefs...even emotional responses."

I nodded, having already lived through many such shifts. "Just because we are brought up in a certain religion and assigned a sex at birth doesn't mean we aren't allowed to expand our thoughts as we mature."

"Exactly," Hanson agreed.

"I no longer attend mass like my parents, sister, and her daughter do," I continued. "It took moving out on my own, away from their influence, and studying science and history while in college to redirect my system of belief."

"Sexuality is no different," Albert said. "Fluidity reflects one of many changes some go through in life depending on their circumstances. For me, it was like waking after a long slumber." He shared a smile with Hanson, and they both moved in as though of the same mind, their lips pressing lightly together.

I considered Albert's words rather than diving deep into the envy that snaked through my chest at their display of affection.

Sean's presence had brought a tingling warmth that messed with the molecules in my body. I hated comparing his effect on me to that of the wife I'd lost, but the attraction was so damn similar it raised the hairs on my nape.

I rubbed over the back of my neck while slowly emptying my lungs. A sip of my beer wet my throat. "It kind of is." I finally agreed with Albert's suggestion of his evolving sexuality and how it felt like every day was a new beginning. I picked at my bottle's damp label. "I've been... merely surviving the past three years, and he walked into my life like a breath of fresh air I hadn't realized I've been gasping for."

Yes, I realized as I stated the words that summed Sean up perfectly.

Nodding to myself, I lifted my focus off my drink.

Albert and Hanson studied me from across our booth where they sat shoulder to shoulder, both offering encouraging smiles. I'd always admired their level of comfort in each other's spaces while admitting to jealousy.

And a sense of loss.

I heaved an exhale, slouching a little in my seat.

"It's not just okay," Albert said, his blue eyes understanding but intense, "but healthy as well."

"You've been taking good care of your body, but maybe you ought to consider that poor muscle attempting to survive inside your chest," Hanson suggested, draping his arm over his husband's shoulders and tugging him closer.

My chest ached to do the same to a needy soul.

"It's finally shown a hint of stirring from beneath grief's shroud," Hanson continued, "but that doesn't mean you have to pursue an off-limits young man."

"There are dozens of dating apps," Albert said. "Maybe join a few, browse, and see if anyone else rouses similar feelings. But experiment and don't limit yourself to one gender."

I nodded absently at Albert's suggestion but had zero interest in finding a man to explore with or a woman to replace my wife. No one would be able to do so, and I'd never been one for hookups during my pre-Katie days.

"What matters is that you're finally attempting to move on like you'd promised Katie you would do," Hanson said, his voice quiet and kind as always.

She'd been mere hours from leaving me alone on the

earth, and in that moment, I would have agreed to anything she'd said. Rob a bank. Shoot myself in the foot. Jump out of a perfectly safe airplane with nothing but a sheet of thin material to keep me from splattering on the ground.

But allow myself to love someone else?

I glanced around the bar, needing distraction from the troubling ideas and emotions roiling inside my guts like a bubbling cauldron. Sean was nothing but trouble regardless of the lightness of his smile and flirty eyes that filled my lungs and warmed my face...along with the rest of my body.

While I could understand that sexuality might be fluid —evidenced by Albert—pursing a student in my classroom was forbidden.

And Katie still owned every part of me.

My thoughts returned to the heaviest, most life-changing reason Sean and I didn't make sense.

He's male.

I'd never touched another man's cock, had never felt inclined to even consider such a thing. But I could admit the idea of watching Sean strip, unveiling his young, lean form didn't exactly turn me off like it would have done in my teenage years.

I'd never had the curious era in college either. I hadn't jerked off with a friend out of boredom, nor had I watched a single porn video that didn't include a leading lady with a handful of breasts and lush softness between her thighs.

But Sean definitely had roused something inside me that called out to my baser instincts, demanded I heed its draw regardless of the other two reasons I ought to avoid him.

My cell buzzed in my back pocket, still on vibrate from my day in classes. Since my social life consisted of the two men I sat with and family, I retrieved my phone to check who'd texted me.

Kenzie.

My stomach dipped at the notification on the screen, all traces of arousal vanishing along with the blood from my face. Experiencing life-giving force to the reminder of what I'd lost whiplashed me in less than a heartbeat. It almost felt as if...Katie had prompted the text from the grave.

Did she not approve?

"Matteo?" Hanson's voice held a hint of concern as my face fell.

"Katie's sister," I whispered, guilt crashing down over me and leaving me hollow inside once more.

My hand shook as I swiped my screen to life to read the message.

Kenzie: **It's check-in time again. I want to make sure you're looking after yourself. We are all healthy but still picking up the pieces and grieving. I honestly hope you're faring better than we are.**

Unlike my ex in-laws, Kenzie didn't blame me for her sister's death. She was the only one to keep in contact with me after Katie's passing.

I understood a mother and father needing to hold someone accountable, to find a focal point for their anger over losing a child. Katie had been the love of my life, but they'd had their own flesh and blood ripped from them. Surely, they suffered more than I did, and I couldn't fault them for their feelings toward me.

Even if they were wrong.

"Is everything okay?"

No, it wasn't, but I nodded at Hanson's question before

shoving my cell back in my pocket. "She reaches out on occasion to see how I'm doing." I tried for a level tone of voice, but the upheaval of emotions within the previous few seconds didn't allow for calm, the same as it always did whenever Kenzie reached out to me every couple of months.

"You're not going to respond?"

Shrugging as though indifferent, I exhaled until my lungs attempted to collapse. "After Katie's death, her parents carved me from their family with a blunt knife. Kenzie still cares about my wellbeing, but I sometimes wish she wouldn't jolt me like this with reminders of what I lost."

My beer bottle's label became a distraction again for my fingernail as I struggled to settle my mind from the roller coaster Kenzie's text had tossed me onto. "Honestly, I wish Kenzie would let me go like her parents did. Choosing to continue breathing is tough enough without her rousing my grief and bringing up their continued negative thoughts toward me. I would rather be free to enjoy the *good* things I cherish about the only woman I'll ever love."

Tipping my beer upward, I took a few heady swallows in attempt to change my focus back to where it belonged.

I'd had my chance at happily ever after, and I had no wish to tarnish our pure love by exploring with another man in order to make sense of or prove my sexuality.

I knew who I was, and my faithfulness to the memory of my wife wouldn't waver.

Even if I ended up dreaming about him every night in the coming weeks.

Chapter 9

Sean

I didn't remember my failed year at college being so damn hard. Who knew sitting in classes and studying shit that at least *somewhat* interested me would be exhausting to the point I didn't want to go out? The first time around at college, fuck all, but now? I *wanted* to succeed and still struggled.

It was difficult enough having to perk up my dick for clients two to three times a week when back in early August, I'd been ready to fuck at the drop of a hat. I dragged ass, actually popping little blue pills to please EEMM's needy holes and swollen balls. I still got off. Enjoyed the release of tension, but the drain on more than just my nuts weighed on me.

Sleeping didn't come easy even though tiredness toppled me onto my bed when the sun went down. With the three mil of hard-earned cash I'd dropped on my corner condo overlooking Boston's wharf, I should have found contented rest every damned night. Vivid dreams visited regardless of exhaustion, not allowing me the drowsy relaxation my body required while cradled in satin sheets.

Damned bags hinted beneath my eyes that no expensive-as-shit cream erased too.

After only ten fucking days of school!

Friday, I had a rare evening to myself. No clients. No need to fuck for cash. No desire—yet again—to even go out. I just wanted to curl up in my bed and sleep without dreams about sexy Teach and what I wanted him to do to me.

What he never would do.

Ugh, the life of a gay man falling for the straight professor sucked ass but in the worst way possible. There was no tongue action—licking or probing either—to make my crush bearable.

My cell pinged in the stillness of my second bedroom I'd turned into a home office, and I lifted my weary head off my desk where I'd been attempting to write a paper for the previous couple of hours.

BetsyAnne, EEMM's secretary had texted, alerting me to the fact a client had cancelled last minute. The rare occurrence left my buddy free.

Drake himself texted me before I shot off a reply to BetsyAnne, thanking her for the update.

Boo: **Client backed out. What are you up to?**

I glanced over my workstation—textbook, pad of paper with a bunch of illegible scribbling, two broken pencils, and one pen. My laptop sat open, its dark screen reminding me I hadn't accomplished shit. While a few minutes earlier I'd wanted to crawl in bed and call it a night, I hadn't enjoyed any actual fun in far too long.

The stirring of interest for something outside school lit inside me, and with the decision for procrastination made, a grin roused to life on my face.

Me: **Nothing of importance.**

Total lie, but what the fuck ever. I needed a break.

Drake: **I'll pick you up in twenty.**

I took the fastest shower known to man, not bothering to spend extra time on the sexy bits since I was off the clock and unable to hook up. Tight jeans snuggled against my thighs and ass, and I went with a T-shirt that hugged my lean torso and showed off my pierced nipples with hot as fuck bumps beneath the cotton.

While fixing my hair, I wondered what sort of a response I would get from Teach if he saw me in my nightlife clothes rather than the more subdued attire I wore to class twice a week. Even in baggier shirts and jeans, I still caught him looking my way with a *what-if* lingering in his eyes. What would he think of my piercings? Would he want to feel up the globes of my ass so lovingly encased in faded denim?

My dick stirred, but I shut that shit off since I wouldn't be seeing any action from him or anyone else until the following night. I was booked with EEMM Saturday and would hopefully get dicked down by a visiting dignitary from some foreign country in Europe I'd never heard of.

Drake texted to let me know he waited out front of my condo building, so I grabbed my keys and wallet before hurrying into the elevator.

My paper due the following Wednesday could wait.

I had beers with my name on them and a few hours of letting go from responsibilities I'd been dutifully focused on for almost two weeks. To say I was proud of myself was an understatement. I deserved a night just chilling with my boo and enjoying local brews.

Drake's silver Mercedes Roadster purred alongside the curb, and I climbed in with a grin still plastered on my face.

"Hey, boo." I leaned over the console and kissed the air

beside his cheek, causing him to back off with a grimace. The guy was an affection whore but pretended to hate when I got all up in his face.

"Jesus, you have no sense of personal space," he muttered the absolute truth while pulling out into traffic.

I pinched his nipple, which earned me a hiss, and reached for my seatbelt. "And you love me."

"Unfortunately."

Laughing, I settled into the red leather seat, filling my lungs with the new car smell he'd somehow managed to retain after owning the Roadster for over a year. It had been his first big purchase as an Elite, even before the small condo he'd bought. His home had cost a fraction of what mine had, but I enjoyed the evidence of how far I'd come, how much I'd accomplished before hitting thirty. So what if I'd paid an arm and a leg to own the place?

It had felt good to spoil myself for a change even if Pop had grumbled about poor investments and wasting my money. He hadn't stated the same to Micah when he'd bought his mansion.

While my pad wasn't near my big bro's square footage or had a plot of land with it like his, I didn't require anything more since I had zero plans of having kids. There was no need for a sprawling lawn that would demand upkeep. No huge outdoor living space when my condo's small balcony provided salt-scented breezes and room enough for a grill and a couple of lounge chairs for kicking back and chilling out.

And if Pop didn't like it? I didn't give a shit.

Lies, lies.

"Where are we going?" I asked glancing once more at my friend, ready to eradicate everything from my brain but a good time. "Dancing? Drinking? How about both?"

Drake wasn't a club type but often relented to my manipulations when I was in the mood to get my groove on, sweat, and grind all over hot bodies.

"O'Malley's."

Drinking it was.

Our knuckles met in between us for a bump. We shared a love for hops, and thank fuck for fast metabolisms and extra hours available for the gym, or we'd both have beer guts.

The gym.

I didn't really have much time for that anymore with my new school schedule. Maybe I would need to lay off the booze a bit.

But with Drake driving? I was free to let loose for the first time in two weeks, and I wasn't going to refrain from sucking down extra useless calories. The man was a tank and had the tolerance of three men, so I had zero issue with him enjoying a few before driving us home. Fuck knew we'd be sitting at the bar for three to four hours, so plenty of time for him to switch over to water before heading back to our responsibilities.

Not me though. I was going to do as I pleased, and getting drunk sounded divine. Everything else could wait until tomorrow.

We bullshitted about the Sox, Pats, and work, sharing more than we should about the final topic considering the NDAs Elites had to sign. While we didn't exchange the names of clients, I wouldn't have had any problems finding out exactly which ones Drake referred to since, as manager, I had unhindered access to all of EEMM's files and often-times handpicked Elites for new clients.

"How was last night?" I asked as we sat at a high top in O'Malley's bar. I expected Drake would give me all the details like he always did. I hadn't gotten to enjoy a customer since the weekend before, so the dry spell was starting to make me restless for dick. Maybe I wouldn't need pills to please the dignitary booked with me tomorrow night.

"It was the same guy I told you about a few weeks ago." A corner of Drake's lips curled, and he glanced at the TV screen that showed a repeat of the Sox game from earlier in the day.

"Our age, black hair?" I asked, remembering how Drake had gone on and on about him. "On the slender side? Gorgeous green eyes?"

Drake dipped his head, a slight pink stain spreading over his cheeks.

"The fuck, man?" I sat back, hands on my thighs and eyes wide. "Don't tell me you're falling for him."

"I'm not." Drake met my stare head-on. "Promise. But if he had red hair?" My best friend feigned a shiver/swoon moment, eyes rolling and everything, a rare display of playfulness. Thank fuck he had me as a sidekick to chill his seriousness. "That would be a different story altogether."

He had a thing for gingers. They were his kryptonite, he'd stated on more than one occasion. Even had gone so far as to say he hoped to fall in love and have babies with one someday.

I cringed at the thought of both. Being tied down with extra weight shackled to my ankles? No fucking thank you.

"How are classes?" Drake asked as our waiter approached.

We gave our order for a bucket of IPAs, and I turned back toward my friend to answer. "Exhausting. I'm fried before six every night. Haven't been to the gym in too fucking long. Took two magic pills last weekend in order to satisfy the customer."

Drake blinked his baby blues at me, making me jealous for the umpteenth time over his thick, black lashes. And the fucker had muscles to spare too. Thank fuck there wasn't an ounce of attraction between us, or our friendship would have failed years ago since I was a one-and-done kind of guy.

Freedom was my mantra. Nothing better than a buffet of man flesh to gorge on until sated—

The memory of my hot professor knocked on the door of my lifelong stance, halting it in its tracks.

"Sean Fox needed help to get his dick hard?" Drake asked, pulling my focus off whatever the fuck had me thinking exclusivity might not actually be so bad.

I picked up some popcorn from the bowl the waiter had placed between us and tossed it into his face.

He snickered.

I didn't, still unsettled by whatever the stirring inside me might mean.

The bucket of beers landed in front of us—the perfect diversion—and we both muttered our thanks. We each took one and tapped the long necks together.

"To freedom!" I said, my backside restless on the chair even though tiredness still clung like a bitch beneath my eyes.

"To life," Drake added.

I enjoyed a long pull, loving the coolness sliding straight into my empty stomach.

"Forgot to eat," I noted aloud.

"Wings?" Drake suggested our usual.

"Fuck yeah."

He flagged down our waiter, and I sipped again,

glancing around O'Malley's packed bar in an attempt to keep my head quiet over the whole Teach and ball-and-chain thing I would usually avoid like the goddamned plague. Chatter and the clinking of glasses filled my ears. A few booths lined the far wall, all with couples dedicated to their conversations. Every stool at the bar itself cradled an ass, some more interested in the handful of TVs hung overhead.

The larger seating area over to my right included over a dozen tables and a few more booths, most of which were also occupied—

Well, fuck me sideways.

Twice.

My heart tripped over its own chambers at the sight of Teach with two other guys who sat opposite him at a table. The two gray-haired men cozied together, one of which I recognized from college, but I focused on Professor D'Angelo. *Matteo,* I tended to call him in my fantasies.

Now, he was a man I wouldn't mind sinking my dick into more than my usual one and done. Would gladly have my hole filled up by him a baker's dozen times too. My not-so-sweet Prince Charming must have felt my stare on his profile.

He turned, our gazes connecting, and I made an *oomph* noise as the breath left my lungs.

"You okay?" Drake asked.

"Hmm?" I couldn't tear my eyes off those chocolate orbs even though I couldn't peer into them from the distance separating us.

"Earth to fucking Sean." A boot kicked my shin.

"Jesus!" I jerked my head back toward Drake. "The fuck, man!"

"Who's the hottie glowering at me?"

I glanced over to find Matteo doing exactly as Drake had said—frowning at my boo.

Little bursts of electrical currents rippled through me, making my stomach flutter. I fucking giggled like a goddamned kid.

"Professor D'Angelo," I murmured through my chuckles as he once more focused on the men he sat with.

Sighing over losing the man's attention, I turned to find Drake studying me. "What?"

"Someone is hot for teacher."

A barked laugh tipped my head back. Couldn't fucking help myself. "I thought the same exact fucking thing. He teaches my first class on Monday and Wednesday mornings. Hot as fuck. Built like the perfect man. Gorgeous shoulders. Those lips...that ass." I had to adjust myself.

Drake snickered. "He didn't seem too happy to see you sitting with another guy."

I allowed myself to pretend Teach was jealous even though I hardly believed that fantasy. Digging had awarded me some intel on him. He'd been a professor for twelve years, had grown up in Boston, and had recently been widowed.

No kids.

There wasn't much on social media presence to give me insight into his daily life either.

Since I'd told him that I would be a good boy, I hadn't taken advantage of having his cell thanks to that syllabus, nor had I done any serious stalking. He didn't want my dick or any other part of my body. The man was straight, even if his lingering, somewhat hungry, and curious gazes argued with my assumption. He was also my professor and a widower who didn't need to be bothered by someone my age.

"Think he's into you?"

Fiddling with my cell on the table with the sudden urge to text Teach to find out, I shook my head at Drake's suggestion. "Only in my dreams, boo."

Unfortunately.

Chapter 10

Matteo

Of all the people I could run into at O'Malley's, Sean Fox showed up. I'd been aware of him within seconds of him walking in with a beast of a man, well over Sean's five-ten or thereabout height. Dark and broad to Sean's slender, lighter appearance, the stranger waltzed in with a familiarity alongside my student that made my lips purse.

But like sunshine, Sean broke through the clouds lingering around my head as usual and heated my body with addictive warmth.

Whatever Hanson and Albert had been discussing faded into the background along with the other noises emanating from the busy bar. Silence settled in my ears as I watched Sean slide his fine ass onto a chair across from his... boyfriend?

A muscle ticked in my jaw at the same time my stomach tightened. I fought to keep my hands from fisting and settled back in my chair in an attempt to relax muscles that had tensed from neck to thighs for no reason whatsoever.

Once their waiter left them alone, the two leaned

toward one another, talking with an ease that suggested they weren't out on a first date. Sean tossed popcorn in the man's face, so the two were definitely friends at the very least.

I finally took stock of Sean, checking his profile out from his perfectly mussed blond hair down over a T-shirt entirely too formfitting to be considered modest. But he looked good.

Real good.

Swallowing a rush of saliva, I noted his tighter than normal jeans, which led my mind to wander toward what else I might see wrapped up in the denim if he stood close enough for me to reach out and touch.

The light on his face, regardless of the haggardness I'd taken note of while in class earlier in the week, shone bright as always.

He couldn't sit still, something else I was more than aware of. And yet he managed to pay attention in class and to that point had a one-hundred percent average on both assessments I'd done.

The bob of his throat as he swallowed a long pull of beer captured my focus. What would his skin taste like? How would his scruff feel on my tongue or his muscles under my hands?

Life stirred in my groin, and I stifled a groan.

"Matteo?"

I tore my gaze off Sean, attempting to realign myself with reality as the bar's sounds filtered back to my ears.

Albert looked at me expectantly.

"I'm sorry...what?"

"I asked how you've been doing with the whole sexual fluidity thing we discussed when we were here last."

"Oh." I cleared my throat before sipping my beer to ease the dryness lingering from watching Sean for too long.

Heat seared the side of my face, and I couldn't help but

glance his way. Those crystalline blue eyes of his held my stare. I cursed beneath my breath without moving my lips. The young man was absolutely stunning, and a sense of powerlessness swept through me. My body ached to be near him so thoroughly that my feet slid over the floor with the intent to stand.

But his friend kicked him beneath their high table, and Sean's barked curse could be heard across the bar.

I took a better look at the man in the chair I wished I sat in. He was easily taller than my six feet, broader, much younger, and hot enough to grace covers of magazines. I didn't compare...not that I should have been thinking such thoughts.

Like Sean, he glanced by me, and I was struck by the vivid blue of his eyes.

Shit.

"Matteo."

Jerked back to the present once more, I turned to find both of my friends staring at me. "I'm sorry?"

As one, the couple peered toward what had caused my distraction twice in a matter of minutes.

"Who's the cute blond?" Albert asked, approval in his voice.

"Sean Fox," Hanson replied, his tone and *ah-ha!* inflection telling me he'd figured out who the guy was I'd told him about two weeks earlier. Seeing as how my co-worker also taught first-year students hoping to graduate with an MBA, I shouldn't have been surprised to find he knew who Sean was.

Releasing a heavy exhale that sank me into my seat, I closed my eyes.

"A student of yours?" Albert asked, sounding clueless. Two seconds later, his quiet, "*Ooooh...*" reached my ears.

"Yes," I responded before either could question me further. Forcing my eyelids open revealed what I'd expected.

Both men studied me, one with a smile—Albert, the French lover—and his husband with a concerned, arched brow.

"That boy has trouble written all over him," Hanson declared, and I couldn't argue. "The way he's looking at you..."

Not glancing at Sean was a feat I somehow managed to accomplish. "How?" I pushed, needing to know.

"Like he wants to devour you from head to toe and go back for seconds."

"Thirds," Albert suggested with a chuckle.

Rarely did I drop an F-bomb, but *fuck* whispered a few times in my mind at the image painted in my mind from my friends' words.

"Life is too short," Albert continued as imaginary Sean licked down my happy trail toward my leaking cock. "I say ride him hard for as long as you can."

"Albert!" Hanson admonished, his tone incredulous. "He's our student!"

Only one of the reasons my conscience insisted I keep my distance even though every cell in my body vibrated with the need to attach to his.

Quietness slid over the table, and I rubbed my nape, attempting to tame the hairs Sean's stare made stand on end. Regardless of why I needed to stay away from Sean, my body ached for a taste of him too.

"I'll be right back," I mumbled. The issue inside my slacks needed taking care of so I could sit and visit with my friends without behaving like an immature, lust-filled teenager.

The ruckus of people enjoying a night out faded as the bathroom door closed behind me. Ignoring the man at the urinal, I slipped into a stall and gave myself some privacy. I didn't bother dropping my pants to my knees, just fished out my hard cock and palmed the throbbing head, grabbing a wad of toilet paper with my free hand.

While the man outside finished up his business, I stroked my length with the pre-cum oozing from my slit, my arousal already on the edge of release. Once allowed full ownership of the bathroom, I focused on my need.

Lips pressed in a thin line and nostrils flaring, I gave in to the fantasy of Sean on his knees, mouth open and waiting, pink tongue wet and hungry for my seed. The vision in my mind consumed my thoughts and senses. Ears ringing and thighs tightening, I ignored the guilt wanting to entwine through my guts like an invasive vine intent on choking out the bit of pleasure I allowed myself.

It wasn't the first time I'd jerked off while thinking about my student, nor did the quick release surprise me.

Heavy exhales accompanied my ejaculating into the toilet paper, and I clenched my teeth against groans wishing to erupt from my mouth. Sean's eyes would be darkened by lust, his throat bobbing as he swallowed my cum.

A quiet gasp escaped my lips with the final euphoric spurt from my slit that Sean would lick from his lower lip.

"Whatcha doing in there, Teach?"

Sean's suggestive question kicked me in the stomach, and I dropped the soiled paper in the toilet and flushed it with my foot. Curses rang in my head as I attempted to calm my racing heart. Cock tucked back inside my boxer briefs and slacks, I unlatched the stall door.

Sunshiny energy radiated from the young man leaning

against the wall in a tight shirt that showed off...nipple piercings?

My dick attempted to twitch, and I clenched my jaw, turning away from the knowing look in his eyes.

I pretended to pay him no mind while washing my hands and grabbing a few towels.

He stepped in front of the door as I reached for the handle to escape his presence. My hand fell shy of his abs by a mere foot.

Our gazes connected, an ocean of blue tempting me to dive in beneath the surface and never come up for air.

"You smell like cum."

I gulped at Sean's murmur, hating and yet loving the slow curl of his lips.

"What had your dick so hard that you had to jerk off in a bathroom stall? Talking dirty with Professor Martin and his husband? Or was it the sexual tension I feel sliding over my skin like a silken tongue every time we share a room?"

"Mr. Fox..." I attempted a firm tone but failed. His blunt words did strange things to my brain.

Sean stepped closer, and my body refused to back away even though my subconscious demanded I do so. His chest brushed against mine, his head tipping to the side. He leaned in even more, placing his lips near my ear. A hot exhale ghosted warm wetness over my lobe, and I shuddered.

"I'm trying very hard to be a good boy around you, Teach, but you're just so. Damn. Hot." He whispered the words, nothing more than moaned caresses that urged my dick to life again.

The bathroom door swung inward, slamming Sean in the back—and into me.

He was hard, his hands suddenly on my waist, and my cock swelled against his.

"Oh, shit!" The guy who'd barged in stumbled into us in a drunken lurch forward. "My bad."

I pulled from Sean's grasp and slipped around him. Rapid beats of my heart pounded in my ears and in my groin.

I am most definitely not *straight.*

The truth continued to repeat in my head as I hurried toward O'Malley's back exit on shaking legs.

My hands trembled as I texted Hanson, letting him know I wasn't feeling well and that I was leaving. Seeing as how we'd already finished dinner, I'd treated, and we'd been on our final drink, I didn't feel as bad for bailing on him and Albert.

I worried they had seen Sean follow me into the bathroom and speculated over the truth, but I needed space from my temptation. No way, no how could I be alone with that boy behind closed doors ever again.

He was still forbidden as my student.

And my heart would never belong to anyone but Katie.

Chapter 11

Sean

Oh, the joys of being a student.

The days seemed endless, and the work bogged me down like damned quicksand. I suffocated beneath the worst kind of load in history while anxiety due to falling behind tangled me up inside.

My mind raced at all hours of the day and well into the night. I couldn't find a few spare moments for the gym, and the lack of exercise made me feel powerless to ignore the overwhelm that dragged me under.

I swore I lost weight in the two weeks following that delicious moment in O'Malley's bathroom with Teach. It had been the most sexually charged handful of seconds in my entire life. Dick straining and heart racing, I'd been desperate for a hit of him.

But my intentions had been cockblocked by some drunk asshole who'd at least allowed me to appreciate the thickening swell in my professor's slacks.

Teach had escaped me, and I lusted for another chance to misbehave, even though I'd promised him I wouldn't.

But in the four days I'd seen him in class since that

night, I began to recognize what I felt for him, the draw and desire, went far beyond lust. He was mature. Steady. I wanted to sit at his feet and just listen to his voice. He could quote fucking scripture I despised, and I would probably swoon and stare at him with hearts in my eyes.

I didn't know what the fuck was wrong with my fickle ass, but I went with the flow, since I didn't have extra energy to spare while fighting the draw.

Unlike me, Teach still appeared calm and fine as fuck in front of the class, droning on about something I couldn't focus on other than how his low voice soothed me like a cool glass of water on a hot, humid day.

While he flooded my body with delicious tingles, my stomach didn't feel right and hadn't for days. A low burn in my belly, probably from too much caffeine and not enough food, distracted me as much as Matteo's fitting slacks.

That ass...

My mouth watered, same as it had that night he'd fled from our near kiss.

He'd taken off like his ass was on fire, and that image in my head had me thinking all kinds of naughty shit. What I wouldn't do to burn inside those slacks along with him.

A frown flitted over my brow at that thought of me attempting to climb into his pants, and I chuckled. Better I stripped him down...but that would be *escaping* the flames—

"Is there a problem, Mr. Fox?"

I blinked, realizing Teach had addressed me. "Huh?"

"You laughed. Does summarizing and reporting transactions amuse you?" His dark eyes bored into me, and I shifted on the hard seat like I had ants skittering over my backside. My dick also perked up with natural interest for the first time since I'd last sat in his class.

"Um...sorry? Just got a little lost in my head."

His frown deepened over my slow smirk, and I added a teasing glint to my eyes to suggest exactly where I'd gone in my imagination. A very pregnant pause settled between us, the silence as thick as molasses in winter.

Teach cleared his throat and shifted his gaze from my face. He returned to his lecture as though we hadn't just enjoyed a sexually charged stare off.

Damn, the man is luscious.

Sighing, I propped my elbow on my desk and rested my chin in my hand. Even though my stomach continued to burn with discomfort, I enjoyed drinking in the sight of Professor D'Angelo.

His hair hadn't been cut since the first class, and I wanted to sink my fingers into the thick dark strands atop his head. I would hold him still and devour his mouth. Swallow his moans while we frotted together like a couple of horny teenagers. Was he cut or uncut? A leaker like me? Would his mouth taste sweet as candy or hold a hint of depth and darkness I craved like another cup of coffee?

An elbow in my side jolted me out of my fantasy.

I raised an eyebrow at Jazzie, and they grinned with a knowing smile.

Heat rose to my face, but I stuck out my tongue like a kid before turning once more to face front. I hadn't taken a single note from Teach's lecture.

Fuck, I was going to fail if I didn't get my shit together. Thank double fuck for Jazzie and their kick-ass note-taking. We'd met up at the library the week before to go over the information they'd managed to capture that had eluded me. I hoped their tutoring would be enough to help me earn a passing grade on the test we'd had the Friday before.

"As a whole, you all did better than I'd expected last

week." Professor D'Angelo retrieved a stack of papers off his desk and began handing them out. "Two students aced the test, doing away with the curve I usually implement. I suggest those of you who struggled with the first half of this unit go back and study what we've covered up to this point because it will be on the final."

Here it comes.

I'd been nervous as fuck, staying up well past midnight Thursday the week before in attempt to soak in Jazzie's notes through osmosis. Had it been enough? Would I earn a grade I could brag about to Pop?

My heart rate kicked up a few notches as I waited, Teach's voice a low hum in my ears that didn't articulate into words.

He paused in front of me. "Good job on your first test, Mr. Fox."

His words of praise stroked over my mind like a firm grip around my thickening cock. And his raspy voice delivering the gift sent tingles racing down my spine.

I grinned up at him, my face hot.

Goddamn, those dark chocolate orbs sucked me in like a vacuum, tumbling me toward...I wasn't sure, but I fucking loved it.

Wanted more of it.

He tore his focus off me for Jazzie, and my hand shook as I turned over the paper Teach had handed me.

B+.

I got a motherfucking B+!

"Ha!" The sound ripped from me, but I kept the *Take that, Pop!* to myself.

A few snickers sounded, but I didn't give a shit. I bounced a bit on my chair, giddy as a third grader on Christmas morning. Elation ran through me for the final moments of class, and the second we were dismissed, I bolted from my chair.

Same as Professor D'Angelo had done the previous couple of weeks, he hurried through the door ahead of his students as though desperate to escape the room.

Was it the temptation of lingering with me like our first day that sent him scurrying?

I stalked after him with sure steps, desperate to get him alone again for just one minute. My soul craved more of his affirmation. His attention. Feet as determined as my dick, they propelled me forward through the crowded hallway.

I'd already snooped out where his office was, and I knew he didn't have much time between classes. Sure enough, though, he slipped behind his office door.

Fifteen minutes wasn't near enough a number to do everything I wanted with my obsession.

Not bothering to knock, I walked in unannounced.

Professor D'Angelo stood with his back to me facing a sunlit window. His shoulders sagged. "I'm failing," he muttered as I quietly shut the door behind me.

"In what?" I asked, and Teach jolted around, quickly glancing down over my not-so-relaxed posture.

"What are you doing in here?" he asked, that low tone of his doing yummy things to my balls.

I shrugged, quickly taking in the office he obviously shared with someone since two desks occupied the space. Professor Hanson, I assumed since they both taught in the same department and they'd been out for dinner together two weeks earlier. I also recognized the navy cardigan dropped over one of the rolling chairs as Professor Hanson's favorite.

"You need to leave." Teach's tone wavered, the *wanting*

in his eyes suggesting he hoped I would do the exact opposite.

So, I moved inward, strangely desperate to please his instinctive craving rather than his words.

"Sean..." he whispered and swallowed hard, backing against the window as I closed in on him. "What are you doing?"

I dropped my bag and reached for his face. His scruff scraped at my palms, waking my nerve endings and shooting a weird tingling throughout my body. "Kissing you," I murmured, my heart in my throat.

His lips parted, but I didn't give him a chance to talk me out of what I needed more than breath. Teach's hands grabbed hold of my hips as I pressed my mouth to his.

A rushed exhale of relief emptied my lungs at the softness of his lips.

Professor D'Angelo groaned and yanked me closer rather than pushing me away.

Internally squealing with glee, I flicked out my tongue.

He let me in.

Chapter 12

Matteo

The warmth of the sunbeams caressing my back through the window didn't compare to the heat of Sean's lean, tight body pressed against my front. His mouth on mine turned my blood incendiary in a flash. My face burned where his hands touched my skin, and I whimpered...*whimpered*...as I tasted him for the first time.

He was sweet as caramel with a hint of bitter coffee, and I licked into his mouth, addicted after a single stroke of my tongue along his.

A ravenous hunger awoke inside me with roaring force, swelling my cock to the point of aching in seconds. I'd been starved for touch for so damn long, without affection or intimacy of any kind...every inch of me yearned for more.

Ears ringing in a rush of lust, I clutched him closer, hands sliding to his ass for something to hold onto, a grounding force to keep my mind from scattering to the ends of the earth.

Hardness met mine, and our desire doubled, his fingers finding purchase in my hair. Panted breaths accompanied our lashing tongues dueling for dominance. Fingertips bruised. Teeth nipped. Groans and gasps filled the heated air around us.

It had been decades since I'd come hands-free from dry humping, and my balls raced toward a collision course with release.

"Matteo," Sean whispered against my lips, and pre-cum slickened my throbbing cockhead.

Not professor. Not Teach.

He called me by my name with heady desire as though he needed to taste all that I was, every hidden part of me.

Sean shoved his hands between us to get at my belt, and I sagged against the warm window, defenseless against the onslaught of lust coursing through me.

It had been years since someone visibly wanted me, since I'd heard my name spoken with such reverence and yearning.

Breathing heavily, I did nothing to stop Sean's deft fingers from unbuckling my belt. He unzipped my slacks and shoved his hand beneath my boxer briefs, unhindered by my better sense.

"Fuck," I whispered as his hand closed around my aching length.

He took my mouth again, swallowing my moan, devouring the noises rising from inside me.

I trembled at his firm grip, the way his thumb caressed over my slit, spreading the welling slickness I imagined painting over his puckered hole.

While I'd made peace with no longer identifying as straight, the mutual hunger between us slammed the truth home for good.

Sean reached deeper to cup my drawn-up sac, and I

grunted against his mouth. His fingertips toyed with my taint. I widened my stance, pressing up onto my toes on instinct. I'd never taken part in ass play, but the thought of him touching me there—

He massaged over my hole, pulling a low groan from my chest. "Jesus," I whispered harshly against his mouth.

"Hmm," he hummed, continuing with slow strokes until my head spun.

My heart raced, my pulse pounding in my ears as I rutted into his hold on my cock, surprised by how good his touch felt in that forbidden place.

I was going to come...

Sean tore his lips from mine and dropped to his knees, taking my slacks with him.

"Wha—"

The question ripped from my head as his wet mouth engulfed my cock to. The. Root.

"Ungh," I grunted, thrusting, and he swallowed around me.

I grabbed his hair, hissing as he hollowed his cheeks.

He sucked, backing off until my glans kissed the inside of his lips.

But I wasn't having it. I yanked him forward, fucking into his throat, and he took every thrust with grace, moaning like the greedy boy he was.

I got off on the noises of pleasure he made, lusted to empty my balls and fill his belly with my cum.

He didn't gag a single time but grasped at my ass, yanking me forward, fingertips digging into my skin as he swallowed me down.

I'd never...let loose...

Jesus, Sean was killing me.

I shuddered, nearing my end and yet desperate to stay

in the moment of perfection forever. I peered down at where he knelt, intent on taking every inch of my throbbing length into his mouth. Saliva smeared down his chin, his lips reddening from the friction along my cock. The desperation in his lust-hazed eyes, the way his slick tongue worshiped me was nothing short of euphoria. My feet walked on clouds, my soul flying through the highest reaches of heaven as he loved on my body.

Tongue swirling over my cockhead, Sean moaned, his hand once more finding my balls to give them a little tug as though aware I reached the pinnacle of falling into oblivion.

"Sean," I croaked, my knees weakening. "I'm gonna come."

He popped off, a string of saliva connecting us, and he licked it free while glancing up at me. Sky blue eyes full of sunshine and lust met mine and stole my breath.

"I want it," he whispered.

Groaning, fucking powerless against the draw of his desire, I guided him forward once more.

He opened for me.

"Fuck!" I hollered as my taint convulsed and balls erupted. Spurt after spurt of cum hit the back of his throat, and he swallowed around my pulsing girth shoving over his warm tongue. Sounds of gratification leaked from his lips, accompanying my release.

Elation rippled through me, the likes of which I'd never felt before, addictive power and yet soothing liberation.

I held Sean tight against my groin, one more shudder wracking my body as the last of my climax leaked from my shaft. "God," I croaked, gasping for air, my extremities tingling from the mind-numbing pleasure.

He tapped my thigh, reminding me how I'd gotten to such a blissed-out state.

"Sorry—fuck, I'm sorry," I blathered, pulling him off my cock so he could breathe.

Pink flushed his gorgeous face, his eyes watery and luminous as a glorious sunrise after dreary darkness.

I caressed over his flushed cheekbones, lost in a pool of blue, a vast ocean of gentle waves and peaceful depths. A shiver slid down my spine at how beautifully he knelt before me, how much I appreciated his submission. "Sean..."

"Yeah, Teach?" he rasped as though I'd abused his vocal cords.

Teach. Professor...

Reality jolted clear through my brain, slammed against my chest, and stole my breath.

I released my hold on Sean's head too quickly—harshly —and he tumbled onto his ass, hands hitting the hardwood floor to keep himself from falling onto his back.

We stared at each other as coolness from the air-conditioning humming in the background caressed over my wet cock dangling between my thighs. The scent of lust and cum lingered—*poisoned*—the air. Panted breaths escaped me from fucking my *student's* willing throat.

Guilt doused over me like a waterfall, blinding everything—drenching me with unease and the instinct to escape him.

"Y-You have to leave." With suddenly shaking hands, I yanked up my pants, as desperate to right myself as I'd been to shove my cock past his lips. I swallowed hard against the stirring in my guts threatening to erupt up my throat.

Sean slowly pushed to his feet. Hands fisted at his sides, he disobeyed my order. A violent energy rippled between us, a mixture of lust and anger, but I didn't know where either feeling spawned.

"Matteo—"

"No!" I clenched my jaw and lifted my focus to his face even though I feared the outcome of seeing the effects of what we'd done in his eyes.

Those beautiful orbs still shone bright with lust, but hurt radiated from a deeper level.

I bit back a whimper over the insistent desire inside me to pull him against my chest and erase the pain I'd inflicted on him.

"We can't do this," I managed to croak through the panic swilling in my core and mind. "It isn't right."

"Nothing has ever made as much sense as you do," he argued. "I don't know what it is or why I'm drawn to you, but I can't stop it. Can't fucking fight it. I need you, Matteo." Sean stepped closer, but I lifted a shaking hand, halting him as he made contact with me.

The heat of his chest, the hard thumps against my palm gave me a sense I held his heart in my hand.

My eyes stung as he studied my face as though searching for the truth of what I longed for compared to what I'd stated.

He would find me wanting. Desperate for more of him —his taste on my tongue, his touch on my skin.

I licked over my lower lip before swallowing against shards of glass cutting at my throat. "Please, Sean. What we did goes against school policy. I could lose my job." My stomach cramped at the thought.

Still, he stared, unmoving, a willful soul who fought my reasoning.

But I'd caught wind of his other needs while handing him the test he'd surprised me by passing with ease when I'd expected him to fail.

"Be a good boy for me like you were in studying for that

grade, Sean," I whispered, hating myself for manipulating but having no other choice. "Make me proud again."

He melted, his eyes going soft exactly as I'd expected.

Guilt shot through me. I wanted to reach into his chest, inside his mind, and lavish everything he craved on his insecure soul but refrained.

"Be my good boy," I reiterated, not intending to be possessive, but the rasped word sounded so damned right on my tongue.

An image flashed in my head of Sean kneeling at my feet while I sat after a long day at work. His cheek rested on my knee, a smile of contentment on his face.

Katie had been that for me—not a too-young man with more than enough willful sass to share.

The comparison hit like an earthquake, shaking the foundation of my entire being. Not only was he off-limits to me as a student, but Katie owned my heart.

"You really want me to go, Teach?" Sean murmured, his steady gaze still searching my soul as I fought through conflicting emotions.

"Please," I whispered, not sure what I begged for. My fingers itched to curl into his shirt and pull him against me again while my better sense and guilt for being disloyal to the memory of my wife pushed him toward the door.

A slow smirk curled his lush mouth still reddened and swollen from being a fuck toy for my cock.

I tamped down a moan at the memory of his blue eyes staring up at me with delicious hunger.

"I'd rather *come* than *go*," he stated, taking my hand from his chest to lift my knuckles to his lips, "but I'll do as told." Sean pressed the pillow of his soft lips to my skin. "This once."

A jolt of lust swept through my groin. My entire body

tensed at the tease of his tongue between my first two knuckles as though he licked over my asshole.

Jesus...was that something I wanted? Would I ever allow someone to...

No. Absolutely not.

I yanked my hand from his, and he chuckled, adjusting his bulge.

"Until next time, Teach." He grabbed his bag off the floor he'd dropped and sauntered away. The fine globes of his ass flexed beneath his jeans, and I curled my hands into fists, hopelessly hanging on to the memory of how those cheeks had fit in my palms.

My imagination ran away from me.

Taut yet juicy, his ass would jiggle from a healthy slap. Bounce beneath my grasping hands as I pounded into—

I clenched my eyes shut to better enjoy the idea of owning him. Fucking deep into his body until he begged me to let him come.

My lips would spill countless words of praise while he coated the sheets with his release. His hole would squeeze me like a vise, milking every drop of my cum until I filled him full.

The door shut quietly, and I stumbled to my desk, the rush and wane of adrenaline making me weak.

I slumped into my chair, my head falling forward to thump against oak—I didn't feel the pain, simply reminded myself to inhale.

A squeak of hinges and the change of air pressure notified me my too-short moment of privacy in my shared office had ended, but I couldn't be bothered to lift my eyes. No tingles raced over my skin as I'd identified too late when Sean had joined me.

"Hanson," I muttered, my voice as wrecked as my aching insides.

"What did you do, Matteo?" His low, quiet voice whispered his suspicions, without doubt having scented sex on the air.

"Something so very, *very* wrong."

Chapter 13

Sean

I ceased to exist in Matteo D'Angelo's world in the weeks following our little naughty blow job in his office.

He ignored my presence every time I walked into his classroom. He avoided eye contact whenever I stared him down, desperate for a single second of his attention. He dismissed my raised hands and my attempts to talk to him in the crowded hallway.

I'd given in to the urge and finally texted him for clarification on something he'd stated in class—just like he'd told us to do that first day of introductions—rather than asking if he missed my mouth like I wanted to.

He did as asked but never answered my follow-up question about his day.

No longer did he rush to escape the room either. He simply stepped outside the door and lingered where students leaving and coming in for his next class didn't allow anyone a moment alone with him.

Short of getting in his face and pressing against his hard

body again, I couldn't figure out how to break through his walls.

He'd called me his good boy, his voice wrecked as fuck, but I hadn't been able to tell if it was from coming down my throat or a sense of guilt over what we'd done—something supposedly forbidden by school policy.

There was no denying the chemistry between us, the desire born of instinctively knowing a good time could be had by all.

If only he wanted more of what we'd shared, which he obviously didn't.

He'd asked me to make him proud, but I fucking struggled, same as I always had with doing what was proper in others' eyes. Dad had countless rules in his household I'd attempted to obey, but I always failed then was reminded about how much of a disappointment I'd been.

I did not want to have Matteo look at me in the same way, but...

Oh, the but of that truth was powerful as fuck.

His feeling *right* to me, like I'd told him, went bone deep, and not just to my hard dick whenever I remembered dropping to my knees to get him off free of charge. I'd been so needy for him, I'd gone against EEMM's rules, hooking up with my goddamned professor, for fuck's sake.

Wrong on more than one level probably, but I couldn't find a single fuck to give, nor guilt to bother me.

I'd had Matteo's taste on my tongue. His cum inside one of my two holes I wanted him to fill up over and over again.

Jesus, I'm a mess.

I blinked in bleary, tired-as-hell movements that did nothing to bring Teach into focus. It had been a long night, a demanding Tuesday booking that had squeezed every penny's worth from my body.

The client had been rough too, something I hadn't been in the mood for, but the rich prick from overseas wouldn't have understood my pleas to go easy if I'd asked it of him. He'd barely spoken a lick of English, but his hands and dick had stated enough for his mouth. Wanting what he'd paid for, he'd taken his fill of me until I'd sprawled on the hotel bed like a rag doll, drained and wasted.

I'd found release with the help of a little blue pill once to his three climaxes? Four?

My ass ached, and I shifted on the hard chair that offered zero comfort to my sore backside.

For the first time since selling my body for cash, I hadn't enjoyed myself. It had been a chore to bend over, and after getting off, I'd counted down the minutes until the guy's night with me ended.

I hadn't told a soul—not even Drake. The last thing I needed was a reason to catch shit from him or Micah. And if Dad found out I grew weary with whoring myself out?

He would probably laugh or mutter something about not being surprised.

Huffing, I attempted to pull my attention back on where it needed to be, but the sight sent my libido into rev mode.

Professor D'Angelo stood a few feet in front of me, leaning against his desk like he was fond of doing while lecturing, and all I could think about was *him* using me how my client had. All. Night. Long. Insatiable as fuck with grabby hands.

My dick plumped up at the thought, and I sighed, wishing I could bust a nut with Teach, close my eyes while wrapped in his arms, and sleep for three days straight.

My stomach paid for the lack of rest too, burning and roiling from downing a shit ton of coffee. Even though I wanted to pass the fuck out, jitters from too much caffeine twitched my muscles and made sitting still even more difficult than usual.

Teach actually glanced my way, and our gazes entangled in knots after too long of not connecting. My dick plumped up with true arousal, and the slight smile I offered turned as feral as my need. Tension, hot and thick, swelled between us, and I lusted to get on my knees right there in front of everyone and suck him off. Drink down his cum, my ears filled with the sweet curses then praise falling from his lips.

Jesus, I'm fucking obsessed with him.

He turned away, and I heaved a sigh, dropping my focus to my empty notebook. Those delicious few minutes in his office had been a one and done in his eyes...but not mine.

And I was fine as fuck with wanting more. A *shit* ton more of that man. Up my ass. Down my throat. In my bed, on my couch. Hell, in my fucking car. He'd crashed straight through my stance on freedom for life, instead making me wish for exclusivity and permanency.

The girl on my left cleared her throat quietly, and I glanced at her. Lips pursed, she sniffed at me before turning away.

Guess she caught onto that little...whatever it was between Teach and I.

Once class ended, I lagged in packing up my stuff—my notebook as blank as when I'd opened it to a clean page almost an hour earlier.

"Thursday?" I asked Jazzie quietly as they readied to head out too.

"Sean." Their smile looked pained, their dark eyes concerned. "You need to take better care of yourself. You're going to burn out at this pace."

I guessed I still appeared haggard as shit, same as when I'd peered with bleary eyes into the mirror that morning.

"Don't have a choice." I shoved to my feet, my entire body at war with itself. Restless energy and exhaustion. If Jazzie could do it with their crazy-assed schedule, I could too. "So...Thursday?"

They sighed and nodded.

"You're the best."

With a squeeze to my forearm, they left me alone.

I slipped into the less crowded hallway to find Matteo leaning against the wall, arms crossed over his chest in a closed off position if I'd ever seen one.

His reason for keeping distance between us I understood, but the brat in me hated he had to be so goddamn ethical. Strait-laced. A solid, mature man who didn't waver from his morals. But the newly awoken part of me who longed for something more than a plethora of dick was also drawn to Matteo's maturity. He would be the perfect balance to my wildness, the darkness to my light that often shone too bright for many people's comfort.

Taking a risk by hitting on Matteo could have me ending up worse off than I already was: uncomfortable in class with difficulty concentrating.

Was he aware of what I did for work? Had he found out I sold my body for cash, and that became yet another reason he avoided me? Unsurprisingly, my insecurities came up with answers all on their own.

He saw me as lesser...grime under his shoe.

Our eyes connected as I stepped into the hallway, and that last thought dissipated.

Matteo's dark orbs shot through with desire. Troubled want he hadn't allowed me to see earlier in class in front of all his students. The same pained expression after I'd swallowed his cum.

I stepped closer, breathing in the scent of the soap that had set my mouth to watering the night I'd longed to kiss him in the bathroom...and the day I'd dropped to my knees to taste his cock in his office.

Clearing my throat, I grinned. "How's it going, Teach?"

"Mr. Fox." He bit the greeting out, removing his focus from my face to the people in the hallway I couldn't give two shits about.

"Been thinking about you—but I've been a good boy just like you told me to be," I stated quietly, leaning close enough I caught sight of the shiver that raised goose bumps on his forearm.

A muscle ticked in his jaw, but he didn't reply.

"Haven't I?" I pushed, needy as fuck for one word of praise from his delicious lips.

"You have," he conceded quietly.

My heart fucking *soared*, a grin trying to split my face in two.

"Now make my day and tell me how cute I am," I whispered, "how you can't help but remember how I swallowed your dick—and cum."

"Sean," he croaked but refused to give me his eyes or what I'd asked for.

Still, elation swept through me over his cracked façade, like ice water trickling down my throat on a hot day. I leaned in even closer. "What about you? Been behaving yourself—or spending too much time dreaming about me kneeling for you again?"

A shudder ripped through him. "Excuse me, please." Matteo strode down the hall, shoulders tensed.

Exhaling a heavy sigh, I watched him enter the lecture hall next door—Professor Hanson's.

A safe place for him where I wouldn't follow and tempt him. I scowled.

Goddamn it all to fucking hell and back again.

My cell buzzed in my pocket, and grumbling beneath my breath, I pulled it out.

BetsyAnne: **We have a problem.**

"Fuck." I swore internally a few times at my secretary's text.

Me: **Give me a minute.**

Leaving my fantasies behind, I hurried toward the building's rear exit, shoving the door open to a blast of warm, early fall weather. The sun hit my face, and I blinked a few times before I could see well enough to dial the office at Micah's mansion.

She answered with her sex hotline voice any straight man would enjoy the fuck out of.

"What's up, B?" I asked.

"We got a package today that you need to see ASAP." Her tone lost its purr for a hardness I'd never heard from her before.

"New toys?" I joked.

She muttered beneath her breath. "Photos. Lots of them —and they don't cast EEMM in a good light."

My brow furrowed, and I started toward the parking lot rather than my next class, feeling more awake than I had in weeks. "Who the fuck is it from, and what do they want?"

"One of Zack's clients from last month—and he's demanding two mil, or he's leaking these images to the press."

"The fuck did Zack do to him?" I shot out, my blood

injected by a rush of adrenaline as I slammed my car door behind me.

"I called you first, so I have no clue what went down," she said, "but these pictures aren't good, Sean—at *all*."

I roared my car's engine to life and tore out of the parking lot, quickly calculating the fastest way to Micah's, which housed EEMM's office. "Call Zack and have him meet me there. I don't care where he is or what he's doing—tell him it's urgent."

"Should I get in touch with Micah too?"

My lips pursed for a few seconds as I considered her question, my guts suddenly roiling twice as violently. My brother and his wifey had jetted to some island in the Pacific for one reason or another. "Not yet," I answered, my voice shaky at the prospect of facing the shit alone—but wanting to prove myself at the same time. "They're halfway around the world and probably still sleeping."

"See you soon." BetsyAnne hung up.

Had I somehow fucked Elite without lube? Had I not vetted Zack properly before hiring him? Checked into the client enough?

"Shit!" I punched my steering wheel.

Zack had been employee of every month ever since Kellen had retired a year earlier. The tall, dark, and quiet man never complained. Got raving reviews. Kept to himself and didn't cause any drama.

So what the fuck had happened?

The client had pictures, BetsyAnne had stated...something that went against Elite's contracts. No video recordings were allowed, either.

"Hey, Siri—call the office." At least my damned voice didn't shake.

Seconds later, BetsyAnne answered again, her voice smooth as silk as she asked how she could help me.

"What kinds of pictures?" I abruptly cut her off, my patience gone.

My secretary's heavy exhale tensed my already strung-tight shoulders. "It looks like Zack kicked the shit out of him."

"No way." I shook my head, sure I spoke truth. "No fucking way, B. Zack wouldn't do that."

"He's a teddy bear, but the pictures are graphic, the bruises too *real* to be painted on."

As a former social media diva who had made good money as a makeup artist, she would know. BetsyAnne had gotten caught in a compromising scandal that lost her the endorsements she'd been blowing through every time a deposit landed in her bank account. She'd been Elite's gain though.

BetsyAnne liked to talk amongst the employees too, thus my knowledge of her personal life. At least, she didn't gossip outside the office walls as required by the NDA she'd signed when taking the position.

I'd done my homework before hiring her, checking her background thoroughly as Micah had taught me for every new employee of our company, and I trusted her implicitly.

"I don't know, Sean." Her tone worried me. "There's a grainy picture of Zack holding him up against a wall by his neck—and another image shows bruising exactly where his fingertips gripped the guy's throat."

"Fuck!"

"What should I do?" she asked quietly.

"Nothing," I barked. "And keep your mouth shut—don't tell a goddamned soul. Not even the other employees."

"I won't."

I believed her since she'd proven herself as my secretary.

Pain ripped through my guts after we hung up, and I spewed a few curses into the silence inside my car. I probably had an ulcer the size of a hockey puck.

Couldn't one thing go right in my life? My plate was fucking full. I couldn't even find a few spare minutes for the gym, for fuck's sake!

"Goddamnit!" I slammed my fist onto my steering wheel again, nauseous as hell, a migraine brewing behind my eyes.

Something had to give in order for me to not lose my sanity while attending classes atop work—which I had somehow seriously fucked up a week after Micah left the country, putting me in charge.

Balancing it all was proving to be hard as fuck, damn near impossible for my scattered brain.

Jesus fucking Christ.

For the first time since I'd decided to try my hand at college again, I questioned my choice. Was showing Pop that I had everything to classify me as good a man as Micah worth it? Because I'd been falling short since that B+, no matter how I tried otherwise.

I remembered a lifetime of being compared to my brother and always found lacking—the driving force for me to get that damned MBA when I'd failed in my first go-round. I needed validation. Wanted it more than anything.

"Fuck yeah, it's worth it," I growled at myself even though my gut didn't trust the statement.

And the mess boiling around Elite?

I would figure shit out. Had to.

Or I'd prove myself a failure to Micah and all our employees as well.

Chapter 14

Matteo

I'd woken that Wednesday with a raging hard-on that refused to wilt on its own. Vivid dreams had inspired my body's wakefulness, and no matter what I did or didn't do prior to crawling into bed, I couldn't stop the straining morning wood from happening.

But it hadn't been soft flesh and feminine curves haunting me during the night that moved my hand down over my stomach before the sunrise. It wasn't Katie's eyes like I used to see while fisting my cock. She'd been replaced in my dreams by a young man full of sass and brilliant light who kissed with life-giving passion.

Lean muscle and wide shoulders moved beneath me in my mind's eye regardless of the guilt wanting to creep in and stop me from pleasuring myself. A backside made for plundering became my focus as it always did when I failed to stay faithful to the memory of Katie. My strokes intensified with firm intent. He was warm and tight in my fantasy, a perfect sleeve of lubed slickness to take my entire length deep inside his body.

My breath had caught that morning over the thought of

his scruff on my face as I devoured his mouth. Tasting. *Owning.*

I'd grunted while releasing over my flexing abs, repeating my obsession's name with every spurt on my skin.

Sean.

The boy who'd promised to be good, the flirt who'd kept his lips shut but used his eyes to speak to me without care of being found out by those around him. Hunger radiated from him when I'd made the mistake of allowing our eyes to connect. His knowing, secretive smile as though telling me he thought about me earlier that morning as much as I did him. He'd shifted on his seat as though the mere clashing of our eyes had hardened his cock.

Sean exercised more restraint than I'd expected upon first meeting him, but he pushed buttons that morning as his voice had taken part in tearing down my stoic reserve.

His questioning if I'd been behaving or thinking about him on his knees for me created cracks in the walls I'd attempted to build in order to keep my job and my sense of loyalty to Katie.

"Excuse me, please," was all I'd managed to rasp from my working throat before turning away.

Cursing, I strode up the hallway, needing space to escape the temptation of him. His stare burned my backside, and I longed to spin back around, to tell him how badly I wanted him, how he haunted my dreams while sleeping and awake, fidelity and propriety be damned.

For the previous year, I'd honestly tried to get back into the land of the living, Hanson and Albert attempting to help, but I hadn't found anything to interest me. None of their outings, not a single suggestion to set me up on a blind date with a woman had stirred desire inside me.

But Sean did so in spades.

Sexuality was definitely fluid, but strangely, only he pulled my attention in such a way.

Every day since that heated moment in my office, I had covertly checked out other male students of all shapes and sizes, coloring too. I could admit to many being good-looking, but zero trace of sexual-related need buzzed through my blood. Not a lick of lust suggested I rip off their clothes, slam them against walls, or bite the sly smirks off their lips.

And every day Sean Fox had entered my classroom with his magnetic pulses of warmth wanting to entice me closer, my body came alive with the desire to do those very things and then some. Never mind the memory of his blue eyes sucking at my soul as thoroughly as he'd done to my cock.

Stirrings of guilt hadn't allowed my gaze to linger on Sean that moment in class regardless of his magnetic draw. Katie was no longer with me, but I couldn't help feeling like shit whenever I woke and took care of my throbbing balls thanks to the blond boy slinking into my dreams.

Hanson eyed me from where he gathered his belongings, late in leaving his classroom. Two students still remained, deep in discussion at the back of the room.

At the look on my face, Hanson pursed his lips and shook his head as if recognizing I needed to unload—and shouldn't in public.

I nodded and followed him to our shared office a minute later.

Our door shut us in privacy. "What's happened now?" he asked.

I slumped in my chair, head tipped back and eyes closed. "The temptation of him..."

"Matteo."

"I know." I scrubbed a hand over my scruff and exhaled loudly.

"Had anyone else walked in here a few minutes earlier that day..."

Swallowing hard, I acknowledged what he'd reminded me of before. Hanson was a good friend to protect my secret, my moment of weakness in crossing a line that would terminate my employment.

"Do you enjoy teaching eager minds? Encouraging them to pursue their dreams?"

"You know I do," I muttered the absolute truth, the passion I held for my job. But oh, the sweet lure to taste Sean's mouth often filled my mind, making me forget how much I valued being a professor.

"Remember Joe Barkley," Hanson reminded me, his tone kind yet firm—same as he'd done that morning after I'd confessed to what I'd done with my student while the sunshine had warmed me from the back—and front.

No college would trust me with another students if our mistake had been found out by someone other than my friend. Getting off, exploring the newborn desires inside me wouldn't be worth the cost to my professional life.

Period.

But damnit, I was tired of fighting and even more exhausted from sleep that hadn't proven restful thanks to intense dreams that left me hard every morning. Even my pre-dinner jogs hadn't deadened my mind from lingering on Sean.

My jaw cracked on a yawn. The night before had been riddled with images of the many ways I wanted to explore his body. Monday and Wednesday were the two days I looked forward to most—and dreaded.

His eyes had appeared wearier than normal, and I

wondered if the stress of going back to college affected him. I didn't know him outside the classroom or what he did for work. How did he provide for himself? Did someone else? Family? A sugar daddy?

I frowned at the thought, my lips tightening as Hanson shuffled things around his desk, allowing quietness between us for me to consider his reminder about Joe that I'd disregarded within seconds of him saying the man's name.

My focus remained on the one I couldn't keep from my mind.

Who was Sean Fox beyond a sexy young man who'd awakened feelings inside me I'd never expected or considered possible as a widow?

I'd made the mistake of catching his gaze within minutes of my lecture that morning.

A slow smirk had warmed his blue eyes—more sweet than his usual sassy—but still, a zing had gone straight to my groin, stirring life I'd extinguished earlier that morning with my hand.

I hadn't been able to look away, but I'd managed to withhold my desire from my eyes. At least, I hoped so.

Still, he'd seemed to know, the little brat, as his smile had turned...coy. Like the mischievous creature that shared his surname, he'd flicked his tongue over his lower lip, the hint of pink promising warmth I remembered too damn well. Wetness I wanted to taste again regardless of it being wrong.

I had stumbled through my words, my groin stirred to life, and I fought to keep from displaying it through my slacks for the class to see.

His bowed head in my periphery had begged me to see the action as submissive when I expected he would be no such thing in bed. Even still, his mussed hair had called to my fingers to grab hold and own like I'd had the opportunity to do in my office.

A slow exhale lowered my shoulders as I admitted to my powerlessness. That stir of anger or perhaps annoyance I'd felt when I'd first laid eyes on the kid returned. While I didn't consider myself a Dom, I disliked not being in control —during intimacy and otherwise.

Sean Fox knocked me off-balance and had made me question my identity.

Although I'd come to terms and accepted the fact I found myself sexually attracted to a male, I disliked the continued unrest he caused me. Thoughts of him pushed me to set aside Katie and the loving marriage we'd had.

"Matteo?" Hanson broke the quietness.

I heaved a sigh and pushed to my feet. While he got to enjoy a break, I had another lecture to give.

"You could be open with the dean and explain the situation minus your moment of weakness. I'm sure she would have no issue with a request to have Sean's schedule changed."

I nodded as though assuring him I would consider the idea, but the thought of not seeing my obsession again, not having the radiance of his sunshine on my face twice a week sent an ache through my chest.

Somehow, I managed to keep my mind off my addiction throughout the remainder of the day.

Once enclosed in the privacy to my too-quiet home that night, I did my usual routine, putting my things away while seeing memories of Katie in every corner of the home we'd rehabbed and made our own.

The empty hangers in the coat closet that used to hold her outdoor clothing. The mat beneath where only my shoes now sat awaiting a run or work the next morning. The lack of a savory meal in the oven lovingly prepared by her soft hands. Her smile and soft kisses she offered when I'd returned home every evening.

I couldn't imagine Sean being in our space no matter how hard I longed for his presence beside me. I also couldn't help doing what I'd withheld from since the day I'd met Sean Fox.

I collapsed in my favorite recliner where I'd sat whenever Katie needed to kneel for me. Pushing aside lingering sadness over my loss and the too quiet living room, I logged into the first of two social media sites I used to browse years earlier. Over a dozen accounts came up at my search for his name, but the sixth profile pic revealed a grinning face I'd seen behind closed eyes too often and yet not enough.

His background image had recently been updated, showing him with five other guys, all dressed up and holding beers, arms slung around one another. The man beside him in the center wore a tux, a rose pinned to his lapel.

The picture was from a wedding, most likely.

A scroll through Sean's feed revealed other images of get-togethers, plenty of beer bottles, and tagged friends—but nothing indicated he was in a relationship of any sort. He tended toward affectionate, though, hugging some and sitting on others' laps. He smooched a guy's cheek who pushed at him in one image.

Jealousy rushed through me, but I appreciated the guy had attempted to get away from Sean.

I read the name listed of the man...Micah Fox.

He was definitely a relative seeing as how they looked somewhat alike with their blond hair and blue eyes, similar smiles, and square jawlines.

I clicked on Micah's name and scrolled through his

profile that hadn't been updated in a couple of years beyond a single picture. He'd married and had posted a family photo. Sean stood on his right along with whom I assumed were their parents and Micah's bride.

Once back on Sean's profile, I didn't find anything surprising. He enjoyed partying, mostly with men. He was out and proud, loud too from some of the videos he'd been tagged in from earlier in his twenties.

His active Instagram account included updates on college he obviously felt proud of himself for attempting to tackle, almost daily postings of him in the gym up through the beginning of school, and a dozen images from that wedding earlier in August. Summer adventures he bragged about included a trip to some tropical island, deep sea fishing, and mountain biking up in the White Mountains. I'd never done the first two, but the final used to be a favorite outing for Katie and I. I considered my bike that sat in the basement collecting dust, but the depressing thought diminished at the next image.

Sean dressed up in a black on black tux and heading to "work" he'd said.

My cock perked up as I imagined peeling the clothing off him one item at a time. Unwrapping him would be the perfect Christmas present.

But what sort of job required putting on such tailored to fit clothing? The fine tux molded to his body hadn't come from a corner rental shop.

Diving deeper down the rabbit hole didn't reveal how Sean filled his bank account, but the boy definitely had money, as did his brother.

Their mother was on social media but rarely posted. Enough though to let me know their father was a blue-collar worker rather than the type of parent who could afford to spoil Sean with the Ray-Bans or fancy watches he wore in every picture.

And Sean's swanky condo on Boston Harbor he called *home sweet home* after closing on the place the year before? The boy made bank somehow.

Maybe an inheritance, I mused, or a lucky investment.

Heaving a heavy exhale, I shut down my phone and rubbed my eyes. What did it matter who Sean was outside a sexual being, a flirt I couldn't rid my mind of? What drove my curiosity about him and his life?

Maybe I ought to download one of those dating apps my sister had suggested last time she'd visited with her daughter. Perhaps I needed to do what Katie told me to and find someone to help me learn how to smile again. I could look for something casual to help me break through the restrictions I'd placed on myself.

I didn't believe in any afterlife that would allow me to hurt Katie's feelings, so why did the idea of being intimate with a female other than my wife make me sick? Why did my insides clench up and threaten to hurl at the mere thought of another woman's flesh beneath my hands and mouth? Why did I glance around our home, imagining her in Katie's place and shudder with vile revulsion?

The idea of *Sean* in my space, however, didn't cause my body to react in the same way.

Strangely, my groin roused yet again at the fantasy of trailing fingertips over his skin as he sprawled over my bed. My blood heated over slipping my tongue into his mouth and swallowing his moans as he came undone beneath me. I yearned to explore him and the unexpected desire he'd lit inside me with driving force I failed at ignoring.

He was all sorts of voodoo I didn't believe in but couldn't deny with my body's response.

But codes of conduct and the fear of somehow hurting Katie remained.

I would do well to remember both so I wouldn't do something stupid again and end up living with even more regrets than those that already littered my soul.

Chapter 15

Sean

"**I** didn't do that."

I believed Zack's adamant response to the pictures I had sprawled over my desk.

He leaned forward from where he sat across from me and picked up the two I tapped at, lifting them closer. "Little fucker had a hidden camera." Lips pursed, he shook his head while studying the grainy image of him propping the young client against the wall by his neck. "You can't see it in this image, but his feet were on the ground, and I barely held him. Didn't cut off his oxygen because he'd specifically asked me not to."

Zack shifted his attention to the second, a closeup of the young man's face that showed bruising where Zack's fingers had supposedly been the day before the picture was taken.

Jackson Zerig was a twenty-seven year old waif who'd been a client of Zack's the month before. There'd been nothing special about him...he had brown hair and eyes, a nondescript type of person one would see on the street and immediately forget about, but there was no denying the guy in the both images was the same man.

I always booked new clients. It had been *me* who'd put Jackson in a room with Zack.

"He wants two million in cash or he'll leak these to the press," I stated quietly, my stomach a rock, my shoulders hitched up near my ears.

Zack paled at my declaration, his focus jerking up to my face. "But I didn't do this!" he reiterated, his voice raised to a point I hadn't heard from him before. He'd never even skirted the edge of losing his shit. "I barely put any pressure on his neck!"

"I believe you, so I'm assuming the bruising all over the rest of his body is makeup. We're going to prove it—you have nothing to worry about," I assured Zack even though I didn't feel as though my words held weight, nor did I have a clue how to go about doing what I'd promised.

I'd wracked my brain throughout the half-hour drive to Micah's mansion and the addition which housed Elite's office, and I'd come up with nothing. My brain refused to think of any creative way other than offing the asshole attempting to extort the family business Micah had built from the ground up.

My temples throbbed, but I had Zack recount his night with Jackson Zerig from beginning to end—twice. We went over the contract together where the client's limits listed anything beyond vanilla. He'd wanted to be wined and dined, something Zack excelled at, thus the booking choice on my end. He was the perfect escort for what Jackson Zerig had requested.

Had the asshole planned to do this from the very start?

I'd looked over his paperwork, the contract and NDA he'd signed, but hadn't caught a hint of a red flag. Not even a sixth sense had raised hair on my neck about the guy.

I bet Micah would have sniffed something fishy out

though. He wouldn't have booked the new client if he'd been the one to look over Jackson's application. Surely, I'd missed something.

Guilt and shame sat heavy on my shoulders. The issue facing us was my fault. Plain and simple.

Elite was a legal business, but attempting to fight Jackson would definitely lead to too much exposure and attention that might prove bad for our image.

"The quarterly meeting is Saturday," Zack felt the need to remind me. "When does Micah get back?"

A piece of me cracked inside, but I refused to show how my employee's words hurt. I was the gay branch manager, but I clearly wasn't trusted by more than just myself to take care of shit. "Friday," I bit the word out.

"You'll talk to him as soon as he's stateside?"

Teeth clenched, I nodded.

"Shit." Zack shook his head again and tossed the images onto my desk. He scrubbed a hand over his mouth. "Tell Micah I'll do whatever necessary—answer any questions— go on record, for fuck's sake, if that's what he needs."

I nodded.

What Micah *needs.*

More words to make me feel like an incompetent fuckup.

Hashtag definitely not winning. Better yet? Loser.

BetsyAnne poked her head inside my office door a few seconds after Zack left me alone to stew in anxiety that burned my stomach. "Anything I can do for you, boss?" she asked, her word choice soothing the part of me having a pity party.

"I'm going to call Micah," I said since I'd only failed to that point and had no other options that my tired brain could come up with.

Pay him or off him. I didn't have the means for the first and didn't know anyone capable of doing the second without getting caught.

"I'll see you Saturday at the quarterly meeting?" she asked, studying me as though she could read my mind.

"Noon, right?" I asked absently.

"Yeah."

I nodded. "I'll be there."

BetsyAnne left me in oppressive silence, and I heaved a heavy exhale, slouching in my chair. Damning images scattered over my desk, and fear snaked through my guts at the thoughts of worst-case scenarios.

Something like this can bury us.

No more Elite Escorts, gay or otherwise. No more dick, balls, or holes smorgasbord. No more getting paid for the pleasure of using my body. And definitely no more living the high life as a once again blue-collar worker who stocked shelves overnight at the grocery store.

Micah was going to be pissed...I'd messed up for real this time.

"Fuck." I muttered a few more curses.

Sure, I could wait the two days for Micah to get home, but the sooner I tossed shit out into the open, the sooner he could come up with an answer to protect us.

I swiped my cell to life and called my brother, the golden boy, the one who didn't make mistakes like I did. He would know what to do to ensure Elite would escape this unscathed.

I had a client Friday night, but I couldn't focus worth a shit. A blue pill helped me fumble my way through the first round. Thank fuck the guy was vers and wanted to pound my ass the second time. What sucked a pickled prick was the fact that fuck with me bent over the end of the hotel bed took place at three in the morning.

When I got home at six, I collapsed, passing out before my head hit the pillow.

Micah had calmly assured me during our short phone conversation that he would handle shit but refused to cut his vacation short. He'd gotten into town Friday late afternoon, but I'd already been on the way to pleasing our client so had yet to speak to him about whatever plan he'd cooked up.

I trusted him, so my brain *should* have relaxed over the entire situation. Not so. The whole pile of shit had hounded my mind and body non-fucking-stop to exhaustion like I'd never experienced.

A buzzing noise roused me but silenced before I forced my eyelids open. Sighing, I snuggled deeper into soft sheets and warmth, every inch of me needing to slip back under. But my damned brain got moving on the what-ifs.

The buzzing started up again.

"Jesus fucking Christ," I muttered against my pillow, wanting to cry like a little bitch. "Leave me the fuck alone!"

A third interruption made me lift my head to blink bleary eyes at my alarm clock.

Twelve-thirty.

In the afternoon.

"Oh fuck!" I pushed up to sit on the edge of my bed and grabbed my cell, my insides turning liquid, rumbling in a flash.

Micah: **Where the fuck are you?**

"Shit, shit, shit." Once more, I revealed to the world how much of a fuckup I truly was. When Micah had announced the MM branch of Elite at the Christmas party and put me in charge, I'd promised him I wouldn't let him down. For the first time, I'd really believed in myself, in my determination to grow up and prove I could be responsible.

I doubted Micah was surprised I'd failed, and I could only imagine what Pop would say when he found out about the mess I'd created by contracting Zack with an asshole bent on ruining us.

At least I'd learned to own my mistakes rather than lying to cover my ass as I would have done prior to becoming part of Micah's team.

Me: **Overslept. Late night with a client.**

Micah: **What the fuck?? Get your ass to my place NOW. You're the manager, so fucking act like it!**

Micah never used exclamation points. Ever.

"Goddamnit!" I slapped my cell back onto my bedside table, and my shaking legs took me into the bathroom where my insides exploded outward.

Fucking hell, anxiety was a fucking cunt. But better rumbling bowels than an ulcer.

I was already a disappointment and going to be the last person showing up at the mansion for our quarterly meeting, so what was a few more minutes? No fucking way would I be able to focus without at least showering.

Shortest time getting ready behind me, I sped westward out of the city toward Micah's, my stomach only somewhat settled. Dismay weighed heavy on my shoulders, making me feel even worse than what I'd been dealing with since shit had gone down on Wednesday.

Thanks to an accident and having to be rerouted after twenty minutes of being stuck in traffic, I pulled into Micah's driveway over an hour after he'd woken me up. Only a few employees' cars remained, and I cursed while climbing from mine.

He was going to hand me my ass in front of people. Good fucking time for me.

Stomach churning again, adrenaline making me tremble, I let myself into the office addition I'd parked in front of. A clandestine peek through the opened door leading into Micah's house revealed the meeting had definitely ended.

Micah, BetsyAnne, Drake, Zack, and the new guy, Jimmy, still lounged in the living room on my right, unaware of my presence.

Whatever snacks my sister-in-law had set out were gone, mere crumbs on the three plates atop the coffee table.

"Hey, little brother." Jasmine approached from the kitchen on my left with a sweet smile, offering me a cup of steaming coffee.

Her kindness eased some of my anxiety.

"You're a lifesaver," I mumbled, taking note of her pale cheeks. "You okay?"

"Little stomach bug, but no big deal." She handed over her gift without touching me.

Maybe that was what had plagued me earlier.

"Don't take his pissiness personally, okay?" she whispered. "He's on edge, and everyone oversleeps sometimes."

Forcing a smile, I nodded and headed toward the group of people now eyeing me. "Sorry I'm late," I said, trying for my usual carefree attitude.

"Sit your ass down," Micah ordered, his tone hard. He sounded so much like Pop that goose bumps rippled down my spine and suggested my flight instincts get me the hell out of there.

I collapsed onto the couch beside Drake instead since fleeing the scene would only make shit worse for me.

"You can read the meeting notes from BetsyAnne later. What matters right now is this mess with the Zerig guy. I filled everyone in on what happened since this could affect all of us. While I have the money he's asking for, I refuse to bow to extortion."

"Think we can we prove the images are fakes?" I asked.

"*After* he releases them to the press and brings attention we don't need?" Micah asked, his blue eyes glinting.

"We should cut his legs off before he takes another step," Drake stated, crossing his arms, legs spread as always when on a couch. The dude was a beast.

"We're not going to do anything illegal—no violence," my brother declared, matter of fact.

Drake huffed a snort. "Not *literal* legs. We need to find something or some way to bribe him out of going to the press or threaten to extort him in return if he continues with his plan."

"What do we have on him?" BetsyAnne asked.

"Only the information in his file," I said, having looked over the guy's paperwork a half dozen times since Wednesday.

"What about your friend Reid Sullivan?" Jasmine asked Micah. "Isn't his uncle a detective or something? Some bigwig in the Boston PD?"

"Reid's uncle used to be the Chief of Police," Micah answered. Reid was one of Micah's best buds and a retired Elite who'd found the love of a lifetime like my brother had.

Silence settled for a moment.

"JJ—James Jenner," I spoke up as soon as the thought

crossed my mind. "Kellen's man was a detective before they moved up to Maine. Maybe he can help us find some shit on this asshole."

Micah nodded, his eyes lighting as he pulled his cell from his pocket.

A sense of finally doing something good trickled through my insides, easing my tension the slightest bit. I actually inhaled without my chest wanting to cave in on itself.

My brother put through a call and set it on speaker.

Kellen answered after the third ring. "Micah! What's up?"

"A shit ton," Micah muttered. "Is your man nearby?"

"Yeah—hold on." Kellen's voice had lost its jolly tone. "We're down here visiting Mason and Jasper this weekend. Everything okay?"

"Not really."

"Shit. Mind if I listen in?" he asked, a door closing and another reopening in the background.

"Not at all," Micah said. "Feel free to have Mason and Jasper do the same. We'll take whatever ideas any of you might have."

"It's Micah," Kellen said, his voice muffed. "Sounds like some shit hit the fan. Gonna put him on speaker."

"Micah?" JJ greeted with a question in his tone. "What's going on?"

I fought to sit still and sip my coffee while Micah caught the two retired EEMM employees and their partners up on what Elite faced.

No one spoke for a few seconds once Micah went quiet.

"I was hoping that with being a detective, you might give us some direction on what to do, JJ," Micah finally said, his voice sounding unsure for the first time in his life.

My world shifted slightly off-balance. Since when did the golden boy not have his shit together? The fact he didn't already have a plan in place was more than troublesome to my already worried brain.

"I don't have the kind of contacts you're going to need for something like this," JJ finally said. "And unfortunately, no one on the force owes me any favors I could call in to cross a morally gray line it seems like you might need."

"Fuck." Micah scrubbed a hand over his face.

"I'm sorry," JJ tacked on, obviously having heard the unusual stress in my brother's voice.

"Don't worry about it." Micah exhaled loudly. "I'll figure something out—I always do. Kellen, you guys coming over tomorrow for the game?"

"Yeah, we'll be there," Kellen replied.

"Mason? Jasper?" Micah questioned.

"Wouldn't miss it," Mason assured us, his tone calmer than everyone. I expected he leaned against Jasper, soaking in the peace of his younger man and soulmate.

Envy trickled through my mind, shifting my thoughts toward Matteo.

I sighed, wishing I could just sit at Teach's feet, close my eyes, and fucking *rest*.

"Well." Micah rubbed his hands down his thighs after hanging up. "There's nothing else we can do for now. Drake, you're booked for tonight?"

"Yeah," my best friend said.

"Zack?" Micah asked.

"Just eye candy for me tonight, thank fuck."

My brother turned to the final employee, who'd sat silent since I'd arrived. "Jimmy?"

He shook his blond head.

Micah nodded and stood. "Every one of you had better be on your best behavior, got it?"

Fuck, he sounded like Pop.

"No funny business," Micah continued, "and if you catch a whiff of anything that stirs your sixth sense, call it in, and I'll take care of ending the night's contract."

Both Drake and Zack nodded.

Drake clasped my shoulder before standing. "You need anything..."

I nodded, expecting he could figure out I might require a night on the town with a bottle or two of vodka after my brother reamed me out.

Chapter 16

Sean

I'd avoided Micah's gaze until the door closed behind Drake, leaving us alone. Jasmine tinkered around in the kitchen outside earshot, so at least I wouldn't be too embarrassed by whatever my brother had to say.

Stomach in knots and guts once more churning, I waited for Micah to start in on me—how I'd somehow missed red flags he wouldn't have. How I hadn't done enough to protect Elite.

"You're stretched too thin," Micah stated firmly.

Not what I'd been expecting at all. What happened to *I'm disappointed in you* or *you fucked up?*

"What?"

"Have you looked in the mirror lately?" Micah's forehead furrowed. "You're exhausted, Sean. Worn down. There's bags under your eyes, and you've obviously lost weight from burning the candle at both ends."

I rubbed a weary hand over said eyes, feeling every damned thing he'd stated. While I hadn't stepped on a scale since the last time I'd been to the gym, my tight jeans had felt a little loose when I'd put them on the night before.

And here comes the part where he tells me to go home and never come back.

"You need to give up the partying and focus on work and college."

"That's all I *am* devoting my every waking hour to," I argued, frowning at his comment on my lack of discipline he'd assumed.

"You haven't been out with Drake lately?"

"Three weeks ago."

Micah's eyebrows shot up. "Seriously?"

I nodded, baffled by how the conversation went when I'd been sure Micah would can my ass or at least scream at me like Pop would have done.

Jasmine walked into the living room, disrupting our private conversation. She went straight to Micah, and he stood, his expression growing concerned as he eyed her. With her back to me, she leaned into him, letting out a heavy sigh. He wrapped his arms around her, nuzzling against the side of her head.

"Okay?" he whispered.

"Still feel sick."

"Maybe we should stay home tonight," he said.

She shook her head against his neck. "No. It's been too long," she stated, her voice muffled from her face smooshed against his skin. "We need it. *I* need it."

Micah rubbed her back while I looked on with jealousy snaking through me. All through my teenage years and twenties, I thought for sure my older brother would be a playboy bachelor for life like I'd planned on. No one had tempted him to settle down. It had taken a younger woman with touch issues to snag hold of his heart and ensnare him thoroughly.

Fuck, how my future expectations had flipped—my heart no longer beat for myself.

Even if it meant making do with one man's body for a lifetime, to share in something like Micah and Jasmine did... Yeah. I wanted that.

But with a man who was determined to keep me at arm's length.

Micah pulled back to cradle his wife's face in his hands even though their entire fronts touched from chest to knees. "Why don't you go lie down," he suggested quietly. "I'll finish cleaning up our mess then come check on you. We can decide then if we're going."

She nodded, and he kissed her forehead.

Turning, she caught my eye. I'd noticed she'd seemed a little off earlier, but she'd gone from pale to green around the gills.

"Still not feeling well?"

"Haven't been for a few days, but I'm definitely on the mend." She attempted a perky tone but failed.

"Take a nap for me while you're at it," I said with a grin, hoping to make her smile. It worked just enough to curl her lips upward.

"I'll try."

"See ya later, Sis."

"You too, brat," she murmured, quietly slipping away to leave me alone with my brother again.

"So no partying, huh?" He went right back to it, and once more the muscles in my body tensed in preparation for flight like I tended to do whenever I got into trouble.

"Nope."

"Are you drinking at home instead?"

"The six-pack I picked up Tuesday night is still sitting in my fridge untouched."

My brother stared with widened eyes as though I'd shocked the hell out of him.

I used to down beer every night and partied a few times a week when I wasn't escorting, so he had every right to be surprised. Dry evenings were definitely not my norm unless I was out to prove I could have them on occasion.

I leaned forward, elbows on my knees. "Outside Elite, all I'm doing *is* school shit. Studying. Writing papers. Attending lectures. I even have someone tutoring me on Thursday nights at the library. I haven't been to the gym in weeks, and I'm popping little blue pills to help me please clients." I ended my spewed unload abruptly, my face heating as I shifted back on the couch.

"Damn," Micah murmured, staring from where he sat on the ratty recliner he refused to part ways with. "Maybe you need to take a break."

"The semester is far from over—"

"From Elite."

I snapped my jaw shut.

And there it was, exactly as I'd expected. I was being let go for fucking up.

"Stop escorting until you're settled in with school," Micah continued before I could mutter a word—but again, he didn't say what I had expected. "Or better yet, wait until you're done."

"You aren't firing me for this clusterfuck situation? Or the fact I overslept?"

"Fuck no." Micah gave me a baffled look. "You aren't responsible for what this fucker is doing to us, and considering how you're stretched to the cracking point, I'm not surprised you overslept."

Well, fuck.

I sank into the couch boneless, my lungs emptying as I

stared at my brother. He'd never been outright unkind to me, even while joking, but the blatant...kindness, his under-standing spread warmth through me. Tears suddenly stung my eyes.

"But I'm serious about taking some time off. No more booking yourself with clients until you get your degree."

"That'll be two years!" I couldn't imagine going that long without a smorgasbord of dick to help me get off, since as an Elite I wasn't allowed to browse my old haunts—clubs and apps.

"Are you hurting for money?"

"Well, no."

"You'll still act as manager and get that salary," Micah reasoned. "Just give up the fucking part for a while, so you don't stay out too late and miss important meetings."

I actually considered Micah's suggestion even though he'd tossed it out along with a dig attached. At least he hadn't sounded like Pop, his voice laced with disdain. The sex work had *felt* laborious, like a dreaded Monday morning every night I'd been booked with a client.

"Would that mean I could hook up again just for the hell of it?" I asked, my tone a little cautious along with a hint of hopeful, my mind flitting toward a certain professor. "Because you know I can't go a week without dick."

Micah shrugged, his lips twitching as though he fought against a secretive smirk. "If you aren't available for clients, you'll have to find a way to get off somehow, I suppose. Have at it—just don't pull all-nighters and make this escorting break a waste of your time and energy."

Fucking was *never* a waste of energy.

I focused on Matteo's presence in my head. I would be free to be a naughty boy...to pursue what he denied us because of some silly ethical standards. One glide of his dick up my tight ass and he'd change his tune. I just had to get him between my thighs. Or behind me. Hell, he looked strong enough to hold me up against a wall.

I would take Teach inside me however the fuck I could.

"I'll think about it," I said even though I'd already made up my mind. I opened my mouth to adjust my answer and set it in stone that I was free to fuck around, but in typical ADHD form, a wayward thought shot through my brain. "Preston!"

"Huh?"

"Preston...a client from last year. He was pretty faithful there for a while, and I don't know what the fuck just reminded me, but the guy is a self-proclaimed computer nerd. He's a local private contractor—programmer—all that technology shit that baffles me. Maybe he could help us?"

"At this point, I'm close to desperate," Micah replied. "Can't hurt to see if he'd be able to dig anything up on this Jackson asshole."

"Stay here," I ordered, hopping to my feet. "I'll go grab his file." Excitement fluttered inside me. While JJ hadn't been able to point us in the right direction, maybe my second suggestion could.

I sifted through the folders in alphabetical order in the files beside BeckyAnne's desk, recalling what else I could about Preston. He was a redhead...Drake's kryptonite. Funnily enough, the guy had the same first name as Drake's stepbrother he hardly ever mentioned but definitely different than Casswell, the surname his stepmom had kept when she'd married Drake's dad.

It was a good thing the client hadn't requested my best friend. Drake probably would have fallen hard and fast, adding another Elite to the tumble-into-love bug that had taken so many of our employees off the available list.

Preston Gibbons.

"Bingo." I hurried back to Micah and went to hand the client information form over but paused. "Can I call him?"

Micah nodded. "Go for it."

Even more of the lingering heaviness in my chest eased at the trust Micah showed me.

I dialed and put the phone on speaker before setting both onto the coffee table between us. It rang twice.

"Hello?"

"Preston?" I asked, glancing at my brother who focused on my phone with a grim look on his face.

"Yes—who's calling, please?"

"This is Sean Fox from Elite Escorts."

"Mr. Fox, what a pleasant surprise!" His tone hinted at happiness along with...wariness? Shame, perhaps? He wouldn't be the first that had stopped booking with us due to guilt over hiring a sex worker.

"I'm sorry to bug you," I went on, "but Elite is facing something a little...troubling, and I was hoping you might be able to help us."

"Tell me what the issue is, and if I'm able to be of assistance, and we can come to a financial agreement on the cost, I would be happy to."

The guy was so damn proper and well-spoken. Loaded as fuck too.

I glanced over at Micah again, and he nodded, allowing me to take the lead. The following half-hour conversation centered around Jackson Zerig and all that had transpired since the package had arrived on Wednesday. While we took a chance in spreading information we'd rather not have leaked to the public, we'd done right by Mr. Gibbons and had never encountered any issues with him or the NDAs he'd signed.

Mr. Gibbons informed us of his cost, which Micah agreed to without hesitation.

"First thing you need to do is acknowledge the man's request. Jackson Zerig is an alias, by the way," Preston said. "The guy doesn't exist."

We'd heard a keyboard clacking in the background while I had spoken. Obviously, Preston didn't waste any time and had all sorts of hacking tricks up his sleeve.

I'd gone through Zerig's paperwork again and hadn't noted anything strange about the copy of his license we had on file. That shit looked authentic as fuck.

"It sounds as though you've done some digging like this before," Micah said, grinning across the coffee table at me, hope in his eyes.

"A time or two," Preston admitted, "but same as Elite, I require NDAs. Seeing as how you have enough information on my closeted ass to make waves in my life, I believe I can trust you and vice versa."

"You have our word we will not speak of your involvement with anyone," Micah assured him.

"When he gets in touch with you like he promised to do, tell him you'll need some time to get the funds together," Preston continued, all business. "Use whatever stall tactic you can. Get him to hold off as long as possible so I can work my magic."

"Will do," Micah said, and I nodded.

"I promise I'll find out who he really is. What he's hiding and how you can use that information to hopefully dissolve the situation Elite is facing."

I hung up and once more glanced over at my brother.

"I'm glad you remembered this guy from…" Micah looked over Preston's information form, which listed the two Elite's he'd booked with—Mason and Kellen. "Last year?"

He glanced up at me, surprise lifting his eyebrows once more. "Good job, Sean."

I soaked in his words of praise, a sweet sting stabbing my chest. "Thanks."

My footsteps no longer dragging, I walked out Micah's door ready to head home and study while we waited on Preston to work his magic, as he'd said. Fingers crossing, I shot off a prayer to whatever saints might actually exist.

A cardinal flitted across the sidewalk on quick feet, chirping at me with a side-eye glance. A grin split my face as I thought of my mom's father, Grandpop. Cardinals had always been his favorite bird. He'd even turned his back on the Red Sox to follow the baseball team from St. Louis, the traitor. We'd had plenty of fake arguments when I'd been a kid.

I drove toward Boston, my stomach calm for the first time in fucking forever and headache gone. I hadn't gotten reamed out like I'd expected, and Preston's confident tone had given me hope everything might actually turn out okay.

While the rest of the day lay open ahead of me with hours available to focus on school, I decided to take a few for myself. But not to drink.

I pulled into the cemetery where Grandpop and Grandma rested. It had been months since I'd last visited. The skittering bird looking at me like I was trouble reminded me too much of my childhood hero and a proper father figure to ignore the sign I felt sure he'd sent me from over the rainbow bridge.

A slight chill clung to the late afternoon air, but the sun still hung in the sky, warming the patches of brown grass not in shadow.

"Hey, Grandpop," I stated, patting his headstone. "Grandma."

Sighing a lungful of fresh air, I sat cross-legged on the ground in front of their shared marker. Tranquil silence settled over me like it always did whenever I took a moment to reflect in quietness. Cemeteries freaked a lot of people out—my mom and brother included—but something about the cold stones and dying flowers soothed me. Morbid, but I'd never claimed to be normal.

Besides, Grandpop had requested while on his deathbed that I swing by every few weeks to share the latest baseballs stats just in case heaven didn't allow sports talk.

I hoped wherever he'd gone allowed what had made him happiest on earth outside Grandma.

He'd found peace after old age eventually took him away from his family. If only my soul and body could know that kind of rest in life.

Chapter 17

Matteo

"I have a confession to make."

For late October, the sun still warmed my face as I sat with Katie, my eyes closed since I couldn't bear the thought of looking at her name etched in granite while I spoke what I'd been keeping from her for far too long.

I knew she wasn't there, that she wouldn't actually hear me, but I needed to unburden my heart for my own sake.

"I've been unfaithful." I huffed an exhale and shook my head as I lowered my chin to my chest. "You told me to live, to find love again, but I'm struggling with moving on since it feels as though I'm betraying what we shared. There's this... young man."

I cringed against both arousal and a sense of grief.

Of course, my dead wife didn't speak aloud or on a breeze like I would have preferred as I spilled my secrets. I told her about Sean and how he affected me. I even went into detail about the kiss we'd shared and when he'd gotten on his knees with eager determination to make me feel good.

He'd blown my mind, pun intended, and I admitted to that fact aloud too, my cock thickening and face growing hot from embarrassment.

"What should I do, Katie?" I muttered, needing a sign, something to help guide my steps. The ethical choice would be to stand firm in denying what I felt, but I grew weaker with every moment I spent in Sean's presence.

I want you to be happy.

Katie's last words whispered through my mind. What caused me to experience those feelings these days?

Sean—but he also turned my life topsy-turvy, making me desire things I shouldn't as his professor.

Quiet moments slid past as they always did whenever I sought answers from a silent grave. Lingering sweat on my underclothing cooled as the sun slid behind the looming tree, leaving me in shadow.

Disappointed in the lack of answers I sought for, I pushed up to my feet, cursing my knees yet again even though I knew better than to sit on my haunches like I'd been for the previous half-hour or so. I kissed my fingertips and lay them atop my wife's headstone. "See you next week, my love."

Turning, I caught sight of a blond head I recognized regardless of the fifty or so feet separating us. Adrenaline leaked into my bloodstream. Had he followed me and pretended to spend time beside another grave? Or was he truly there for a loved one, a mere coincidence when I hadn't run across him in the three years I'd been visiting Katie's final resting place?

Perhaps his presence was the sign I'd asked of my dead wife...

Swallowing hard, I started his way, studying Sean's slouched form. He picked at the grass and didn't turn as I approached even though he had to hear my footfalls on the dry ground.

I stood behind him, unsure what to say, wondering why he hadn't looked over his shoulder to see who stood behind him. No earbuds blocked his hearing, so he must have been aware someone drew near.

"Sean?" I murmured, not wanting to startle him just in case he *hadn't* heard me for whatever reason.

"Is it strange that I knew it was you?" he asked, still facing forward. "That I could literally feel you? My skin prickles with awareness anytime you're nearby."

I could relate but wasn't sure what to make of it for myself, so I kept quiet.

Sean heaved a loud exhale and tossed a blade of brown grass to his left. "My mom's dad was the only man who loved me unconditionally and tempted me into believing I was a good kid."

My gaze flicked over the gravestone, noting the same last name as my student. "I'm sorry for your loss," I offered, meaning so much more than for the death of his grandfather. Sean's tone had held too much grief, an unsettledness I often experienced whenever I thought of Katie.

"I've been visiting my wife's grave for three years, and I've never seen you," I went on when Sean didn't speak.

He sat with his legs crossed and leaned forward, elbows on his knees. "That's because I don't visit Grandpop and Grandma nearly enough."

"Do you believe they're still here? Watching and wanting our happiness?" I questioned as a few remaining leaves rustled on a nearby tree.

"I like to think so," he murmured.

Silence settled for a few minutes as I warred over what to say. We hadn't shared a moment of non-sexually charged space before, and I found the passing minutes to be...pleasant. Comforting, even.

"I've never loved anyone but her," I finally shared what I thought he had the right to know. It was a day for confessions, after all. "I've never experienced instant attraction, the kind of connection that binds two souls together from across a room before her either."

Sean remained still, as though his breath held for the beat of ten long seconds. "And since her?"

I released a slow, steady exhale that took enough time Sean finally twisted his torso to look up at me with hope-filled eyes.

"You stated it better than I ever could," I whispered the truth of how he made me come alive, how he made me *want*.

The hunger in his gaze was subtle for a change but kicked me in the groin as it always. He might not be on his knees, but those blue orbs peering up at me caused my usual craving for him to rise in more ways than one.

"I'm struggling, Teach," he said rather than expanding on what I'd stated. Zero trace of flirting or teasing lined his face—he spoke of something deeper than the shared lust between us. "I'm so damn tired and incredibly unhappy."

I sank onto the ground beside him, careful to keep space between us, thankful the sun still lit his grandparents' part of the cemetery. "I'm a good listener."

He chuckled quietly and turned back to face their headstone. "Believe it or not, Matteo, it's your maturity that haunts my mind and makes me question my desiring you so desperately when I've always loved my freedom."

I wanted to push for more of those *feelings* but bit my tongue. Was it from being off-limits? I didn't believe so since a taste of me hadn't quelled his yearning.

"It's strange…" Sean plucked more grass and tossed it to his other side. "I've been a playboy my entire life, and this older guy ensnares the fuck out of my mind to the point work sucks."

Again, I craved to question him, to get answers, but chose not to. "So you're saying *I* make you unhappy?" I tried to help him explore where his emotions came from instead.

"Fuck no," Sean muttered and lay back on the ground, legs stretched out and ankles crossed, his eyes focused on the cloudless sky above us. "Shit hit the fan for me and my brother's business, and true to my weak-assed form, I'd backed out to let him handle the problem. I might have come up with a possible solution, but none of this would have happened if I hadn't fucked up to begin with. I'm nothing compared to Micah—never have been. He's the golden boy, and I'm the wild child who can't do anything right."

Empathy welled inside me as he bled his insecurities without hesitation to a man he barely knew. Who had caused him such low self-esteem? Both parents? One? Or did he simply compare himself to his older brother without prompting outside his own thoughts?

I doubted he lacked in any way. Sean Fox shone like the summer sun, brilliant and smile-inducing. He'd proven himself to be dedicated to his education even if he occasionally arrived a few minutes after I'd begun lecturing.

Katie had been much the same with low confidence, but she'd found peace and felt good while on her knees submitting to me. Would allowing my student to do the same give him the quietness of mind he sought?

Lust stirred in my groin, but I pushed it away along with

the image of Sean before me, soaking up all the praise and edification I wanted to pour down over his head.

He huffed a sarcastic laugh, his eyelids shutting, forehead furrowing. "I decided to get my MBA to show Pop that I'm every bit a man as Micah is, but I'll admit the hours, the workload, is a lot. My stomach burns all the damn time, like I've got an ulcer from anxiety. Can't seem to catch up on sleep either. And don't get me started on how much it sucks not having the energy to drag my ass to the gym these days."

Even though pink tinted his cheekbones, the rest of his face was pale as it had been the previous month or so. His words assured me of what I'd suspected.

"Your persistence is admirable, and you're doing well in my class," I offered.

He perked up a bit, offering me the grin I'd expected from that tiny bit of positive reinforcement. "Only because I'm determined to prove to you that I can be a good boy."

Fuck. I rubbed a hand over my mouth and tore my focus off his flirty gaze. A cool breeze slid over me, and I shivered along with the dead leaves on the tree to my left. He wanted to prove himself to me, same as he did to his father.

The poor kid was desperate for positive attention and affirmation, and I wanted to give it to him. Doing so, I knew from experience, would fulfill a part of me that had been buried along with Katie. I missed my wife, but I also grieved losing that caretaker piece of me along with her.

"Maybe you should lighten your course load," I suggested rather than admitting my true feelings and flirting back like I wanted to. I half hoped he would drop my class so I could pursue the desire he'd unearthed inside me.

But Katie...

I pushed aside the guilty thought, sure in the deepest

parts of me that she would...like Sean. Perhaps even approve of him since he made me smile again.

"I'm taking a break from work at Micah's insistence." Sean shifted on the ground, drawing my focus once more.

He'd closed his eyes, fingers laced behind his head. His hoodie pulled up enough a hint of skin peeked above his waistband.

My mouth watered, and I curled my hands into fists to keep from tracing over what I would have preferred to lick. Would his skin be salty? Sweet? Would he submit to my loving? Beg for more? Or would he allow me a taste before grappling for dominance?

A shudder rippled down my spine, and I bit my tongue to keep from emitting a moan.

"You're staring."

I jerked my eyes back up to Sean's face.

Those blue orbs of his laughed at me—called me out with a knowing glint. "Tell me about your wife, Matteo," he said, his voice as warm as my blood.

I lay back onto the cool ground and gave him his wish.

Chapter 18

Sean

"She was the light of my life. My biggest supporter. A sweet, submissive soul who relied on me—fulfilled me in ways I never knew possible."

Grief laced Matteo's every word, and my heart broke for the man who'd lost the great love attainable only in poetry and romance books. His dark eyes peered off in the distance, hazed over as though lost in years past.

"She was diagnosed with cancer, and her parents blamed me for not sending her to the doctor sooner. It was too advanced to save her, and she suffered terribly." Matteo heaved a despondent sigh, his broad shoulders slouching.

I'd been blamed throughout my life for all sorts of shit I wasn't responsible for but nothing that severe. I reached over, laying my hand on his forearm. Even through his sweatshirt, electrical currents slid between us.

Matteo didn't pull away but closed his eyes and swallowed audibly. "My parents and sister moved to South Carolina years ago, so I have no family here. Katie's sister reaches out once every couple of months to share about their continued mourning, but other than that, I'm alone in my lingering grief."

I squeezed his arm, and he shifted to lace his fingers through mine.

My heart rate picked up but different from the usual lust I experienced whenever a man of interest touched me. The connection between Matteo and I ran deeper on a level I'd never felt before. The pulses of energy were...addictive in a non-lustful way. Life-giving.

Matteo stared at our hands, lifting them slightly while rubbing his thumb over the back of mine with gentle caresses.

Muscles melting, I submitted to his touch, allowed him to lead since he seemed to prefer having control. And Katie's gifting him that part of her had fulfilled him...fuck it all, I wanted to do the same for him. The desire to ask more about her, learn her ways, flooded through me—but emanating his dead wife wouldn't give me what I wanted.

His appreciation for *me*. Sean, the wild, little shit, not some lovely, sweet woman he still held on a pedestal. I'd had enough comparison to those types throughout my life.

Flight instincts demanded I withdraw my hand and take the fuck off, but I held steady, soaking in every second of his attention I could even if his mind rested elsewhere.

"Tell me about your childhood," I said instead of continuing on learning about a female I would never live up to. "Your likes. Dislikes. What you do for fun and how you spend your evening hours."

He obliged me, and I did the same with his questions, explaining about Pop's negativity and Micah having my back more often than not. I avoided discussing Elite since I wasn't sure how he would take my being a part of an escort business—and selling my body alongside the other employees. I used the old communications description for the family business I helped manage. An ease of words flowed between us, unhindered by the guilt, fear, or discomfort that seemed to plague him at the college.

We sat in the cemetery and talked until the sun sank, leaving us both chilled through. Although I wanted to spend the entire night beside him beneath the stars, I'd grown too cold to stay any longer.

Matteo ambled alongside me as we made our way through headstones to my car. Exhaustion still clung to me, but being with him had boosted my spirits even further than they'd been earlier.

"If it wasn't October," Matteo said, "I'd see if you wanted to mountain bike with me sometime. Katie and I used to go every weekend, and now my bike sits unused in the basement."

"Why, Professor D'Angelo," I teased. "Were you thinking about asking me out on a date?"

"What? No! As *friends*," he hastened to add, his cheeks flushed in the darkness.

Goddamn, did I want to kiss his face off. "So." I chuckled, bumping his shoulder with mine as we walked. "Checking me out online, huh?"

He coughed.

"I'm not at *all* offended, Teach. Can't say I'm innocent in doing the same with you. Couldn't help myself any more than I can stop dreaming about you every night."

Matteo cursed quietly, and the tension intensified between us in a heated flash.

We stopped by my car, and I toyed with my keys. He'd told me he'd jogged to the cemetery, but it had grown too dark for him to be running without some sort of reflection on his clothing. "Can I give you a ride home?"

He eyed me, his face in shadow from the lack of daylight. "Will you behave?"

"Hmm." I checked him out from head to toes, itching to touch every inch of him. "Only if that's what you really want."

The energy between us rippled back and forth, attempting to draw us together like a couple of magnets, unable to deny the force of nature.

"I can't *have* what I want," he whispered.

I nodded at the answer I expected. He *could*. He just didn't have the balls to take it.

But walls had tumbled down between us, so I couldn't complain. And no way in fuck would they be erected ever again. The only two things I wanted *erect* between us were our dicks. Mine was half there, so I adjusted myself, drawing his gaze downward.

"Sean..."

Laughing, I pulled open my driver door. "Get in the car —I'll keep my hands to myself. Promise."

Matteo muttered something while rounding the front of my Audi. He shut us together in close proximity that made my mouth water and skin tingle with awareness.

I got the engine going and shivered against the cold and the potent attraction I felt for the man beside me. Hints of his soap lingered beneath musky sweat from his earlier run. I lusted to lick all the fuck over him, to taste the salt on his skin. Swallow around his glans and fill my belly with his cum.

Clearing my throat, I pulled out of the cemetery, determined to behave. I wished I could invite Matteo to grab something to eat for dinner since both of our stomachs had grumbled in the previous hour, but our shared time sitting in the grass hadn't changed Matteo's stance.

Being seen out with me by anyone he knew from work wouldn't look good and might cause problems for him. Something I refused to do.

But goddamnit, I wanted to.

He directed me to the curb in front of the home he'd shared with Katie for over a dozen years. The wooden stoop was lit from its roof, bathing the stairs in a soft, welcoming glow. Two planters flanked the painted door, both a more vivid blue than the door itself. No plants peeked from their rims. They sat void of life, same as the rest of his yard in the cold October night.

Matteo didn't make a move to exit my car, his gaze on his home. He finally turned toward me. Sexual energy ramped enough my pulse picked up, my heart beating hard.

His focus dropped to my mouth.

I flicked the tip of my tongue over my lower lip before sucking it between my teeth.

"Tease," he murmured, his low, rasped tone swelling my dick.

A smirk popped my lip from my mouth.

He huffed an exhale, lifting his gaze to my eyes. I wished for my interior light to flicker on so I could read the hunger in his dark orbs. "If you ever need to talk, I'm only a text away. My door is always open too."

The man didn't know the temptation he offered, but I didn't tease or flirt. "Thank you—and same."

Matteo nodded, another quick glance at my mouth making my dick buck for escape from my jeans. "I appreciate the ride home, Sean. I'll see you Monday morning."

"Yeah," I agreed as he opened the door, allowing a rush of frigid air to fill the space he left empty.

He shut me in, and I stared after him, soaking in the sight of his shoulders, his trim hips...his ass flexing as he climbed the stairs. He paused, hand on the doorknob, to turn.

Even though space separated us, I could feel his gaze on me as gentle as the caresses he'd painted over my knuckles while sitting in front of my grandparents' gravestone.

A shiver raised the hairs on my arms, and the goose bumps lingered long after he shut his front door between us.

My breaths came easier on the drive back into Boston, my pulse fluttering like a newly morphed butterfly's first flight regardless of what Elite faced. Grief weighed Matteo down, but he'd brought to life something inside me I couldn't name. Some delicious force that made me hunger for more. To persevere. To find answers. To conquer.

I collapsed on my couch, cell in hand. He'd given me a green light of sorts, so I took total advantage of it, hoping to make him impossibly hard and need release as badly as I did.

Me: **Good night, Teach. I hope you dream about me. Fuck knows I'll be seeing you when I close my eyes—same as every night since I met you.**

Chapter 19

—————

Matteo

I climbed out of the shower to find Sean's text waiting for me. Thankfully, I'd already emptied my balls down the drain along with the soapsuds I'd used to clean my body. Still, my groin attempted to rouse at his words.

Instead of explaining in detail all the images in my head I'd been having of him while sleeping, how he made me wake up every morning aching for release, I went with something a little more professional.

Kind of.

Me: **I thought you promised to be a good boy.**

My heart raced as I waited for his reply, a mixture of excitement and adrenaline pumping through me from skirting a line I had no right to toe.

Mr. Fox: **Deep down, that's not what you truly want.**

Rather than agreeing to his assumption—the truth he clearly saw through my attempt to hide it—I set my cell on the bedside table. Flirting with danger would only leave us both burned and hurting.

The first reason I'd attempted to keep my distance from Sean, my being straight, had been obliterated. And while that second out of loyalty to Katie had settled somewhat in my mind during Sean's and my time at the cemetery, the third reason remained strong as ever.

I glanced at the book alongside my cell. I'd dug out the employee handbook just to double check my employer's stance on becoming involved with students. The rule was etched in black ink, too direct to argue or find some way around.

I respected—loved—my job and needed the salary to survive.

Slumping onto the edge of my bed, parts of my body still beaded with water, I glanced around the rest of my room. I'd long since boxed up Katie's things and donated them to charity, but her dresser still sat on the wall opposite mine. A single dried rose rested in a glass vase atop it, the only flower I'd kept from those that had adorned her casket before she'd been lowered to her final resting place. The leaves had dried brittle, sensitive to touch. No matter how little I tried to jostle the vase while dusting, a single petal would fall, reminding me of Beauty and the Beast.

I'd always found the beast alluring, his sharp edges and broken bits more lovable than the outward perfection of his human form.

Only one petal remained.

Once it fell, I expected to be condemned to a solitary existence where loneliness would be my only companion.

Sighing, I closed my eyes.

Sean found me in the darkness behind my eyelids rather than Katie, and for the first time, guilt didn't rouse. I allowed my thoughts and feelings free rein to do as they pleased.

I didn't believe Katie would be jealous over a younger man stepping into my focus that used to be solely on her.

What about Sean got to me? What trait drew me in? It went beyond physical attraction, almost like a sense of knowing him outside time and reality.

Scrubbing a hand over my mouth, I glanced at my clock. Eight—on a Saturday night.

While I would normally sit on the couch and watch a show to pass the time, my feet itched to move. I should have run home from the cemetery and finished off my body to the point of exhaustion like I usually did after visiting Katie's gravesite rather than taking Sean up on his offer of a ride.

I remembered where she and I would go when feeling a little...restless or adventurous, and the similar itch had me considering heading back out. I'd allowed my membership to expire but could pay a drop-in fee.

An urging welled up inside me, and I moved on instinct, sending a text to a number I hadn't utilized in years. I had no urge to interact, simply *be* in an atmosphere Katie and I used to enjoy together.

The club owner replied before I crossed the room to grab a pair of slacks.

I've been waiting for you to return to the land of the living. You're always welcome, Matteo.

A part of me settled at her assurance, but something deeper resonated with the first part of her message. I had been stuck among remnants of memories that ought to be cherished rather than wallowed in. Doing so had held me back from exploring once more...possibly finding happiness.

Twenty minutes later, the buxom blonde met me at her office door, a force to be reckoned with. "Matteo."

"Mistress Chantelle." I kissed her cheeks as she did mine before sitting on the chair she motioned toward.

"I wondered when you would grace us with your presence again," she said, settling behind her desk across from me. "How are you, Matteo?"

"Still grieving but feeling as though I want to live again."

Her knowing gaze slid over my face, her Domme instincts reading with ease even if I'd attempted to shield myself from her. "You're not ready for more than finding your place though, are you?"

"I'm not."

She nodded. "Masters Cooney and Kaden are here tonight with their partners. I'm sure they'll be happy to see you."

I entered Chantelle's lounge a short time later, memories swarming my mind. The air scented of leather and sex, and a blood-stirring mixture of lust and longing flooded through me at the images in my head of years long past.

The place was packed far beyond when Katie and I used to frequent the club when she would kneel at my feet and gaze up at me with grateful adoration.

As promised by Mistress Chantelle, Master Cooney sat far to my right in a chair with his back to the wall. His thighs were spread wide, and Becky was seated on the floor between them, her lush curves hidden by a silk shift. Her cheek rested on his thigh, and ropes bound her from wrist to elbow, the lead rope in Cooney's massive paw. He toyed with the ends of her dark hair, softness on his face when he'd used to be so damn hard before she'd crept into his life, a timid, abused woman. He'd been happy to be her rigger and master, the safe place she'd needed to heal.

Feet lighter than they had been in years, I made my way

toward them, having to politely decline three other members' requests to play as I crossed the lounge.

I'd never been into giving or receiving pain, was as far from a sadist as a man could be. But while I wasn't one with a heavy hand, I enjoyed having someone to care for, a person to pamper and lavish with love. And their submission in return fulfilled me with heart-wrenching joy.

For the first time since Katie's death, my chest didn't ache at the memory of her. My inhales weren't hindered by grief, and my eyes didn't sting from heartache as I remembered the love we'd shared in and outside of Chantelle's club.

Master Cooney raised his focus off Becky, and his gaze landed on me, a wide smile cracking his facade. He didn't stand to greet me, and a quick glance down at his wife let me know why.

She rested in near subspace, eyes closed, a contented smile on her face from kneeling and being bound by her Sir.

Master Cooney lifted his free hand, and I shook it firmly, grinning.

"Master D."

I snorted a laugh at his greeting, a name I hadn't heard in I couldn't remember how long. Only those friends I'd left behind after Katie's passing called me a Master even though I didn't identify as such.

"Sit." He gestured to the empty leather chair beside him, and I did as told by the red-haired giant of a man I'd lost touch with.

"I never thought I would find my way back here," I said, settling in beside Master Cooney.

"It's good to see you, Matteo."

"You too," I stated, meaning it with my whole heart.

He caressed a hand over Becky's head, a loving touch I

envied his being able to gift.

My heart did ache at that but with longing rather than loss.

I'm moving on, Katie, just like you wanted.

The realization of the choice I'd made, the determination I felt inside to live again, hit me with a bittersweet pang. I would never set aside my sorrow over losing Katie, but I finally felt free to seek out intimacy—emotional and otherwise—once more. She'd wanted that for me, had asked for it on her deathbed, and if nothing else, I had trusted her with my whole heart. I had to believe she was smiling down on me from wherever she'd gone.

Filling my lungs fully, I gave the scene taking place in front of us my full attention.

Master Kaden's Bella rested on her knees, reddened ass lifted high, her lips pressed to his boot. Livi Risso had been a brat of the utmost grade when she'd first sauntered into Chantelle's looking for a little fun years ago.

She'd gotten what she'd wished for and then some. Master Kaden's sadist side matched her needs, and their love of exhibition and sceneing in Chantelle's lounge had always brought smiles to other patrons' faces and releases to sexual needs.

The sassy brat had handprints on her lush backside along with lashes up her back that had probably come from a flogger.

"I missed out on the fun," I said, turning toward Master Cooney.

"He finally put her out of her delicious misery about five minutes ago," he replied, his focus flitting to Becky's calm face. The man was still smitten, his eyes warm with longing.

We got caught up over the next half hour, and my desire

for someone to kneel for me intensified with every passing minute. Envy for the dominants littering Chantelle's lounge area filled me to the point I allowed myself to imagine a needy Sean at my side.

While Chantelle's was inclusive, more straight couples than queer paid the fees to be club members. Katie and I hadn't been rich by any means, but she had used part of an inheritance from her grandmother to gift me a membership after we'd begun to explore aspects of BDSM that fit us. We'd been enjoying monthly visits at Chantelle's for two years before she'd fallen sick.

Master Cooney's attention shifted to the doors, and I followed his gaze.

The couple stepping into the lounge looked familiar, and I studied them as they drew closer, the man grinning at Master Cooney.

His blonde partner clung to his arm, her cheek resting on his shoulder. He wore leather pants and chose to go bare chested like quite a few of the Doms littering the lounge.

The same he'd done with me, Master Cooney stuck out his hand but didn't disturb his wife from where she continued to rest. "Micah."

The blond returned his greeting as recognition bloomed in my brain.

Micah Fox. Sean's brother, the one whose social media I'd browsed through.

Well, damn. Small world.

"Matteo D'Angelo," I said when Micah turned toward me. We shook, but Micah's touch didn't rile me up like his little brother's did.

"Micah Fox," he introduced himself, "and this is my wife, Jasmine."

I noted the collar around her neck and bit my tongue to

keep in the *I know* that threatened to spill, which would have turned the moment into an uncomfortable one. I chose to greet his wife with a smile and nod since I wasn't aware of their dynamic and didn't wish to overstep possible boundaries by offering her my hand.

Micah sat in the empty chair on Cooney's other side, and his wife curled up on his lap, her face buried in his neck. Someone was feeling needy.

Again, my heart ached with envy as I watched her snuggle in her Sir's arms.

"Are you new to Chantelle's?" Micah asked, his blue eyes similar to Sean's flitting over me without a hint of interest, simply sizing me up.

"No, but this is my first time back since my wife passed three years ago."

A frown dented Micah's brow. "I'm sorry for your loss."

"Thank you."

"For what it's worth, welcome back, and I hope you find what you must be feeling you need once more."

I appreciated Micah's bluntness. "I'm not sure I'll ever truly be ready, but the stirrings are definitely there."

He smiled, popping a dimple just like Sean's.

Arousal slid through my veins and not because of the man sitting across from me.

"Did the rumor mill find your ears?" Micah asked Master Cooney.

The giant redhead simply raised an eyebrow.

"A client is trying to extort Elite."

Master Cooney's eyebrows furrowed deeply, denting his forehead. "What?"

Micah glanced at me, but I sat still and unassuming, hardly a threat—that he knew of. His Dom intuition must have found me to be someone he didn't need to worry over because he went on to explain to his friend about a past client delivering images depicting a beating that one of Micah's employees claimed didn't happen. The man wanted two million, or he was going to leak the photos to the press.

I wasn't a detective, but it didn't take long for me to figure out exactly what kind of business Micah and Sean Fox ran. No judgment swam through my mind. Everyone had to make a living, and some people required the privacy of secretive hookups in order to find release denied to them in their day-to-day living.

Did Sean's exhaustion come from managing Elite outside his schoolwork, or...

The memory of him in a tux headed to "work" detoured my mind down the second path. With his blatant sexuality and his love of men, I realized he must take an active part in Elite outside the office.

I readied for disgust to fill me, a turning off of the switch Sean so easily flicked on inside me.

Nothing happened other than for acceptance to settle more firmly in my mind. I didn't care how Sean made his money, only that he didn't burn himself out between school and his responsibilities for Elite.

"What do you do for work?" Micah interrupted my thoughts, and I realized I'd sat in silence for a lengthy time.

"I teach finance at Boston College."

A grin split Micah's face, yet another expression he shared with Sean. "My brother Sean went back to school this year for his MBA."

"Sean Fox," I stated his name, feeling as though hiding the truth of knowing Micah's brother might prove more troubling than not. "He's in my Financial Accounting class on Mondays and Wednesdays."

He's also the delicious bane of my existence, the reason I realized I'm not as straight as I'd always assumed and that I'm ready to move on from consuming grief.

"How's he doing?" Micah asked. "Is that something you're able to discuss with a non-faculty member, or am I overstepping a moral code of sorts?"

I wasn't allowed to talk about my students' grades, but that didn't stop me from building up the young man in my class. I hadn't expected him to excel in it, considering his inability to sit still even when exhaustion clung to his shoulders.

"He's one of my most dedicated students." I didn't mention my wondering if he might be ADHD, but by his B average grade, he'd somehow found the ability to focus enough to study.

"He hasn't given you any shit?" Micah chuckled. "He's a brat and needs a firm hand."

My groin woke back up. "He did in the beginning," I admitted, "but he's...worn thin."

Lips pressing tight, Micah nodded, adjusting his wife slightly in his arms. She sighed and kissed his neck. "I told him that he had to take a break from—" Micah cut himself off.

"I suggested he drop a class or two," I said rather than focusing on or pushing for what Micah had been about to say. I didn't need to be a genius to guess.

"He won't." Micah shook his head. "The kid is so damn stubborn. Why the hell he's doing this to himself is beyond me. He's got a gorgeous condo overlooking the harbor, a brand new Audi, cash in the bank, and even if Elite gets fucked over by that fucker Zerig, he's still set for life with the investments I pushed him into."

"He's doing it to prove himself to be every bit the man

you are, Micah," Master Cooney interjected. "To your father and to himself."

"What?" Micah turned toward his friend.

"You're intuitive as fuck, but you don't see your own brother's insecurities."

"The fuck are you talking about?"

"He's lived in your shadow his whole life, Micah. Your dad is a prick about it too. You know how many times I'd have enjoyed laying him out on his ass for being negative about every damn thing your brother tries to do?" Cooney shook his head. "I'm proud of the little shit for what he's attempting—but he's got nothing to prove. It's too bad he doesn't see himself for what he is."

Master Cooney went on to reiterate what resonated in my brain. Sean's pure sunshine brought light and laughter to those around him. The kindness and attentive listening he portrayed when so many people lacked those characteristics. He had a determination I admired and stubbornness I respected. The love reflected in his voice when speaking of his family, those living and passed, I remembered well from our time in the cemetery together.

Sean Fox was a good man.

And the neediness in him called out to every part of me.

I took my leave not much later, reflective and restless.

While I wasn't free to fulfill him or the hollows inside my soul that would undoubtedly find contentment in him, I'd fallen for the young man.

Too many weeks remained in the semester until I could set aside the final reason Sean and I couldn't be together.

I just had to play things safe and keep my hands to myself, until he was no longer my student.

Chapter 20

Sean

Matteo and I had a major breakthrough in *whatever* we were, but shit wasn't progressing as I would have liked. We texted a few times a week, and I still flirted when I managed to get a private minute with him amidst the hallway full of students.

It physically hurt to respect his boundaries, and because of the constant ache for him, I pushed every chance I got.

But fucking hell, the stress of the Jackson Zerig situation ate at my insides, keeping me on edge.

I did as Micah had suggested, giving up escorting, and my wrist hurt from all the action since I had zero interest in hooking up with anyone but Teach. Thanks to Matteo and the nightly dreams he visited, I took great pleasure in releasing pressure from my balls every morning and some-times immediately after his class in a bathroom stall. Unfor-tunately, I had to keep quiet rather than moaning out his name while coming around other students.

Zerig had called on the day he'd said he would, but he caved to Micah's pleading, agreeing to give us another week to finish getting his money together. Preston had informed us Tuesday night that he'd found the asshole's true identity and the fact his attempt to bribe money from Elite wasn't his first go-round at extortion. Three other people from his past had been victims, and Preston had also learned there were warrants out for his arrest in two other states.

But the address Jackson Zerig had put in his contract with Elite, while an actual house, wasn't his residence.

JJ had agreed to take the information of Zerig's real identity and warrants to Boston's PD, but their detectives had yet to find the fucker.

Thus the reason for my sleeplessness and dragging ass to the point I couldn't even make myself go to the gym. Anxiety over Zerig releasing those faked photos to the media kept my gut in a state of unrest too. If shit went badly for Elite, we could easily face being shut down. I would lose out on the enjoyment and satisfaction of helping to fulfill closet case dick-lovers' fantasies.

Stomach burning from too much coffee, I stared at Matteo as he lectured from his leaning perch against his desk. His low, raspy voice coiled around the nerve endings in my groin and nipple area, making all my good parts tingle and harden regardless of my nausea.

Fuck, the man was so goddamned fine, more potent than a shot of caffeine to my lagging system.

Keeping my fingers to myself was proving more difficult with every passing day. I just wanted to curl up against his side or starfish over his body, soak in his warmth, and fucking *rest*. Sure, I lusted for him to fuck my brains out, but more than anything, I yearned to feel the same contentment I'd experienced while sitting on the cold ground as evening had settled over us. I longed to lose myself to the huskiness of his tone outside the classroom where I was free to interact with him in whatever way I wished.

Refraining from pursuing what I wanted sucked ass and not with spine-tingling arousal I preferred to bring to life during a good eating out of someone's hole.

"How are you holding up, Sean?" Matteo asked when I exited the lecture hall and sidled against him for a quick exchange like I'd been doing for the previous two weeks.

"Tired as hell."

Matteo's gaze flicked over me, probably noting the bags beneath my eyes that had become as permanent a fixture on my face as my nose.

Weakness rushed through me, and I wanted to lean into him, bask in his heat and strength. Allow him to hold me so I could steal some of his sturdiness I needed in my life.

"Sean."

I blinked, having lost myself for a moment. "Yeah—I'm okay, Teach." I forced a grin he didn't return.

"I'm here for you," he reminded me quietly.

His door was always open…

Nodding, I left him for my next class. But afterward? I allowed my feet to take me to the place I'd avoided out of respect for his wishes regardless of his assurances he was available should I need an ear.

What exact door he'd been referring to that night in the cemetery, I wasn't sure, but there was nothing wrong with a student seeking out their professor for help. What I required from him just didn't have anything to do with his class.

Same as the first time, I didn't knock, simply let myself into Matteo's office. Thankfully, he was alone.

"Sean." His gaze flitted over me, concern in his dark eyes.

Sighing, I slumped in the chair across from him rather than onto his lap like I'd have preferred. My eyes closed against his steady study of my face, and I tipped my head back, slouching down enough I could rest against the seat.

"Sean?" he repeated, a question in his voice.

"I know you don't want me here, Teach, but I just... need a minute of your energy. Your class is strangely the only place I feel peaceful even though everything about you vibrates the atoms in my body to the point of erupting."

Matteo didn't chuckle or make a joke about my word choice like I'd have done, considering the image in my head of my dick *erupting* cum all over his chest.

Huffing an annoyed exhale, I pried a single eyelid open. "You're so fucking gorgeous," I murmured while taking in his dark eyes and those lush lips I wanted to suck on again. "My Prince Charming come to life." He'd look even better covered in my spunk.

Pink flushed his cheeks, and he cleared his throat, glancing down at the papers on the desk in front of him.

"I'm not sorry for being honest," I stated, opening my other eye to trace my gaze over every inch of his face.

"I'm glad." His quiet statement hit me hard, stirring interest in my balls.

A slow grin lifted my lips. "Professor Stoic is softening toward me, folks."

"Not all of me, unfortunately."

I barked a laugh, butterflies taking flight in my stomach as blood rushed southward. "Teach has found his flirting game!"

"Shut up," he muttered, glancing at me, his face still pink, his eyes hungry.

"Fuck." I pressed down on my suddenly aching groin.

He licked his lower lip but on instinct, not with teasing intent.

"I have to taste you again," I gave him more honesty to see how he would respond.

He swallowed audibly and shifted on his chair.

"Want your cock down my throat—fuck that. How about I lock the door and you let me eat your ass this time around? Or maybe you'd prefer to get on your knees for me?"

His eyelids fluttered shut. "Sean."

"Yeah, Teach?" I whispered, my exhaustion long fucking gone from this game we played. Fuck, was he addictive.

"We can't."

"You mean you *won't*."

Matteo straightened his shoulders. It took him a few seconds, but he finally met my gaze straight on. "I ran into your brother a couple of weeks ago."

"Micah?" I stupidly asked in my surprise over the abrupt topic change. "Where?"

He hesitated in answering while I wondered over why Micah hadn't said anything to me in the handful of times I'd seen him since whenever his and Matteo's paths had crossed.

"It doesn't matter, but he shared about the situation your business is facing."

My heart stutter-stepped inside my chest.

Matteo knew about Elite—what I'd done for a living up until the day Micah had told me to stop escorting. I'd never been ashamed of how I made my money, but Matteo was so damned wholesome...surely he would—

"I'm not a judgmental prick," Matteo said, obliterating where my thoughts travelled with that simple sentence and releasing the tension that had hitched my shoulders. He leaned forward, elbows on his desk, his gaze intent. "I would never look down on a person for their lifestyle, but taking a break from your work hasn't lessened enough of your stress. I admire you, Sean, you're one of the most focused students I have this year."

I snorted even though those words of his lit me up inside. "Yeah, right."

"I'm serious." Matteo's dark eyes bore into me with understanding and empathy I wanted to swim in. "But with what Elite is facing—I'm assuming it hasn't yet been settled?"

"No," I admitted.

Matteo nodded. "Drop some classes, Sean. You don't have to prove anything to your father—or your brother. In our short conversation, I could sense Micah's love for you, his admiration for your stubbornness. He isn't waiting with an *I told you so* should you decide to quit."

"I'm not a quitter," I stated firmly, annoyed Matteo would even suggest I do such a thing.

Lies—I'd done that the first time around, which had only made me more determined now.

"I know you're not, but I don't believe you're pushing yourself to your limits in order to fulfill a lifelong dream. So, are you slowly killing yourself for *you* or them, Sean?" Matteo asked quietly.

I opened my mouth but shut it once more without answering since I wasn't exactly sure. Part of me wanted to state that getting an MBA to show my family I was something more than a directionless partier *would* be for me. But how long might that satisfaction last?

Would handing Pop a degree with my name on it even change his mind toward me? And what would that piece of paper earn me outside my being able to brag I'd worked hard for it?

Pop didn't respect my lifestyle and never would. Hell, he hadn't said a goddamned word about my lack of escorting or the fact I hadn't gotten wasted since class started, both of which I'd mentioned at the dining room table the last time we'd gotten together at Micah's for our monthly family meal.

Mom had beamed at me for giving up my party boy ways, but Pop?

Nothing.

He couldn't even be proud of my investments that continued to thrive. A lot of Bostonians would kill for the life I had—and I wasn't satisfied, believing a degree would get me further ahead somehow?

"Countless hours of therapy didn't help me realize it was okay to live again, to focus on possible good things I've been missing out on."

I shifted my attention to Matteo, not having realized I'd stared at his desk, lost in thought once again. God, the words off that man's delicious tongue messed with my brain.

He smiled, his focus flitting over my face. "It took a blond, sassy brat to shake me from my stupor, to show me that joy doesn't have to be restricted to the only places I'd known before."

My mind went straight to flirt mode along with my body. "*You want me,*" I sang, running my hands down my chest. "*You think I'm sexy.*"

"Damned right I do," Matteo surprised me with his candor along with a light laugh I wanted to hear more of every single day. "And it's that attitude right there, that confidence, that shines through like sunlight in my world I kept dim on purpose because I didn't believe I deserved to be happy again."

My grin faded, but the feeling of weightlessness his declaration brought to my chest remained.

"What I'm saying, Sean, is that you don't need someone else's approval to find joy. It shines out of you so damn brightly—it's addictive." Matteo sucked in a shuddering breath. "It's a part of who you are, but the contentment part? That won't come from proving yourself to *anyone*. Trust me, I tried with Katie's family. To this day, all but her one sister blames me for her death even though I'd been as powerless as them to save her.

"You walked into my classroom a confident young man bursting with life in August, but you're fading. Tired and unhappy, you said you'd been feeling that day in the cemetery. If people can't accept you as-is, then that's their loss. This human experience is too short to waste your time on what doesn't bring you joy."

Talk about a fucking pill to swallow.

"*That* wasn't a loaded speech at all," I whispered, shifting with restless energy while trying to hold myself back from attacking the man I more than merely lusted for. His attentive gaze, the solidity of his older soul tugged on the strings of my heart.

Fuck it.

Deciding to act on his advice to take what would make me smile, I hopped up and rounded his desk, spinning his chair toward me.

Matteo went to hold up his hand, but I swooped in and planted my lips on his before he could stop me from going for what I wanted.

Fucking hell, his mouth was divine. His rushed exhale was sweet in my nose, filling my lungs. I grasped his scruffy cheeks and held him still while sliding my tongue inside to taste him. *He* was happiness and sunshine, a soothing warmth I would never get enough of.

"Need you," I murmured against his mouth, groaning when he grasped my hips and tugged me closer.

I climbed aboard the Teach train, making myself comfortable as hell on his lap even though it was a tight squeeze between the chair's arms. Mouth glued to his, I writhed atop him, loving how his dick swelled against mine with matching hunger.

"Sean." He gasped as I bit at his jawline.

"Please." I wasn't above begging, claiming his lips again to keep him from denying me.

His hands grasped my backside, a deep groan rumbling his chest as he thrust against me.

Fuck yes.

I grabbed at his hair, his shoulders, desperate for an anchor in the sea of desire threatening to drown us. "Matteo," I whispered his name—and abruptly erupted like a pubescent teen. "Oh God—fucking Christ." I choked on a hard swallow, grinding my pulsing dick against his, cursing the clothing between us. "You made me come. Jesus," I hissed and grabbed his face again, devouring his mouth.

My pulse raced as aftershocks ripped through me.

Matteo hugged me tight through my release until I collapsed against his chest. Nuzzling against his neck, I exhaled a shaky breath and rested. Sated. Fucking happy as shit in our stolen moment.

The door opened, but neither of us moved.

Matteo faced whoever had entered—probably Hanson —but he didn't tense, didn't push me away or hop up to defend himself. He simply held me, allowed me to feel peace in his firm grip for a moment longer.

A quiet snick sounded without a word exchanged, and we were alone once more.

"My naughty, naughty boy," Matteo murmured against my ear, his warm breath sending a shiver down each verte- brae of my spine. "You're going to get me in trouble, but I can't find it in myself to care when you're so sweet and pliant in my arms."

I loved being his good boy, but in that moment, nothing sounded better than naughty.

But we couldn't linger.

He had class, and I had soaked underwear that would grow cold and uncomfortable as fuck sooner rather than later.

Chapter 21

Matteo

Hanson had walked in on me in a terribly compromising situation but had backed out after making eye contact with me. He'd shaken his head, his disappointment in me apparent, but had left without saying a word.

I trusted our friendship, but how far would he go to protect me from the same fate as those who'd failed before me in touching what was off-limits according to school policy?

"Sean," I whispered, running my hands up his back.

He sighed and slowly sat up. Sated, beautiful oceans of blue tempted me to sink beneath the surface of his soul. "I know, Teach. You just...what you said..." He swallowed hard and climbed off my lap, leaving me cold regardless of my hard cock throbbing between my thighs. "I won't apologize."

"Neither will I," I murmured, adjusting my aching length.

A slow smirk curled his lips but more from inner pleasure than flirting. "You make me feel things. Good things.

And someday soon, this semester will end, and there'll be no stopping the collision course we're on." He turned to leave.

"About that."

He paused, glancing over his shoulder.

"You're right—we *can* do this, but I won't. Not here on campus. Please, Sean. It would be best to wait until you're no longer my student. I'm begging you to not tempt me again past what I can handle."

His jaw worked as he struggled to accept the boundary I set between us, and even though he eventually nodded, I didn't trust him to respect my wishes. He hadn't been able to prove he could thus far.

I tipped my head back against my chair and watched him pick up his bag he'd dropped beside the chair opposite my desk. At the door, he grimaced even though that damned glint lit his eyes. "Thanks for the orgasm at least."

"You're welcome," I teased, withholding my smirk at the thought of his groin covered in cold goo—but he'd asked for it.

Sean huffed, obviously hesitant to leave. "Damnit, Matteo."

"Go home. Rest."

"I've got too much studying to do."

Lips pursed, I nodded. My little speech obviously hadn't changed his mind about dropping out of college, but I hoped the words would echo in his mind in the days to come when he felt overwhelmed again.

"See ya around, Teach."

I nodded and closed my eyes as the door shut behind his fine ass I wanted to feel in my hands again.

Hanson walked back in a few seconds later, too soon for me to gather my thoughts on what to say to him but long enough my erection ebbed. I'd assumed he had slipped off to allow Sean and I time to finish, so his reappearance didn't catch me off guard at least. "I forgot my briefcase," he explained, returning to the office when he had class starting in a few minutes. "Are you okay?"

Exhaling slowly, I forced my eyelids up to face my friend. "Better than."

He studied my face while retrieving his bag from behind his desk. "Should I be worried?"

I rubbed a hand over my scruff. "I told him we had to wait until the semester ends, but I can't say no to him. He throws himself at me, and I'm powerless against the draw. He's given me something I never expected to find again after I lost Katie, and denying those feelings, those needs..." I shook my head, at a loss for words. I wanted to be strong, but goddamnit, that boy made choosing right near impossible.

"Please be careful," Hanson urged, heading once more toward the door. "Maybe keep these little trysts to places *off* campus. Meet at your house instead—or you go to his. Crossing lines here is dangerous, and while I have your back, I would really rather not be in the position where I would have to lie about my knowledge of this situation."

I nodded my agreement. I wouldn't expect him to put me above his job, nor would I ask him to, but he had a point. "No more in-office shenanigans. Promise."

"Thank you."

My friend left me for his next class, and since I didn't have one until later in the afternoon, I pulled out my cell and called my little sister.

"What's wrong?" Alessia answered with rather than saying hello.

I laughed for the second time in one day.

"Oh my God. Who is this, and where is my brother?" she demanded.

"It's me, and I'm fine."

"Well, it's about fucking time," she stated with a rushed exhale as though she'd been holding her breath for me for the previous three years. Knowing her adoration for me, I wasn't surprised at her obvious relief. "Who is she, and when do I get to meet her?"

"What makes you think someone has caught my eye?"

"Pah-lease, Matty." I could hear her eye roll. While only four years younger than me, she acted a hell of a lot like a teenager in many ways, language included. "Your down-in-the-dumps voice wouldn't change overnight unless some woman swept into your life and shook shit up."

Bracing myself, I spoke the truth that might shake *her* up a bit, but I wasn't going to beat around the bush. "He's one of my students."

That got her tongue.

"Alessia?" I finally checked in to make sure the call hadn't dropped.

"Explain," she ordered in her usually bossy manner, and I didn't catch a hint of what she might be thinking about the bomb I'd dropped.

Wariness tightened my shoulders.

"His name is Sean. He's a first year student—and yes, I've recently discovered I'm bi. Or demi. Not sure which, really, and I can't say I care about labels all that much."

"Sean-sexual." She snickered with a teasing lilt to her voice that brought my smile back firmly into place and relaxed my tensed muscles.

Of all my family, I'd held hope she would be the one to not frown upon my straying off the straight and narrow.

"Is he hot?"

"More than the sun," I admitted.

"Someone's got it bad." She had no idea. "Send me a pic. I gotta see the guy my big brother fell for."

"How's Claire?" I asked about my niece.

"Nuh uh! No changing the subject! Tell me all about this younger man—I'm assuming you're robbing the cradle if he's your student?"

"Fourteen years difference."

"Oomph." She snorted as though I'd knocked the wind out of her sails. "He's a baby. Mom's gonna love him."

She would—if she could accept the fact he wouldn't be the woman she'd been hoping for my future.

I kept to the facts but filled my sister in on what had transpired since Sean had first walked into my classroom. He'd spun my world off its axis, casting me once more into the blinding radiance of the living. When with him, the sense of emptiness that had plagued me since Katie's death disappeared.

"He sounds lovely, Matty—truly."

He was, and I would count down the days until the semester ended while trying to keep my hands to myself in the meantime.

"What's the policy on fraternizing with students though?" Of course, my lawyer sister would think to question me on that subject.

Unease weaseled its way back into my stomach, clenching it tight. "Doing so could mean my job if we're caught."

"Fuck—Matty, please tell me you're being smart about this."

That was the problem though. Sean made me feel... stupidly unable to control myself. The need he exuded, even beyond the physical, called out to me in many aspects.

It went deeper on almost a soul-ish level where two people bonded together without sex.

"I'm trying," I stated quietly, all too aware of my weakness. Sean and I had to avoid one another while on campus, but outside the college would be just as dangerous if we were seen in public. Sneaking around would be an option, sure, but would the anxiety make his stress worse? Would it put me on edge until I too suffered emotionally as he did with the mental load he carried?

I'd set the boundary, and I needed to hold firm for the next six weeks.

"How's my little pumpkin?" I asked since time ran short, and I didn't want to talk about myself the entire time I managed to keep Alessia on the phone.

"Claire-bear is still a pain in my ass and the light of my life."

I snickered. While Sean was quite a bit older than my only niece, I could appreciate the contradicting statement.

"Seriously though," Alessia said, her tone calm after attempting to make me laugh with stories of her four-year-old, "be careful. Your job is more important than climbing aboard his dick or giving him yours."

"Oh God, Alessia," I groaned, shaking my head. "The way you speak. Mom would clutch her pious, Catholic pearls."

"Someone had to be the black sheep of the family, since it sure as fuck wasn't going to be the golden boy."

Her never-before-stated label of me had me sitting up straighter. "The golden boy?"

"Yes—you, Matty. You always behaved. Well, until now, that is. I can't wait to see what Dad thinks about you boning a dude."

"I'm not boning—" I cut off, shaking my head.

Alessia snickered. "Don't worry, I'm not jealous. I am who I am, and I happen to love the shit out of myself."

My smile returned, and I thanked Mom and Dad's God that she'd had a strong sense of self that hadn't been overcome by insecurities brought on by others. I'd never once heard our parents put her down or compare her to me, but my sister's words proved that Sean too could grow his confidence in all areas of his life, not just his sexual side.

I hung up a few minutes later, my smile fading along with a heavy exhaled sigh. While my sister tended toward crass, she'd been on point in the way she'd warned me. I wasn't independently wealthy and couldn't afford to lose my income over my obsession, no matter how much I wanted to *bone* him.

But if Sean and I were meant for more than flirting and fantasizing, our time would come.

That truth, the fact I'd made strides in moving forward, had me reaching once more for my cell. It was time to text Katie's sister and sever the connection that did nothing but stir up the past. I was ready to place grief in the backseat of my life.

Chapter 22

Sean

"Twelve hours," Zerig snapped, and the line went dead.

"Jesus fucking Christ, that was too fast a conversation," Micah muttered, rubbing a weary hand over his face. "Were you able to trace the call, Preston?"

"Hold on..." Preston responded from my cell on speaker where we'd had mine sitting beside Micah's atop his desk.

Zerig had set a date for the cash exchange, but we grasped at straws while waiting for the police to locate his lying ass.

I sat across from my brother, his office door left open behind me. Both his secretary and BetsyAnne shared the reception area but had left for the evening. It was past seven on a Tuesday night, just shy of one week from my little lap ejaculation atop Teach that had made me miss an afternoon class.

I'd texted Matteo about his friend walking in on us, and he'd told me not to worry about it. But, he reiterated the fact we had to keep our distance from each other on campus grounds.

Respecting his boundary pushed against my instincts. I wanted to be his good boy, but the strong desire to lose myself in him so I could just stop *thinking* for a while poked at my naughty side.

"Fuck," Preston muttered the nonanswer we hadn't been hoping for.

Micah released a long line of curses harshly enough even I grimaced.

I swallowed hard, eyeing my brother who always had his shit together. Rarely did shit get beneath his skin and even more rarely did his face betray concern. He always had answers...

"What if we released the story first?" The idea left my mouth as I thought it since I kind of felt as though I'd been on a roll with doing things right for a change.

"Why the fuck would we do that?" Micah asked, sounding annoyed rather than interested in my suggestion.

"Hear me out." I leaned forward so Preston would catch my words over speakerphone too. "You're friends with that exec over at NBC, right?"

"Yeah." Micah eyed me without a hint of trust in his frigid eyes.

"What if we gave him everything we have—unveil Zerig for the shady douche he is? What if we press charges for defamation or whatever? You know...turn the tables type shit."

"He hasn't committed any acts of defamation yet, and spilling the story ourselves still brings the unwanted attention we're trying to avoid." Micah's disinterested voice—blowing me off—made me want to curl in on myself

"It was just a suggestion," I muttered. So much for being helpful.

"I'll keep searching. We'll find him," Preston said, his

confident tone doing absolute shit to boost my spirits as I took it too as a brush-off.

"Do so, and I'll owe you one—hell, ten."

We hung up, and Micah muttered a few more curses. "How the fuck have we remained untouchable for so goddamned long, and suddenly this young, greedy fucker thinks he can steal from me?"

Elite had been good until Micah had placed the management of the gay branch into my hands. He hadn't stated the words, but I felt them. And the stealing from *him* rather than *us?*

Cramps stirred once more inside my guts that had already been knifed to death by stress.

Losing Elite meant I would be jobless with a shitty resume that included stocking shelves, waiting tables, and a short stint of trying to sell windows. That sweet feeling I always got in knowing a customer was satisfied in the best way possible would be gone. All those numbers ratcheting up in my bank account. The crisp bills offered in tips. And forget the sense of accomplishment of having done a good deed for someone in need. That sense of...pride I sometimes managed to hang onto for longer than a hot minute.

Pushing to my feet drew a fleeting glance from my brother, but I could tell by his scowl he couldn't give two shits about what I did or didn't do in that moment.

"I'm heading home, but I'll stop by in the morning."

College classes would take a back seat. No way in hell would I be able to focus on a lecture while waiting for the shit to hit the fan if Zerig wasn't found and arrested before dropping that discriminating package off to some news outlet.

Micah nodded and picked up his phone, clearly already having forgotten about me.

I let myself out of his mansion's addition and climbed into my Audi. The engine purred to life, but I took no pleasure in the proof of how far I'd come in a few short years. What did my condo and all the money in my account gain me if I didn't have Micah's thankfulness or respect? I felt helping to grow Elite's gay branch into a thriving business had earned both, so why did Micah dismiss me so damn easily tonight?

I spiraled into my usual insecure funk I thought I'd been clawing my way out of.

Had my brother offered me the job to simply make me quit asking? Fuck knew I was a relentless prick. Pop used to give in to me a lot when I'd been a young, annoying brat. *Anything to shut him up*, I'd heard our father mutter too many times to count. Manipulation had become an art form for me as a kid—I'd been accused of being spoiled rotten when utilizing those skills for my benefit.

Perhaps Elite's growth *wasn't* my doing...maybe Micah had been working behind the scenes, behind my back, to make it appear I'd been the one to expand his gay branch into something lucrative as fuck.

Stomach bottoming out, I glowered but more pissed than hurt.

My exhausted mind raced in overthinking shit, and I might have taken that aggression out on the streets leading me back to Boston. It had been months since I'd drunk hard liquor, but I bypassed the two bottles of beer still in my fridge for the vodka in the freezer before my tossed keys even landed on the island.

Two shots slid down like water but settled in my stomach like pure poison.

"Fuck," I muttered with a grimace while pouring a

third. I was beyond concerned about the pain burning through my guts. I needed to forget for a while.

My throat tightened, but I swallowed down a third shot. Eyes stinging, I slammed the glass onto the counter. "Can't fucking do this shit anymore," I muttered to myself, blinking to keep the tears contained.

Even though my head and body dragged ass and wanted to collapse into oblivion for a few days' worth of rest, my feet refused to stay still. The type of peace I needed could only be found in one place, and I wasn't giving him a chance to turn me down.

I showered quickly, cleaning up all my bits with care—just in case.

Three shots atop exhaustion assured me I couldn't drive, so I called an Uber once ready to roll. My knee bounced the entire ride, my mind racing over insecurities and fears. Old hurts rose to the surface as I remembered time and again our father giving in to my whining so I would be quiet.

I'd thought I was a smart shit back then but recognized how the lack of discipline had crafted me into the spoiled brat most saw me as. Twenty-eight and I was still as selfish as a goddamned toddler, further evidenced by where I headed uninvited and unexpected.

Matteo ought to turn me away since my relentless pursuit disrespected the boundary he'd set between us the week before.

I stood on his stoop, shoulders slumped and heart racing as he pulled open his front door to my knock.

A quick glance past me to make sure no one saw me enter his home and he stepped back, a clear invitation to cross over the threshold. "What are you doing here?"

I stumbled inside, desperation and a little buzz urging

my feet. "I just need—" My voice broke, and Matteo cursed quietly, locking the door behind me. I couldn't see through the welling of tears I fought to hold back.

Strong fingers wrapped around mine, and I followed him like a little lost puppy, desperate for direction. The other half of me wanted to act up and be disciplined until I learned my lesson, but I had no energy to do more than go where he led.

Need so far beyond sexual desire prompted my actions, and I was powerless to choose otherwise.

"I told myself I wouldn't do this," Matteo murmured to himself while hesitating inside the living room, eyeing his recliner. He released a shuddered exhale and bypassed the chair for the couch. Releasing my hand, he sat. "Kneel for me, Sean."

My dick perked up at his low tone, and I sank onto the hard floor beside him, wrapping my arms around his sweats-covered calf without hesitation. I clung to his leg like he was a buoy in an angry ocean.

Matteo stroked his fingers through my hair, and I closed my eyes, the tension slowly releasing from my body. He manipulated my head without resistance on my part, and I rested my cheek on his thigh where he directed.

Silence settled over us as I sank into the peaceful energy flowing from him, through his fingertips into my scalp. Down over my shoulders, relaxing them...into my chest, easing the ache there.

And my dick? The fucker loved the act of submission I'd never shown another soul. I could live here, sitting at Matteo's feet for all of eternity, slit leaking, blood stirring with life-giving force.

The heat of Matteo's thigh radiated through the cotton of his sweats, warming my cheek. I burrowed in closer, wishing I could rub my face all over his skin. His fingernails scratched over my scalp, pulling soft sighs from my parted lips as I sank into quietness regardless of my arousal.

My mind rested for the first time in I couldn't remember how long.

No deadlines blared in my head. No responsibilities vied for my attention. No one could touch me while I was being Matteo's good boy.

"Talk to me, Sean. Tell me what made you break my rule and why I shouldn't punish you accordingly."

A shudder ripped through me at the thought of being put over his lap.

That sounded hot as fuck.

I hadn't actually *broken his rule*—he'd requested space while on campus, and he'd said his door was open so...

Instead of arguing, I went with flirting, which might get me what my dick wanted. "Are you referring to spankings or..."

"Sean," he growled, pulling on my hair.

I moaned at the slight sting and ran one hand up the back of his calf to shove between his thigh and the couch cushion he sat on. While I'd rather have just gone for the goods between his spread legs, he'd relented in letting me in. The least I could do was unload like he'd offered his ear for rather than taking advantage of the situation.

The twelve-hour time limit loomed, and I told him my fears concerning Elite. I even blathered on about Pop again, repeating how I'd been nothing but a bother to him my entire life. Sharing what Micah had said to me an hour earlier in his office brought back that sense of smallness and reminded me so much of how Pop made me feel that I wanted to puke.

My damn eyes got all stingy again, and I swallowed

hard. "I'm sorry for coming here—putting you in this situation. Especially when this is Katie's and your space. I-I'm not trying to be a brat. I just needed you, Matteo," I whispered as a tear slid down my fucking cheek, revealing my weakness I'd fought so hard to keep hidden.

He released a slow hiss, and I lifted my watery focus to his face. Dark eyes studied me in the dim light from a lone lamp across the living. "You know what a safe word is, Sean?" he finally murmured.

Oh shit. Fuck yeah, I did. But was he into that stuff?

Blood rushed south with a vengeance, even though I'd never been interested in any play that required a safe word.

"Yeah, but what do I need one for?" I asked, my thoughts at war with my damned dick.

"You disobeyed me, and you need to escape for a little while, don't you?"

Fuck arguing semantics. Maybe he was just looking for an excuse to get his hands on me.

"Yes. Yes, goddamnit," I rushed to say, the lust winning over whatever my concern about safe words. "I'll take whatever you'll give me."

"I've never done this before, but..." Matteo patted his lap with a resigned sigh. "Lie down and make yourself comfortable. If it's too much, say red, and I'll stop."

Goose bumps rose along my arms, and I scrambled over his thighs from a shot of pure adrenaline to my bloodstream.

"Good boy." He soothed his hand over my denim-covered ass, giving me a little squeeze. "But you need to lose these. I want to see the handprints I leave on your skin."

My balls pulled up tight in a flash.

Fuck. Yes.

Chapter 23

Matteo

I'd expected a slow striptease with Sean's twinkling eyes full of suggestion.

He pushed off my lap, shoved his jeans and boxer briefs to his ankles, quickly flopping back onto my thighs before I got a proper look at his cock. The boy was desperate, and the ethical line I'd been toeing had already been crossed.

I'd also expected guilt to swamp me or at the very least shame over even considering sexual acts with someone who wasn't my wife in our home. My spirit felt strangely quiet and peaceful having Sean there in the safe space I'd only ever shared with Katie.

If she hated what I did from beyond the grave, I didn't sense her anger or jealousy. In private, I would give Sean what he needed, what I craved.

But first...

I slid my palm over his smooth backside, swallowing a moan over how soft his skin felt beneath my fingertips.

"Ready?" I asked rather than repositioning him so his

ass was in my face where I had full access with my tongue. I'd never rimmed a guy before, but my watering mouth assured me I would enjoy eating Sean out.

Later.

"Yes—please, Teach. Give it to me."

I held his hips firmly with one hand, and teeth gritted, I let loose rather than acknowledging his tone or words.

"Fuck!" He jolted forward at the heavy blow I landed on his right cheek.

The sting on my palm felt delicious.

"Got anything to say?" I asked, soothing over the quickly reddening mark, loving how a print of my hand bloomed on his backside.

"More."

Brat.

Grinning, I slapped his other cheek, my cock swelling fully at his low moan. Perhaps I was a bit of a sadist after all.

Sean shifted his head so he faced me, cheek resting atop his folded hands on the cushion to my left. "More, Teach. Want to feel you tomorrow every time I sit down."

A groan escaped me at the thought of shoving into his ass and making him *feel* something other than just a spanking. Two more swats pinkened his flesh as I imagined him hobbling around hallways, his backside aching and insides rearranged from my granite-like shaft.

He hissed as I rubbed his red ass, lifting his hips when my palm dragged over his crack.

"I told you to wait until the semester ended." I smacked him hard enough my hand began to hurt, but the swell of satisfaction inside me from the enjoyable punishment couldn't be beat.

"Jesus!"

A squeeze where I'd hit him earned me another cursed groan. My pulse raced, adrenaline and arousal alike sprinting to every cell of my body.

This...this was sweet satisfaction I hadn't known I'd been missing.

"But because you need this—" I smacked again in the same spot. "—and I can't seem to say no to you, the next five are your reward."

Mine too.

All the remaining blows rained down in quick succession while Sean squirmed on my lap as though he wanted to escape. I grasped his waist with my left arm, keeping him still as he whimpered.

"Shh," I murmured, running my fingers over his hot backside, my cock aching for friction. "All done. No more pain."

"How was that a *reward?*" he grumbled through clenched teeth, and I chuckled, too turned on for words.

"It wasn't—not really. But this is." I slid a fingertip through his crack, intentionally avoiding his puckered hole.

Sean groaned, widening his knees and lifting his hips.

"You're such a needy thing, aren't you?" I murmured, loving that part of him since I had so much to give.

"When it comes to you, fuck, yes," he said with a choked laugh. "Stop teasing me and touch my asshole, Matteo."

My cock bucked against his hip, and he hummed while rubbing against me. I hissed and spread his cheeks to look my fill, finding a surprise as I did so.

Sean was waxed bare, a beautiful pink hue around his pucker. He appeared tight. Decadent. But the glint of metal...

"Is that...a piercing?" I lightly touched the ring through his taint.

"Yeah. Flick it a little."

I did as told, and Sean groaned, grinding his cock against my thigh. A smirk curled my lips.

"Got a Prince Albert too."

That type I'd heard about unlike the taint one.

Sean Fox was an absolute delight, and I couldn't wait to play with all his bits and pieces. But first, that sweet rosebud and I needed to get acquainted. "Suck," I ordered as I put two of my fingers in front of Sean's mouth.

He pushed up onto his elbows, grasped my wrist, and took my fingers clear to the knuckles as I'd expected. With steady sucks, he made my slit weep in memory of how that hot mouth had felt swallowing my cock.

"Jesus, Sean." I clenched my jaw, fighting to stay still rather than humping against him. "Get them nice and wet... just like that."

He backed off, a string of saliva connecting us. "Give me both at once," he demanded, but I let him be a little bossy.

I kind of liked his sassy side as much as his needy one.

I pulled his closest ass cheek toward me, once more exposing what would feel like heaven wrapped around my girth. Smearing his saliva over his hole brought a moan to both of us, and he shifted, restless for penetration.

He bore down, and I applied pressure.

Both of my fingers were sucked into his channel like they belonged there.

"Fuck," I whispered at the heat of him, and he shoved back, taking me to my knuckles, same as he'd done with his mouth. "You're so fucking tight," I croaked, twisting my wrist as his ring strangled my fingers. "So damn soft inside."

Silken warmth met my exploring strokes, and I couldn't begin to imagine his insides caressing every inch of my cock.

I eyed his piercing and rubbed over it with my thumb while wiggling my fingers inside his ass.

"Ah, fucking hell." Sean undulated his hips, riding my hand and grinding against my thigh. "You're making me leak all the fuck over your leg, Teach."

Jesus. I swallowed hard at the thought of the piercing through his wet slit—how it would glide over my tongue, how he would taste.

How the hell had I not known this part of me before?

I slid my fingers from his ass and pushed back in, the squelching noise of reaching into his heat tightening my balls.

Luscious, luscious boy. So perfectly smooth—

"Matteo," he whimpered, and I tore my focus off how his hole stretched around my knuckles. He'd contorted his upper body to angle toward me, his blue eyes darkened with lust. "Want you. Fucking need you, Matteo. Please."

Saying no didn't cross my mind.

I shifted from beneath him, shoving my sweats down as I moved off the couch.

As though already knowing my plans, he kicked his shoes and jeans away, hands shaking as he retrieved what we needed from his wallet before tossing that aside too.

Surprisingly steady, I accepted the packet of lube and condom.

Sean twisted to kneel on the couch, arms along the top, and ass right where I'd wanted it moments earlier—in front of my face.

I had no words, simply dropped to my knees and angled my mouth toward him for a slow, probing taste.

"Oh fuck." He arched deeper, reached back to spread

his cheeks, and shoved against me. "More—give me your tongue."

Greedy little brat downright turned me on with his confidence in knowing what he wanted. I set the lube and condom aside and grabbed hold of his hands to keep him steady. I licked him from tight balls and piercing up to the base of his spine and down again. A deep growl rumbled in my chest over the taste of soap and underlying musk on my tongue.

"Play with my piercing."

Another low sound escaped my mouth as I flicked my tongue over the ring in his taint.

"Harder. And stroke my dick."

Jesus, this boy.

I grasped his shaft and pulled in a downward stroke, metal caressing over my palm.

"Fuck, yeah," he groaned, arching his back deeper, presenting his ass like a good boy.

Wetness coated his slit, and drooling like a starved man, I bent lower, angled his cock back toward me, and took the head of his cock into my mouth. His salty musk exploded on my taste buds, and I had to swallow the rush of drool.

"Fuck!" Sean jolted, his cock bucking against my lips. "Jesus fucking Christ, Matteo."

I suckled a little, playing with the piercing through his slit, greedily lapping up the pre-cum oozing like a damned dripping faucet.

"So good," I murmured, stroking his dick and licking back up his taint to his hole.

Addictive didn't begin to describe the young man spread out on his hands and knees for my feasting. Sean was the most delicious thing I'd ever tasted. I licked him again from weeping slit to his sweet pucker before poking my tongue into his tight heat.

"Yes, oh fuck yeah. So good." He gasped as I stabbed inside him as far as I could.

I tongued inside him, my balls throbbing over the act of eating an ass for the first time. And the way he writhed against my hungry mouth made waiting impossible.

"Want my cock?" I asked, nipping at his taint and its tiny ring.

"Fuck!" He jerked in my hold. "Yes. Give it to me."

I backed off, licking the taste of him from my lips while swatting his backside. "Damn, you look so good like this with your ass popped out for me. All sloppy and desperate."

He wiggled his hips, causing his heavy cock to sway between his spread thighs.

"Jesus." I couldn't help myself—I grabbed his cheeks and dove in for one last lick. "Fuck." My voice muffled against his slackened hole as I slurped and rained hard, sucking kisses from his balls to his softened hole.

Adrenaline coursed through me. Opening the condom wrapper proved difficult, but I got the damn thing out, hoping I remembered how to put one on. It had been years...long before Katie—

I shut the thoughts down and focused on rolling the rubber over my length then opening the packet of lube.

One slickened finger rubbed deep inside Sean's ass, causing him to shudder. "Fucking hell, Matteo—right there. Oh, fuck yeah."

I chuckled, slid in a second finger, and stroked his sweet spot again.

"Ung," he grunted, arching deep enough I was afraid he would hurt his spine. "Put your dick in me."

"Have to stretch you," I murmured, weaseling a third finger inside his tight ring.

"No you don't—just shove your dick inside me and pound the shit out of my hole."

"Jesus, Sean...the way you speak." I'd never heard such a filthy mouth—and I loved it.

"Told you I wanna feel you tomorrow. Make it hurt until I blow my load all over your couch."

I slid my fingers free from the heat of his body and moved in closer, bending at the knees slightly to line us up. The condom choked my girth but not enough to lessen my arousal. Pre-cum smeared inside the rubber already, and I hoped I'd left enough room for my ejaculate because there was going to be a lot.

Sean spread himself open again, and I held my base, guiding my cock toward his pucker that looked much too small to take me.

Heart racing, I swallowed hard and flexed my ass, meeting resistance—he bore down, and the tip of my cock breached his ring.

"Oh Jesus—fucking...Sean." I gulped and slid another inch into decadent heat. His pucker sucked at my glans. "Fuck." I grabbed his waist, holding still, just breathing through the rush of adrenaline and lust pumping through me over being inside him. "Sean."

He pressed back, and I groaned as my slickened length disappeared into his stretching ring. My cock tried to buck, but his cheeks rested against my groin.

I was balls deep in one of my students. I clutched him close, trying to regulate my breaths, my racing mind.

Off-limits—forbidden.

Deliciously hot—tighter than any fist..

My entire groin throbbed for release, desperate in a way

I'd never known, and when Sean shifted his hips up and down in a twerk-like movement?

"Oh God." I tipped my head back, eyes closed, and lost myself to the motion of his fucking himself on my cock, the grasp of his slick hole sliding over my girth with his every movement.

I swallowed audibly and returned my hazed focus on where we joined. The wet sucking sounds of his ass writhing on my shaft made breathing difficult, and I stared in amazed rapture as he took every inch of me over and over again.

My balls ached, tight against my groin. "Not gonna last," I hissed through clenched teeth.

"I haven't had near enough of your dick, so think about something gross, will ya?" Sean barked.

I huffed a snorted laugh and shifted on my feet for better balance. "There's always round two," I promised.

"Fuck yeah," Sean agreed, slamming against my groin.

I moved him forward away from me to the point my frenum peeked at me from his hole. "So. Fucking. Hot." I thrust into him, our skin slapping together.

"Jesus fuck," he groaned, face dropping to the back of the couch. "Just like that, Teach—pound the fuck outta my ass."

Teeth clenched, trying to focus on anything but the warmth of Sean's insides, the slickness that allowed me to bury inside his body over and over again, I gave my good boy what he wanted.

"Right there, Matteo—fucking hell, I love your big dick. More..."

I stabbed into him with relentless force, my cock stiffer than ever before.

"Harder. Please." He begged so sweetly, but I slowed...

stopped completely to keep from releasing too soon. "Sadist!"

Chuckling and balls throbbing from edging us, I slid my hands up the muscles along his spine to his neck. "Come here."

He lifted onto his knees, pressing his back to my chest. "Ah, fuck, this angle." He gulped, tipping his head onto my shoulder. "You're so fucking deep inside me, Matteo."

"Feels good?" I murmured against his ear, gyrating my hips in a circular motion.

"Fuck yeah."

"You're so damned sexy, Sean." I explored his firm pecs, his tight nipples, over his rippling abs, and finally looked down along his torso to catch an eyeful of his jutting cock.

His swollen head glistened, pre-cum stringing down onto the cushion.

My cock attempted to buck again, and I took Sean's length in hand, eyeing the sexy silver ring. What would it be like deep inside my throat? I'd only had a little taste before.

"Matteo," he whispered my name, moving his hips once more to fuck himself on me.

While I loved control, I allowed him to have it—let him take what he wanted from my cock and hand.

Sean hissed and reached around to grasp the back of my head. He arched, working his body in a sensual dance of lithe muscle and masculinity that turned me on like I never would have guessed years earlier.

"You're so beautiful." My voice was nothing more than lust and yearning to explore the connection between us in every way. "So good around my cock, Sean. Never...never felt anything like this."

He whimpered, the pathetic sound tying strings around my heart.

Sean let go, lost himself in how we fucked, how he moved against me, body tensing and loosening at the same time. The heaviness that had accompanied him through my front door disappeared in an erotic wave of desire.

And I gave him all I had. Nothing held back.

Chapter 24

Sean

This isn't fucking.

The thought swept through my mind as Matteo began moving with me, filling me over and over with long strokes, his hand in opposing motion along my length. Copious amounts of pre-cum oozed from my slit, making for one hell of a messy hand job, and my hole gladly clutched at his thrusting cock.

But there was no race for the finish. No words spoken that didn't hold meaning. No *yeah, take that dick,* tossed out in the hopes of sounding sexy like we starred in some porn flick. There was no talk of breeding or gaping holes.

Just praise.

"Your skin is so soft, Sean," Matteo murmured before licking up the side of my neck. "And your taste on my tongue?" He growled, burying into my body with a sexy swivel of his hips.

I shivered, allowing him to do what he wanted to me.

"Your ass is so hot around my cock—you're perfect."

I soaked every word deep into my soul, getting off on my need of edification almost as much as I did the feel of his thick length sinking deep enough to rearrange my insides. I'd never had a dick fit me so well, as if he'd been designed to fulfill my ass. Thick girth that stretched me with a delicious sting, luscious length...*Matteo* was perfect.

No doubt, my hole would be sore come morning, and I looked forward to the memory, the reminder of how he'd owned me with slow lovemaking I'd never experienced before. Talk about goddamned addictive.

Matteo and I exchanged control back and forth like the tide, giving then taking in unspoken turns as though our minds connected as physically as our bodies. His heartbeat pounded against my back, his hot panted exhales ghosted against my ear when he wasn't telling me how good I was for him.

My skin pebbled along my arms as I fought off my impending climax. He stroked me just right, tagging my sweet spot like he'd known the inside of my ass for years. His fingertips toyed with my glans and piercing, driving me fucking insane.

Balls aching, I groaned, needing...more. "Matteo," I gasped, my lungs on fire, my skin burning. "Let me come on your dick."

He pulled out instead, leaving me wobbly on my knees and completely discombobulated from reality.

Whimpering, I went willingly where his hands led me— to my back, sprawled on the couch.

"Look at you," he breathed, his hair slightly damp from sweat, his dark eyes wild, and his lips wet from licking them as he ran his gaze over me.

I did the same to him, checking out the hills and valleys of his body, the lean muscle along his torso and thighs. And his dick—goddamn, what a beautiful cock my Prince Charming had. I lusted to feel him bare inside me, something I'd never had with anyone, but before I could speak, he lifted the backs of my knees and sank into me with one slow glide.

"Oh fuck," I moaned, reaching for his head.

"I need to see your face when you come for me, Sean."

"Jesus—fuck yes. Want that—you." I took his lips, a fresh shot of adrenaline racing through my bloodstream making my pulse thrum.

We ate at each other's mouths, desperate and hungry.

Matteo's body took control, and those long, loving strokes turned into heady thrusts that spun my brain and assured me my ass would ache in the morning.

I lifted my hips to meet him, small noises escaping between our latched mouths.

Gone. I was absolutely fucking *gone* on the man. Didn't need another dick for the rest of my life. I didn't even care if he wouldn't bottom for me or ever wrap his lips around my cock. I just desired *him*.

For fucking ever and always.

Matteo lifted onto his elbows, clasping my sweating face in his hands as he continued to thrust into me. We panted together, breathing in the other's exhales, and I still didn't feel close enough. He couldn't sink into me deep enough. *Never* enough.

"Matteo," I whispered his name, an unbearable ache in my chest.

"I know, Sean. I fucking *know*."

A whine built inside me, and my back arched as my balls seized. "Oh fuck. Coming..." I cried out, shuddering as cum erupted from my slit without a hand on my length. I spurted my release all over my chest, some hitting my chin.

Matteo lowered himself, his writhing body smearing my spunk between us. "So beautiful—my goddamn sunshine."

He ate at my mouth as I shuddered, his dick plowing harshly into my sensitive hole.

But I didn't complain. I grasped his shoulders, clutching him close, squeezing my ass around his thrusting dick.

"Sean," he croaked out my name and shoved in, holding still. "Jesus—fuck." He grunted and rumbled nonsense in his chest, words I couldn't make out as his dick throbbed inside me.

My heels clasped at his flexing ass as he emptied into the condom, every brush of his lips over mine while panting through his climax filling me the fuck up. My lungs, my heart, and my mind.

Is this what love is?

The question whispered through my head, but rather than answering or trying to figure out the truth of my emotions, I sank into the euphoric bliss he'd gifted my body.

My first hookup without payment, just for my own personal pleasure in years.

Matteo stilled but didn't make a move to get off me. Still buried inside my ass, he ran his nose along my sweat-dampened neck, soft nibbles of his lips on my heated skin making me sigh.

Eventually, he propped up on his elbows, once more cradling my face in his hands.

There were no words. Nothing worth saying that could sum up what we'd done or how we felt. At least, how *I* felt. But the look in his eyes? The hazed passion, the open vulnerability he showed me promised we walked the same path in our thoughts and hearts.

The Sean from a few years earlier would have made a joke to lighten the moment. Mention something about the next go-round with me bouncing on his dick. I kept silent. Subdued by the best loving *ever*.

I touched a fingertip to his lips, and he kissed the pad of my index, a soft smile curving his mouth upward. We both sighed—and I fucking grinned. Couldn't help the outpouring of light and life he'd burst open inside me.

"There's my sweet, sassy boy."

"Mmm," I agreed, squeezing around his softening dick still lodged in my ass.

"Oh fuck." His eyes rolled back into his head.

"Sensitive, Teach?"

He growled and shoved my hands up over my head, stretching my body out along his couch.

"Fuck yeah," I whispered, my smile fading and dick twitching. "Gonna get rough with me? Hold me down and make me take it?"

Matteo burst into laughter, the beautiful rasp of his chuckles welling happiness inside my chest. "You're insatiable."

"And you're the best lay of my pathetic life."

He eyed me before planting a soft, lingering kiss on my lips. "There's nothing pathetic about you, Sean. And I doubt this middle-aged man blew your mind to the extent you did mine."

"Oh, but you did—and I'm gonna need more." I ran my foot down the back of his leg, and his dick slid from my ass. Pouting, I huffed an exhale.

He chuckled again before nipping my bottom lip. "You're so damn cute. I'm afraid I'll never get my fill of you either."

"Good." I slapped his ass, making him curse and jerk to the side, smearing my cum all over us. "So...shower?"

"Whatever you want, my sweet boy."

I liked the sound of that.

Too damned much.

Chapter 25

Matteo

I hadn't realized so many firsts could be had at forty-two.

Taste a man's pre-cum? Check.

Make love to someone of the same sex? Check.

Run soapy hands all over a masculine body and get so turned on every inch of me ached for him a second time within an hour? Check.

Sean was a gift to be savored in sips and nibbles, and I ingested every little noise I enticed from his delicious mouth. The boy was putty in my hands until he grew restless and desperate.

Our mouths plastered together while the showerhead rained warmth over us. We frotted, the glide of his hard cock against mine quickly taking me to the point of emptying my balls. He released against me, and I shuddered, doing the same.

I buried my face in his neck, attempting to catch my breath, my senses overrun.

Sighing, he ran his hands down over the globes of my

backside before giving me a good squeeze. "Sometime soon, I'm gonna get up close and personal with this ass."

He rubbed a fingertip over my hole, and I shuddered but not exactly from desire for penetration.

"Gonna let me, Teach?"

I hesitated long enough in answering that Sean licked into my ear.

"At least my tongue so I can get a proper taste of you," he murmured. "Maybe slip a fingertip in once you're relaxed?"

The idea of anything up my ass didn't sound pleasant— no matter how delicious Sean claimed it felt. "I don't know..."

"I'll make it good for you, Teach. Promise." He squeezed my cheeks so damn hard I yelped. "Gonna leave hickeys all over you too. Big old purple bruises you can look at in the mirror and blush over remembering how your student got on his knees to eat your ass."

"Sean." I shifted away from him, falling all over again at the endless pool of blue staring at me with unsated hunger. "We crossed a serious line tonight."

"Don't care." He tried to pull me back against him, but I held a palm to his chest. His pulse thrummed beneath my hand.

"I do," I stated quietly even though I wouldn't change the connection we'd made or take back the night we'd had together.

We stared at each other, the hot water pelting our skin and running in rivulets down our bodies. His blond hair appeared darker, plastered to his forehead, his lips red, wet, and tempting.

"But I'm not sorry," I whispered the truth since I didn't want him to spiral in any way. What we'd done...I had no words to explain how full I felt even though I hadn't been on the receiving end. Even the fact I'd had sex with someone other than Katie in our home, my first act of intimacy in three years, didn't dampen my sense of rightness over what he and I had experienced together.

But the timing...*that*, I had issue with.

"I'll behave on campus," Sean claimed, clasping my hand over his chest.

"We can't be seen together off it either," I murmured, searching for and hoping to find acquiescence on his face.

Sean huffed, lips pressed tight.

"I wish I could say that I would give up the world for you, Sean, but I love and need my job—my income. If we're caught, no other college would hire me. I don't have investments to see me through past retirement. There's no inheritance waiting for me to fall back on."

"I have a shit ton of money—I'll be your sugar daddy."

I barked out a laugh, tugging Sean against me once more. He was all warm and hard muscle, perfect hugging material. "A sweet suggestion, but I'm not made to be a kept man. Trust me, you wouldn't like a bored Matteo."

"Is bored Matteo a horny fucker?"

"More like grumpy and antsy."

"Fine," he stated on a sarcastic sigh. "But when this semester is over..."

"Yes, Sean. A thousand times, yes."

I lay in silence, watching moonlight bathe Sean's face where he rested on the pillow beside mine. We hadn't discussed sleeping over. He'd simply crawled into my bed and curled around my back as though he belonged there.

I definitely didn't hate his assumption. And while I'd never been the small spoon, I'd found my new favorite place to be. Wrapped up in Sean's arms was nothing short of heaven. His hairy thigh between mine, his warm, damp exhales on my nape, and his hand splayed over my stomach became a reality I honestly couldn't remember not having. He filled up space around me, inside me, to the point he owned my thoughts.

Once he'd drifted off and rolled away in his sleep, I turned to take him in and memorize how he looked at rest in my bed. Nothing overwhelmed him in that moment, no worry over Elite and what they would face in the morning if Jackson Zerig wasn't found.

We both had classes, but Sean planned on skipping them to be with his brother Micah for when the call came in —either news of Zerig's demise or his unleashing what could be damaging to their family business.

Sean had told me he'd stopped escorting, and I wondered if he missed having men at his disposal. My brain wanted to agonize. What if I wasn't enough for him after the newness of what we shared wore off or if he only planned on fucking me from his system and moving on?

The thought of a Sean-less future?

I went cold, my heart slowing and chest aching. Needing to feel connected to the life he'd created inside my dead soul, I leaned in, uncaring if I roused him from sleep. I had to breathe him into my lungs until he became so damned intertwined with me that he couldn't escape. My lips brushed over his parted ones, and he sighed, shifting in his sleep.

But he didn't wake, and I didn't push to steal his quiet

slumber.

Tenderness swelled inside me, and I moved hair off his forehead.

Sean was beyond beautiful, and even when his spirited nature lay deep beneath sleep, he filled me with yearning.

Life stirred in my groin, but I ignored my cock rising between my thighs.

I wanted him rested for when the sun rose, so I let him be, closed my eyes, and eventually found oblivion.

My senses returned with a jolt as wet heat closed over my cock. Strong hands grasped my thighs, keeping me still, and I groaned at the massive man-made tent between my blanket-covered thighs.

"Sean..." I moaned his name as he suckled on me, enticing my length to swell fully on his tongue.

"Mmm," he hummed a good morning, the bob of his head beneath the comforter a beautiful thing to wake up to. But even better?

I ripped the blankets off him and drank in the sight of sleepy blue eyes peering up over my torso as he sucked on my length. Our gazes clashed, and he stole my breath as usual.

Grasping hold of his face, I enjoyed the hell out of the morning blow job he gifted me.

His tongue toyed with my frenum, a twinkle lighting his eyes.

Feeling a little adventurous, I spread my thighs wider, planting my feet on the mattress and granting him access to what he'd said he wanted. Perhaps I was a little...curious.

Lust darkened his orbs, his pupils swelling. In normal Sean fashion, he didn't ask permission, simply went for it, trailing fingertips over my balls, rubbing along my taint, and eventually feathering at my pucker with a soft tickle.

A rush of adrenaline woke me fully, and I swallowed hard, forcing myself to relax.

Sean popped off my cock and watched me while gently stroking my dry hole.

Shouldn't I have felt lust shooting through me? My dick bucking in his other hand at the very least as he massaged my asshole?

"Sean, I'm not sure..."

"It's okay, Teach. I won't do anything you don't want me to." He held my gaze and started giving me those sucking kisses he'd spoken of. Wet and open-mouthed, his smooches ranged from the back of my dick to my inner thighs.

Legs grasped and shoved wide, he made himself intimately acquainted with my groin. He nuzzled my sac, inhaling and groaning his approval of my musk.

"Fucking hell, Teach, you smell so good."

My entire body flared with flames. Never had I ever considered a man sniffing my balls and getting turned on—

His slick tongue lathed at my pucker. We both made noises in our throats, but mine cut off as he breached me, my pulse jackknifing in discomfort.

Just...no.

I hissed, clutching at his hair. "Sean."

He backed off and kissed my pucker before licking over it again. "Taste so damn good." A few kisses against my taint, and he left my ass for my sac, tonguing and suckling until wet warmth encased one of my balls.

A grunt pulled from my lungs, and I tightened my hold on his hair. "Feels so good, sweet boy...just like that."

He lathed and sucked, loving on my sac until I firmed tight against my groin. Eyes catching mine, he licked up the back of my cock, tonguing my slick slit. "Mmm."

"Suck me."

He did as told, taking me clear to the root.

"Good—boy...ah shit, so good." My hips bucked up off the bed, shoving my length deeper into his throat. "Jesus— fuck!"

I shot like a geyser, unexpected and so damned powerful I lost touch with reality.

I gasped for breath, my pulse rushing in my ears, my muscles relaxing back onto the mattress.

Sean crawled up my body, his lips closed tight but smirking.

My arms were dead weight, but I grasped his scruffy face and parted my lips.

He gave me what I expected—his mouthful of my cum then his tongue to make sure I kept it where he wanted it. While I wasn't a fan of swallowing my own cum, I sucked his tongue clean...licking over his lips to get every drop.

Groaning, he began rolling his hips, sliding his hard length against my sensitive softened one.

"Gonna come all over you, Teach."

"Do it."

I wrapped my heels around the back of his thighs, imagining what it would be like to hold him while he fucked my ass. The thought did nothing for me no matter how I wished otherwise.

Sean shuddered, groaned my name, and wet heat spilled between us.

His forehead tipped to mine, and we caught our breath together, that same sleepy, sated feeling from the night returning to make everything in my life seem right.

I was incandescently happy for the first time in three years.

Chapter 26

Sean

Micah didn't wait for the twelve-hour time limit to pass.

We sat together in his office as he put through a call to Preston.

"Nothing yet," he murmured, and my brother and I both cursed.

We eyed each other over his desk, every thump of my heartbeat like a ticking bomb in my head. Tension coiled me tight even though I'd been as relaxed as a sloth an hour earlier after smearing my cum all over Matteo's torso and watching it dry while we lazed in his bed and chatted, ignoring the clock on his bedside table.

Eventually, the spunk I'd left on him grew itchy. We showered together, but no shenanigans had gone down, simply a thorough scrubbing filled with laughter and teasing touches.

Matteo had radiated joy like I hadn't seen before. The sight of his carefree grin had filled me the fuck up. His dark eyes held light that had been absent in the few months I'd known him.

I'd done that. Me. Sean mother-fucking Fox.

"What do we do now, Preston?" Micah asked, pulling my mind back to the reality of why I had no right to smile in that moment.

"He'll do as promised, or he'll offer a bit more time in the hopes he'll get what he wants from you."

Micah hadn't been interested in the chance of calling Zerig's bluff, but maybe we would get lucky and he was more greedy than vengeful over acts that hadn't really happened. He'd extorted money out of other people in his past, and with Elite being a lucrative business, he would push for that cash.

But should the false news release and go viral?

Zack had stuck to his story, and both Micah and I believed him. If the need arose, we had dozens of clients who could vouch for Zack being a class act Elite. He was a rule follower to a T, kept to himself, and simply got the job done with incredible reviews. Outside mine, his dick was the most requested.

And since I'd dropped clients, he'd become the highest paid escort we had with Drake close on his heels.

"There's nothing we can do but wait," Micah said.

"Unfortunately," Preston agreed.

I blew out an exhale, that sense of being overwhelmed and powerless creeping in to settle on my shoulders. I fucking hated the fact I couldn't find a way out. There was no manipulating the situation to get what I wanted either.

"Go to class. Focus on that degree you're hellbent on attaining," Micah said after hanging up with Preston.

While I wouldn't be able to sit still or focus, I nodded my agreement.

"It's going to be okay, Sean." Micah rounded his desk and ruffled my hair like I was a little kid.

I jerked away from him, scowling.

He actually fucking chuckled.

"How can you laugh at a time like this?" I glared while getting to my feet. Same as whenever we stood side by side, his size intimated my smaller stature. He was broad and thick while I was just lithe.

Sure, I had confidence in how I appeared—but only so long as my big brother wasn't in close proximity.

"Not sure what else to do, to be honest," Micah replied, making toward his office door. "One of us has to keep their chin up, ready for a possible staggering blow."

Well, thanks for that dig, asshole.

Teeth clenched, I followed him out into the reception area.

BeckyAnne's smile dissolved as our eyes met. She kept quiet though, and I left Micah's mansion behind.

Rather than attending classes I'd already planned on skipping, I actually went to the gym. Two solid hours of cardio and weight lifting, and I buzzed from endorphins. I'd missed the feeling.

But my fucking stomach ached again.

I grabbed a bottle of antacids on the way home, popping the fuckers like candy. They took the edge off but not enough to allow me to focus on writing my fourth essay of the fucking semester.

What the fuck did essays have to do with an MBA? Like, seriously? Give me numbers any day of the week. Words and sentences, let alone stringing them together to make sense could eat shit and die.

Once more, I rested my forehead on my desk, not getting a goddamned thing accomplished.

At least my body would pass the fuck out from having beaten it into the ground at the gym. Resting without

Matteo as my body pillow might actually happen on its own. But fuck, I preferred having him beside me.

Blinking tired eyes, I swiped my cell to life and shot off a text of what would make him long for me the same I did for him.

Me: **What I wouldn't give to kneel at your feet right now.**

My heartbeat thumped heavily while I waited for his response, but my patience grew thin.

I retrieved a bottle of water from my fridge and stared at my black laptop screen, imagining what I wanted since I couldn't have it for another...four weeks? Checking the schedule, I noted final exams would take place the third week of December. So yeah, twenty-eight or thereabouts days until I could show up at Matteo's door, and he wouldn't be worried about us being found out.

My cell dinged, and my hands fumbled while bringing life to the screen.

Sexy Teach: **Not the words I needed to read at this moment.**

"Fuck." I swallowed hard and replied, **Sorry?**

Sexy Teach: **Don't be. I'm on the phone with my mom and can't be thinking about how perfect you look when resting your cheek on my thigh close to my aching groin.**

I blew out a breath, settling back in my chair even as blood rushed to my dick.

Me: **There's no place I'd rather be.**

Sexy Teach: **Beneath me.**

"Oh fuck." I stroked over my hard dick, imagining just that. Or...

Me: **Inside you.**

My pulse thrummed and breaths heightened as I waited for Matteo's reply.

Dots appeared. Disappeared.

Minutes ticked passed, and I wondered if he really wasn't interested in bottoming. That wouldn't be a deal breaker for me, but I hoped he was open to exploring. I also reminded myself he was on the phone. Dealing with a boner while chatting with your mom wouldn't be pleasant for someone as proper as my Prince Charming.

Me: **Call me when you can? If I can't sleep in your arms tonight, I at least need to hear your voice so I can relax.**

Sexy Teach: **Still no word on Zerig?**

Me: **No.**

Sexy Teach: **I'll call soon.**

Somehow, I managed to write a paragraph. Not that it made much sense, but at least I'd gotten words scribbled onto paper for a class I barely held a passing grade in. Shit was going to come down to finals in every class except Matteo's. Even though his was the most difficult to pay attention in, I somehow managed to hold that B average. Maybe because I wanted to prove my worth to him just as much as Pop?

My cell finally fucking rang, and I answered, my insides melting at Matteo's raspy greeting.

Curling up on my bed, fully clothed, I closed my eyes, ready for my mind to quiet.

Chapter 27

Matteo

Alessia had a big fucking mouth.

Rarely did I swear when it came to family, but she'd purposefully outed me to Mom about Sean, which in Mom's eyes, warranted a phone call. I ended up listening to a lecture the likes of which I hadn't heard since I'd been a teenager and had gotten caught smoking a joint out behind the garden shed.

"I just don't understand, Matteo," Mom stated quietly, and I closed my eyes, pinching the bridge of my nose. "Katie was the love of your life, a sweet young lady like you'd always talked about marrying someday. How are you suddenly wanting to date a *man?*"

My heart sank.

How did I explain to someone from the generation who didn't believe in sexual fluidity that attraction was a force of nature and simply happened? It had taken some convincing for me, and while Mom and Dad weren't homophobic, they still held backward morals.

"I can't describe what I feel for him in any scientific way that will make sense to you, Mom," I said, pushing the cooled chicken and rice meal I'd made for myself around my half-empty plate.

"Try."

"Remember that instant draw I'd felt for Katie?"

Mom's answering light laugh hinted at continued grief. "Yes. She was all you spoke about whenever I called you those first few months at college."

"It's the same with Sean. He walked into my class, our eyes met, and I was...smitten, Mom. Instantly enamored. It didn't matter what lay beneath his clothing and still doesn't even after getting to know him better. He's...sunshine." My voice cracked, so I shut up from waxing poetic about my student I was falling hard and fast for.

"I just don't understand," Mom repeated quietly.

I wasn't sure what to say, so I kept quiet. What other explanation could I offer? My body and heart wanted Sean Fox, end of story, and outside of the dean where I worked, I didn't give two shits what people thought about me dating him.

"Are you sure you can't come home for Thanksgiving?" Mom asked, changing the topic of conversation, thank God. "It sounds as though you need some time away. John and Janice are coming over for the day. I'm sure they would bring Serena if I extended the invite."

I shuddered at the memory of the woman Mom had attempted to hook me up with when I'd visited after classes had let out back in May. "No, Mom. I'm too busy," I reminded her of what I'd said the last time she'd asked for me to come down to South Carolina for the long weekend. "I'll be there for Christmas though—promise. But please, for the love of all you consider holy, do *not* try to play match-maker. Sean is the only one I'm interested in, and no female, no matter how pretty or smart, is going to change that."

He'd weaseled his crafty way into my soul, and I doubted nothing short of death would extract him from my life if I had any say in the matter.

A cool shiver slid down my spine as the words in my head came to fruition in my mind's eye. Losing Katie had left me deeply wounded, but to have Sean ripped from my life?

I wasn't sure I would survive another heartache.

How was that possible? Why did my connection with a young man I hardly knew seem so...right?

A text notification came through, and I put Mom on speaker as she went on about the holidays.

Speak of the wily devil. Sean's text about wanting to kneel for me shot a rush of arousal through me, the last thing I wanted while Mom prattled on in my ear.

I tried to focus on what she said about Claire-bear's Christmas list, but thoughts of Sean on his knees proved a distraction I couldn't fight off. Eventually, I responded, and we had a quick back and forth via text.

"Matteo, are you listening to me?"

"Hmm?"

Mom's exasperated sigh on speaker caused guilt to creep in."Is it him?"

No point in lying. She would sniff out the truth just like Alessia always managed to do. "Yes," I said.

"There's no talking you out of this, is there?"

"Why would you even attempt that?" I asked, annoyance denting my brow. "He makes me happy for the first time since I buried Katie. You should be thankful he's come into my life."

Mom hesitated before replying. "You're right, son. I'm sorry. It's just...something I never expected is all. You never liked boys before."

And we were back to her inability to just accept how I felt. Without a doubt, Dad would react much the same since Mom ruled their roost.

"I have to go, Mom."

"Don't forget we're celebrating Christmas on the twenty-third," she needlessly reminded me.

"The last day of finals is the twenty-first," I told her what I'd said already. "I'll be there for the party. Promise—and no Serena!"

I could hear Mom's pout over the line but didn't give a shit.

Two minutes later, I called Sean like I'd promised. "How are you holding up?"

"I'm not. My brain won't shut off, and I can't focus on this damned paper I have to write."

"You don't have anything to prove," I reminded him. "You're perfect the way you are."

"Pop doesn't think so," Sean muttered like a petulant child, but I understood. He'd spilled his heart more than once about his relationship with his father, or lack thereof, rather. "Hold on...Micah texted me...I gotta go."

"Call me back—"

Sean hung up without a goodbye.

I wanted to be just as much of a brat as him and allow my feelings to be hurt for being dismissed so quickly, but I knew what he faced. The trouble Elite might find themselves in should the concocted story of abuse leak to the press.

Sean hadn't held anything from me, explaining in detail about the attempt at extortion, who the client truly was without giving me his name, and the warrants already out for his arrest. I wished more than once I was some tech guru, a computer whiz who could locate the asshole and end the nightmare haunting my sweet boy.

The waiting proved difficult.

I cleared my plate and poured myself a glass of wine rather than cleaning the dishes.

Sean: **He's in custody!!!**

My breath left like a punch to the gut, and I sank onto the couch.

Me: **I'm so happy to hear it.**

Sean: **I'll call you when I can.**

One weight lifted from my mind, I enjoyed my wine in silence, imagining Sean at my feet, smiling up at me. His relief would have him bouncing off the walls, highly energized, and in the mood to celebrate.

My cock hopped onto that train of thought, but I ignored the fantasies wanting to unfurl in my head.

An exhausted Sean had been tough to keep up with. I couldn't imagine the boy hopped up in full exuberance. He would wear me out.

I grew contemplative, wondering over how deeply I'd fallen with a young man who'd probably slept with more men than I had acquaintances throughout my life.

Would I be enough for Sean?

Would he grow bored with having the same body in bed with him every night if we even got to the point of trying for a relationship?

Would his antsy feet make him seek out new forms of excitement that didn't include his old professor's ass?

I'd never been an insecure man, but the troubling questions littered my brain, and the second glass of wine I enjoyed while waiting for my obsession to call me didn't quiet them one bit.

My cell rang, waking me up. Blinking the living room into focus, I realized I'd passed out on the couch, something I rarely did.

Sean.

Relief washed through my already slackened muscles as I answered. "Sean?"

"Hey, Teach." The buoyancy in his voice roused me from sleep, and I smiled, stretching out into a more comfortable position. "So that fucker is behind bars, but he got in touch with a news anchor before the police busted his door down."

Alarm spread through me, dissolving my smile as I glanced at the clock. It had been over three hours since Sean had texted me. "What happened?"

"Of all people Zerig could email, it ended up being a past, one-time customer of EEMM."

"Get the fuck out!" I huffed a laugh.

"Nope. The guy called me before I could leave the office, and it took a little begging on my part, but he's agreed to sit on the story for now."

My grin faded. "Why not get rid of it altogether?"

"Because he's aiming to become a prime-time anchor, and this kind of exclusive news could pave his way."

"What an ass."

"Micah knows the exec of the station and might be able to pull some strings, but we'll see. While we're far from in the clear, at least we know this shit won't go any further in the immediate future."

"That's good," I murmured.

"So what are you up to, Teach? In the mood for some company?"

I hated to dampen his spirits, but I had no choice, especially after that whole doubt fest I'd had before falling asleep. Sean and I had a taste of each other, but hard boundaries needed to be set to reveal the true nature of what he felt for me.

"Four weeks, Sean."

"Come on!" he whined, and my hands itched to redden his backside again. "You know you don't want to wait. Tell me the thought of my hot ass swallowing your dick doesn't turn you on."

His mouth...

I shook my head, eyes closing.

"Hell, I'd be content to choke on your dick while jerking off. I need this, Matteo."

This, not me.

"Four weeks," I reiterated, standing firm to protect myself. I'd rather have spilled my feelings, how I'd come to the conclusion losing him would kill my desire to live, but that would only encourage him. He would show up on my doorstep uninvited and manipulate his way beneath my skin.

Arousal slid through my veins, but I held firm even as Sean continued to talk me into letting him sit on my cock and lick into my mouth.

"Sean," I cut him off mid-sentence about riding me reverse cowboy so he could play with my balls while bouncing on my dick. "If what we shared is important to you, if I mean anything to you more than a way to find release, please honor my request. Please," I begged, the images in my head he'd painted so vivid I ached for release.

Sean sighed with exaggerated annoyance but stopped

his sexual chatter. "You aren't going to give in just to shut me up?"

"No."

"Have I told you how much I adore your sturdiness, Matteo? How much I crave to be put in my place from someone who won't take my shit even though I really, *really* want you to fuck me right now?"

My cock bucked in my sleep pants, and I squeezed the base to calm myself down.

"Four weeks is a long time, Teach," Sean muttered. "I already feel like I have carpal tunnel. Masturbating is *so* boring."

He hadn't been escorting for just a few weeks, and already he'd grown tired of his hand.

That fear about him doing the same with me returned full force, sending a pang through my chest.

"It's late, Sean."

"Want to have a jerk-off sesh over the phone?"

Goddamn him. "No—I have an early class in the morning, and if I remember correctly, you have an essay due."

"Fuck," he grumbled. "Fine."

"I'll see you Monday in class."

"Yeah, yeah." He sounded like an annoyed kid who needed his ass reddened.

"You can do this, Sean. I have faith in you."

I could sense him perking up through the line, could see his loopy grin over my words of praise.

If only I had faith in the foundation we'd created and our connection wouldn't fizzle out once sated.

Chapter 28

Sean

Talk about a fucking emotional roller coaster. Zerig landed his ass in jail but not before doing what he'd promised. Micah seemed chill about our ability to get the anchor and past client of Elite his promotion, so I tried not to focus on the what-ifs. At least the stress had lessened, and antacids worked a little better at calming my insides. Giving up that third and fourth cup of coffee every day helped too.

But my sexy Teach? He brought on anxiety of a different sort.

He hadn't texted or called over the weekend. Hadn't even responded to my *I miss having your hands on my body* Saturday night or the invitation I'd sent for a FaceTime bust-a-nut-together date on Sunday.

He wouldn't even look at me on Monday morning. During class, he lectured from behind his desk as though a bit of wood and nails could protect him from the want we shared.

Something had shut him down, and I hated how he held

me at arm's length. But like a nagging black fly, I wasn't going to let him shoo me away.

Not being front and center in his thoughts did *not* sit well with me.

At fucking all.

"I'll see you after break! Have a happy Thanksgiving!" He raised his voice to be heard over the others in the room gathering up their things at the end of class. We had off Wednesday, so this was it. The last filling of my eyes with his gorgeousness for a week.

I lagged behind as usual so I could hang with him for a few seconds in the hallway.

"You didn't return my texts." I sounded like a put-out brat as I sidled up to him, but what else was new? Maybe it would make him want to spank my ass. Then fuck it.

"And I asked you to not tempt me beyond what I could handle," he replied, his tone firm.

Why the fuck did his words turn me on but at the same time his stubbornness pissed me off?

I brushed against his shoulder, desperate for contact of any sort.

"Sean," he murmured my name, his dark eyes holding the exact warning as his voice. To back away.

"I'm really fucking needy, Teach," I whispered.

A muscle ticked in his jaw as he looked away, ignoring me.

"Patience is not a virtue I'm well acquainted with."

"So I've noticed," he muttered, arms crossing over his chest. "But in this, you have no choice, Sean. I won't bend."

I considered teasing him about all the ways I would *bend* for him, but I could tell by Matteo's stance that he wouldn't smile or flirt back. And a crowded hallway definitely wasn't the place for me to use my body to manipulate and wear him down.

Nothing sucked more than recognizing my hands were bound tight as fuck with no hope of getting what I wanted before the semester ended.

"Guess I'll see you around, Teach," I said, my heart heavy, my tone snippy.

He dipped his head, lips pressed tight.

It fucking sucked to walk away. We were talking achy bullshit in the chest, dragging feet and all as I traversed a path through other students.

I handed in the goddamned essay at my next class, knowing points would be taken off for it being late, but I didn't care. At least I got the fucking thing written without plagiarizing like I'd been tempted to do.

Matteo hadn't just created space between us physically by holding firm to his stance of waiting, but he'd wedged emotional distance as well. That hurt more than any blue balls ever could.

Sleep? Forget about it.

Burning stomach? Back in full *fucking* force.

Wednesday, I had the whole day off, and with the waiting on Micah's contact at the news station to get back to him, I headed to the gym and killed my body again. Thanksgiving morning, I woke to sore muscles that screamed when I rolled out of bed.

A long, hot shower made moving around my condo a little easier, but I was bored and lonely.

Drake was spending the weekend at his Mom's in Rhode Island, so I had no one to hang with but my family.

I drove over to Micah's earlier than Jasmine had said in her group text inviting us all for the day. Her family would already be there helping prepare the meal for our combined families.

Micah ruffled my hair and earned an elbow to his side after he let me in their front door. "Jerk off." I tried to fix the mess he'd made atop my head.

"Chill out, you little shit. There are no hot men here to think you're any less cute because I wrecked what you probably spent an hour styling."

"Fuck you," I muttered at his back as he walked away chuckling.

"Hi, brat!" Jasmine said from across the kitchen, her face still a little pale as she waved in greeting.

"Hey, Sis. Feeling okay?" I helped myself to the tray of olives on the island since she hadn't approached for a hug.

"I'm wonderful." Pink flushed on her cheekbones, and I nodded, knowing she'd tell me otherwise if she wasn't.

"Mrs. Swift. Liz." I greeted her mom and sister, the latter of which had a whining kid trying to weasel down from her hip.

"Your mom told me you've gone back to college," Mrs. Swift said, her smile kind as always.

"Yeah."

"I can't even imagine how busy your schedule must be." Liz shoved a cookie in her toddler's mouth to keep him quiet and still.

Jasmine's whole family knew about Elite, and while they were more on the conservative side, they thankfully didn't state their opinions. Besides, Micah's money and how generous he was with his in-laws had to be enjoyable as fuck for them. They'd be absolute morons to look down their noses at him after all he'd done for their youngest daughter and how he sent them on bi-yearly cruises.

"It's been tough," I admitted, popping another olive in

my mouth. The burst of saltiness made my mouth water to devour the whole bowlful. "But I'm hanging in there."

"I'm proud of you," Micah said, once more messing up my hair.

While I loved the sentiment, I bit my tongue so I wouldn't curse his ass out in front of Jasmine's family and the mini Cookie Monster in Liz's arms. A growl managed to escape though, and he barked a laugh that didn't sound quite...real.

I watched him head over to Jasmine and wrap his arms around her waist. They had their backs to me, but I caught his murmur against her ear and the flush that spread down her neck.

Tearing my jealous gaze away, I headed toward the living room where Pop and Mr. Swift sat in front of the TV. I greeted them both, but only Jasmine's father felt me worthy of eye contact with his greeting.

I got a grunt from Pop and nothing else.

"So...college!" Mr. Swift stated with a grin as I sat on the couch a cushion away from him.

"Yep—it's going well too," I lied, watching Pop. His stare didn't waver from the massive screen in front of him. "It's a big workload taking classes full time but nothing I can't handle."

Pop snorted, but even though he didn't outright put me down or spew something negative like usual, he'd made his thoughts clear.

Why had I hoped for one positive word? Why did I set myself up for disappointment like this every *goddamned* time?

Throat tight, I left the two older men, cursing myself for showing up early. I'd have been better off staying at home alone until the last possible second.

Hiding away in the half-bath off the kitchen, I pulled out my cell.

Me: **I hope you have a good Thanksgiving.**

I'd considered asking Matteo to join us but knew he'd be spending the day with Professor Hanson and his husband. Being invited to tag along with Matteo would have been heaven.

Maybe next year, because once the semester ended, Matteo would be all mine.

Heart somewhat eased by the light at the end of the tunnel, I returned to the kitchen and made Jasmine put me to work.

Mr. Swift said grace over the meal an hour later, and I busied myself shoving food down my throat until my stomach threatened to spew.

Dina, Elite's original secretary and Jasmine's other sister, had arrived with her husband Aaron a few minutes prior to our sitting down to dinner. I glanced across the table at them, noting how they'd shifted their chairs closer to each other. They'd been married for a couple of years and acted madly in love, like they were still on their honeymoon or some shit.

My gaze roamed around the massive dining room table, my chest caving in as I recognized I was the only single person besides Liz's two kids. Outside Mom and Pop, they'd all found their soulmates, the ones that filled the empty places inside their other halves.

Chatter filled the room, the younger boys loud and demanding regardless of how their parents tried to keep them quiet, distracting me enough I didn't flee the room.

Mom had Christmas carols on in the background—fucking why I didn't know. I enjoyed the Thanksgiving season until Black Friday. Playing Christmas music before that day was just downright wrong in my opinion.

Sudden longing for quiet, the safety of kneeling at Matteo's feet swept through me. My damn eyes stung, and I swallowed against the lump rising in my throat.

Everyone had pretty much finished, but no one made a move to get up and clear the table. I shifted, ready to tackle the chore myself since it would give me something to take my mind off how much I missed Matteo, but Micah clinked the back of his knife on his glassware.

"If I could have everyone's attention."

Voices went quiet as we shifted our focus toward the head of the table.

Micah grinned at Jasmine on his right while gathering her hand. Her smile wobbled.

"Shit," I whispered, and thankfully no one heard my verbal reaction to the thoughts that sprinted through my brain. There was only one thing my perfect brother readied to say.

"We're going to have a baby."

And there it was.

Cries of congratulations rang out, but it was Pop I turned toward at the other end of the table.

Sure enough, a damn smile cracked his face.

Ears ringing and throat swelled shut, I offered my best wishes. Somehow, I made it through helping to clean up the dishes without breaking down. A full-on pity party rioted in my head and heart, and while I took pride in not throwing a temper tantrum, I fucking *hurt*.

While the men grinned and women gushed over baby showers and opinions on breastfeeding and sleep training, I managed to slip quietly out the front door.

Of course, my leaving went unnoticed. Everyone was

too focused on the Fox boy who could do no wrong, the golden boy who financially supported everyone besides me under their roof and wouldn't let our family name fade into obscurity like I planned on doing.

Needy didn't begin to describe how I felt, and there was only one person on the planet I could trust to quiet my thoughts.

And if he turned me away?

Fuck, I couldn't even go there in my mind. Fingers crossed, I headed up the highway, hoping like hell Matteo was home.

Chapter 29

Matteo

"How are you doing, Matteo?" Hanson asked while handing me a beer.

I'd been invited to spend the holiday with them along with a handful of their family members and other friends, but I wasn't in the mood to be thankful. I'd only just arrived and already felt the urge to go back home where I could stew in my misery over my parents' unrest over me falling for a man and the fact I wanted him *now* but couldn't have him.

"Hanging in there," I said.

"Is Sean behaving?"

"Somewhat," I mumbled, lest the others lingering in their kitchen over the appetizers heard.

I'd shared everything with my friend, thinking that unburdening my mind would make the situation easier to handle. It hadn't. I still longed for Sean, even though my sense of self-preservation insisted I continue to hold him at arm's length.

"You're doing the right thing." Hanson clasped my shoulder.

While my head agreed with Hanson's statement, my heart didn't feel as though I'd made the right choice.

I nodded, sipping my beer. The cool liquid slid to my empty stomach without tasting it.

Sean and I hadn't discussed what we were to one another, but I still grieved the absence of him and his light. That happiness I'd felt while lounging in my bed together what seemed months ago rather than a week had faded away to nothing.

I longed for him in ways I couldn't understand, and the possibility of him sifting through my fingers like sand only heightened my discomfort.

While I'd attempted to enjoy the following hours with my friends, I was the first to leave after our late dinner.

Sean had texted me a happy Thanksgiving earlier in the day, but I hadn't responded. Doing so would only open a door for further conversation, and sharing words with him always ended with me tempted to grow lax in my stance on keeping distance between us.

I turned the corner onto my street, my breath leaving in a rush at the sight of Sean's Audi sitting alongside the curb in front of my house.

"Damn him," I muttered even though I wasn't surprised he'd disobeyed me.

Part of me wanted to tear into him for making me feel unsteady, unsure about my choices while the other half desired to wrap him in my arms and tell him I understood.

Once parked in my garage, I waited for him to join me beneath its roof before putting the door down behind us.

He shuffled closer, shoulder slumped and eyes wary as the automatic pulley system squeaked and shuddered once finished.

I didn't speak, simply opened the door leading into the house and motioned him inside.

Sean dropped to his knees on the tile, head lowered.

My chest split, and nothing, no threat of being found out or losing my job could keep me from reaching for him in his time of need. The soft strands of his hair slid through my fingers as I caressed his bowed head, wanting to erase his pain.

Sighing, he wilted beneath my touch.

"Not here, Sean," I murmured, my voice low as I headed for the living room.

I eyed the recliner where I used to sit for Katie, but same as the first time I'd considered allowing Sean to kneel for me, I chose the couch instead. I sat, and he'd followed so closely on my heels that he sank onto the rug before I even settled myself.

He wrapped his arms around my leg and lay his cheek on my thigh, releasing a relieved sigh.

Something more had happened since last we'd spoken, defeat far beyond what had radiated off him earlier in thick waves. He called out to me on that deep level that insisted I take care of him.

"Talk to me, Sean."

"Jasmine is pregnant," he whispered.

The gaps slowly filled in, cluing me in to his mood. He'd told me his mom looked forward to grandchildren, so I expected she'd focused on her older son, without doubt praising him in some way for what his wife's pregnancy meant to her.

Sean sat on the outside in his mind, ignored and forgotten, which had probably dragged up his insecurities.

"I...I'm sorry, Matteo, but you're the only one who can quiet my mind. Discipline me all you want for disobeying your order—deny me the pleasure of you and your body for the next six months—I just..."

I pet over his head, and he shuddered, clutching me closer as his voice ran quiet. Never had someone needed me so desperately to the point I wondered if it ran toward unhealthy. But his statement also quieted the thoughts he simply wanted to fuck me out of his system, that he was only interested in me for the physical.

Sean would benefit from seeing a therapist to work through his emotional childhood trauma, but I couldn't deny how his need created one in me. Yes, he'd gone against my wishes, but I truly wasn't a sadist, nor was he a masochist.

"Come here, sweet boy." I tugged on his hair, and he scurried to drape himself over my thighs. "No." I manhandled him until he realized I wanted him to straddle me.

No trace of sassy brat lingered on his face as he settled where I directed. Eyes downcast, he clasped his hands on his lap rather than reaching for me. Empathy for the pain weighing on him caused my chest to squeeze tight.

I grasped his face in my hands and tilted his chin up until he was forced to meet my gaze. My breath swooshed from my lungs but not from the usual lust when our eyes met. His were anguished, beaten down to the point I worried for him.

"You're perfect," I whispered past the lump in my throat. "Even hurting, you're the light I need to survive and the happiness I reach for in my mind whenever you aren't with me."

Rather than Sean preening at my praise, tears welled in his eyes. "Then why push me away, Matteo? Why deny us when we have no idea when we'll breathe our last?"

His brutally honest question rocked the foundation of

my stance on waiting, the lack of manipulation clear in the deep ocean of his watery stare.

How often had I wished for just one more week, one day, one last fucking *hour* with Katie after she'd left me alone? How many months had I grieved over lost time, wasting time when I should have been living like she'd asked me to?

And I'd been denying Sean what we both drew breath and happiness from.

I'd been a fool.

"I'm sorry," I choked out to both her and the young man killing me with his heartache. "So fucking sorry." My voice broke, and I pulled Sean forward, taking his mouth, pouring every bit of sorrow and desire welling inside me into our kiss.

He fisted his hands in my shirt, whimpering, the desperation in him rolling over me in waves. "Matteo," he breathed against my lips.

"I know, sweet boy."

I encouraged him off my lap but only because I wanted him in my bed. Without words, we stumbled our way upstairs, shedding clothes and sharing hungry kisses as we went. Naked, Sean fell onto my mattress, and I followed him down, blanketing his warmth with my own.

He moaned, arching his back and grinding his hard length against mine. I expected him to toss out orders about putting my dick in his greedy hole, but he held quiet for a change, allowing his body—and me—to lead in every way.

Sean's submission to the energy between us was nothing short of breathtaking. To watch a creature owned by instinct relinquish control filled me up with a sense of rightness I'd never thought I would find again.

Pre-cum smeared between us as we writhed together in heated desire.

I'd been wrong to withhold affection and praise from him. I'd been owned by fear rather than the gift of the bond we shared. Those ideas of not being enough for him? They were shattered by the trust in Sean's eyes. The thought he would grow bored with me was wiped from my mind with his grasp to clutch me closer.

"I will never regret falling for you, Sean—ever. And I'm not going to waste another moment enjoying the gift of your sunshine in my life."

Tears once more filled his eyes, and I kissed him gently before he could reply.

"Let me love you," I whispered against the soft pillow of his lips, and his soft sob broke me.

Chapter 30

Sean

And I'd thought Matteo had made love to me the last time we'd been in his bed.

We went without a condom since we'd discussed clear test results after our first night together, and his slickened flesh stroking into my body as we held each other was beyond blissful. Heavenly in breath-stealing splendor. Other-fucking-worldly with heart-stopping euphoria. The gasps and groans escaping between our mouths plastered to each other turned me on as much as his thick dick filling my ass.

There was nothing between us. Two bodies couldn't be any closer than we were, but it still wasn't enough.

Emotions rolled through me, some glorious and achingly sweet, others tainted from deep wounds.

I wrapped my legs around my lover's back, holding him tight to me as tears trickled from my clenched eyelids. Regardless of the heavy sadness in my chest, I would come from the friction of his lower abs against my aching length squished between us. Having his full attention, his complete acceptance of who I was, flooded me with thankfulness for how fate had brought us together.

Matteo had given in to the pull between us without my manipulating him, and I refused to be sorry for going against his wishes. I would do everything in my power to protect him—

"Sean," he whispered against my mouth, the swivel of his hips while fucking slowly into me sending my eyes rolling back into my head.

He felt so, *so* good inside me...owning me, sinking deep with luscious, slow strokes.

"I'm gonna come," I gasped as my taint starting to spasm.

Matteo lifted his head from mine, and our gazes caught as my release tore through me.

"So beautiful," he murmured, holding my face while I came undone beneath him. "Such a good boy—my sweet Sean." He swallowed hard as I shuddered, still fucking into me with deliberate thrusts bent on driving me insane as my hole clenched around his dick.

I wanted him to breed my ass, shoot his seed deep inside me. Mark me like no one had been allowed before.

Rather than sinking into relaxation, my climax left me feeling edgy. The funk of Micah's news and Pop's reaction roused me, and that life-giving force Matteo gifted me made my hunger spiral higher.

With a lunge, I rolled us. Matteo's hard dick slipped from my body, but I had plans.

"What—"

I spun and sank onto his shaft in one downward thrust, reverse cowboy just like I'd teased him about before. "Oh fuck." I groaned, leaning forward, hands on his knees for a second to catch my breath.

He was so hot and hard beneath me—inside me without a goddamn condom. I shuddered, lips parted as I breathed through the exquisite tingles racing through my bloodstream.

"Jesus, Sean." Matteo grabbed my hips, shifting beneath me as though restless and needing to come.

I started to gyrate my hips, his low, rasped curses spurring me on regardless of how sensitive I was. Settling in, I sat back onto my knees, my thighs spread wide to shove his open as well.

"Mmm," I hummed and stilled on riding his dick, running my hand down over his firm balls and taint. "Lookie here..."

Matteo jolted as I squeezed my ring around his girth.

"Lie still for me," I murmured, drifting down further to ghost my fingertips over his hole. He hadn't seemed into it before, but on the verge of busting a nut in my ass, he might feel differently.

Another curse rose from behind me as I tapped at his pucker. A stroke up my spunk-covered abs gave me the slickness I needed.

"Relax, Teach," I crooned, smearing my cum all over his asshole. "Let me rock your world. You haven't experienced true pleasure until someone makes love to your prostate. Promise."

He released a slow, steady breath, his pucker going soft beneath my touch. "I trust you."

I pressed in.

"Ah, fuck!" Matteo jolted beneath me, but I kept my weight on his hips and began gently trailing my left hand's fingertips over his tight sac while letting him grow accustomed to a fingertip in his ass. "Sean," he hissed through clenched teeth.

"Feel good, Teach?"

"No."

I glanced over my shoulder.

Matteo's brow furrowed, his lips pressed tight.

Wiggling my finger a little only deepened his frown. "Give it a minute—it gets better. Promise."

I shifted over his dick, but he'd softened a little. "You with me, Matteo?"

"Yes, but I don't... I—I can't."

I slid my finger from his pucker and cupped his sac. Someday he might change his mind, but if he didn't?

"No worries, baby," I murmured, meaning every word. "Not everyone likes to be penetrated."

"Sean." Matteo took hold of my arms and shifted me off his cock and around, settling me atop him.

I rubbed my hard dick over his, loving how his semi perked up against mine.

"I'm sorry." His dark eyes still blazed with passion.

Leaning down, I brushed my lips over his. "Not every man who loves dick wants one up his ass. It's fine and definitely not a deal breaker. Honestly. I'll take you whatever way I can, Teach."

We frotted and kissed until he became hard enough for me to fuck myself on him again.

I reached between our sweaty bodies and grabbed hold of his base, shifting his dick to line up with my hole. Sinking back fully onto his length pulled a hiss from me and a grunt from him.

"Fuck yeah," I groaned, swiveling my hips so he went deeper into my guts. "Jesus, you feel so damn good."

Our gazes locked, and an overwhelming desire to sink clear inside him welled up inside me. I whispered his name and leaned down, plastering our mouths together.

My throbbing dick was trapped between sweat-sickened bodies, and I rubbed shamelessly all the fuck over him, smearing pre-cum on his skin. Lusted for it to sink in and mark him for life.

I also wanted him shooting up my ass.

Just the thought tightened my balls and made my shaft ache for release. "So fucking close, Matteo—tell me you are too. Come in me while I paint your abs."

He cursed and shoved his tongue into my mouth, hands grasping at my backside with bruising force as he pummeled into me. His feet found the mattress for better leverage.

"Oh fuck yeah." I groaned, panting as he thrust like a goddamn animal, the noises spilling over my lips sexy as fuck. "Harder, baby—wreck my ass. Fill me the fuck up until your seed is leaking from my hole."

With a shout, Matteo stabbed deep, his dick throbbing inside me.

Warmth flooded through me, making my head spin. My dick shot spunk between us in agonizing pulses.

"Jesus *fucking* Christ," I gasped, shuddering with every spurt, knowing Matteo did the same *inside* me. Wishing I had a plug on hand to keep his seed where it belonged for forgoddamnedever, I propped on my elbows, sucking wind.

I broke Teach. He lay beneath me like a sloth, all lax muscle and soft flesh. Dark eyes, lust drunk and hazed over, peered up at me, full of belly-fluttering emotion.

He took my face in his warm hands and kissed me. Gently. Almost...reverently.

I gave him my full weight, wishing I could sink into his soul and never have to rouse to face reality again.

Chapter 31

Matteo

We spent the weekend in my bed, only dragging our bodies from cum-covered sated bliss for showers and food.

Sunday night, we sprawled freshly showered atop clean sheets. Sean snuggled into my side, a leg thrown over mine, arm wrapped around my torso, clinging as he'd been doing all weekend long.

Nothing had felt so perfect, so right in my entire life. I couldn't even pay heed to the guilt that wanted to push through my happiness, trying to tell me that I'd somehow soiled the memory of my wife by having a young man in our bed.

But I'd enjoyed him outside of it too, many places Katie and I hadn't ever christened with our lovemaking.

I petted Sean's silky, still damp hair, reliving how we'd created the last mess I had yet to clean up. Our Thai takeout dinner had gotten interrupted by my need for his tight hole, and I took him atop the island. Noodles and peanut sauce ended up splattered across the floor, but that hadn't stopped us from finding release.

My hand skimmed down his muscular back, over the swell of his ass. He shifted and sighed as I teased at his crack with my fingertips, remembering how I'd spread his cheeks and watched my cum ooze from his winking hole and down his pierced taint to drip onto the kitchen floor.

I'd never seen such a sexy sight and had decided to rub my spunk all over his sensitive balls and cock until he begged me to stop torturing him.

"You have a sweet little hole," I murmured, wishing I could get hard again just so I could slip my cock inside his body because he was so damn addictive. "You took me so well without complaining about the cold, hard granite beneath you."

He nuzzled my chest, emitting a satisfied sigh, and I squeezed him. I'd forgotten how good it felt lavishing praise on someone who needed to be built up. I'd made sure over the previous couple of days to point out things beyond sex that he'd done which pleased me too.

Clearing his plate and not leaving clothing on the floor, which Katie had often done. He'd insisted on hanging up our wet towels when I'd been ready to let mine lie where it fell when I'd been determined to get him under me again as fast as possible.

I didn't want Sean to leave, going so far as to dread our separating within the hour because I had work, and he had classes in the morning.

He'd filled the emptiness in my home, and I no longer grieved over memories whenever I looked around where Katie used to take up space in my life. I'd never been super possessive over her. When we'd gone to Chantelle's, I enjoyed showing her off rather than growling at other dominants who lingered in checking her out.

But Sean?

Before our weekend together, I hadn't cared too much about him escorting for Elite. He hadn't slept with anyone after we'd gotten together, but what plans did he have for the future? Would he take on clients over break or during the summer months when he wasn't buried beneath his college courses?

Was it too soon to put a label on us that allowed me the right to ask for exclusivity? Was there even an *us*?

I didn't doubt Sean wanted me, but he was young and had fifty times the experience I had. Many years of oat sowing lay ahead of him before he reached an age like me—ready to settle down.

"Sean?" I skimmed my hand up to his lower back, clutching him close against my side.

"Hmm?" He toyed with my nipple, and I grasped his hand to make him stop, threading my fingers through his. In true brat form, he shifted his hips, rubbing his soft cock against my thigh.

I swatted his ass the best I could with my arm tucked around him. "Stay still."

He huffed, and I rubbed the sting away, keeping my palm on his warm cheek.

"What are we doing here?" I asked quietly, my heartbeat thrumming a little faster over a conversation we needed to have but scared the shit out of me.

"Relaxing after one hell of a fuck that finally talked my ass into needing a break," he stated bluntly with satisfaction in every word.

The *finally* bugged the hell out of me. Had it taken three days of orgasms to sate him? At my age, I'd been lucky to get it up. Once the newness of what we did wore off, I doubted my ability to maintain that kind of stamina.

"What about...after?" I asked and tried not to hold my breath.

"After?"

"Will you see clients over break?" I hadn't meant to sound worried or jealous, but notes of both escaped with my quiet words. "I'm not usually possessive," I rushed to add, "but I'm not exactly comfortable with other men having you in the same way I enjoyed you this weekend."

Sean snorted and rolled on top of me, pinning my arms overhead. "*I'm* possessive as fuck," he stated, his blue eyes flashing down at me full of piss and vinegar. "Never have been before, but you... You *touch* someone else, and I'll go batshit crazy on both your asses. We're exclusive if that's what you're hinting at. No one else's mouth comes near you. A dick other than mine even *thinks* about your ass, and I'll burn shit to the ground."

His adamant no-bullshit attitude not only turned me on but settled my mind too. Chuckling, I lifted my head to kiss him but quickly sobered. "Will my dislike of bottoming eventually shift your eyes elsewhere though, Sean?"

"No fucking way. I told you once, and I'll tell you again —I'll gladly take whatever you'll give me and enjoy the fuck out of every second."

"Will you grow bored without having a hole to fill?"

He smirked and licked over my lower lip. "There's always your mouth."

I caught his tongue between my teeth and nibbled gently. "I'm serious, Sean," I stated once I let go of his slick tongue.

Huffing a heavy exhale, he released my hands, and I wrapped my arms around him, not totally convinced.

"You're mine, Teach, got it?" He laid down the law, gaze unwavering as I clutched him close.

My cock fantasized about plumping up but sighed back to sleep against his. "Then that means you're *mine*," I declared.

"Damn right." His grin lit me from the inside out.

"I'm not big on sharing," I said carefully, thinking of Chantelle's and all I'd seen there, "but if at some point you need more, I'm willing to...explore."

He stared down at me, going strangely still. "Care to expand on exactly what you mean by that?"

"Have you ever had a threesome?"

His lips quirked, his eyes turning all flirty. "Why, Professor D'Angelo, what kind of kinky fantasies do you have floating around in your head?"

They weren't exactly mine, but I could read the interest on his face.

"What I'm saying is that if you need an ass to fuck, I'll make it happen for you."

"But not *yours*," he ask for clarity.

"Right," I rasped, really wishing I felt differently about being on the receiving end of penetrative sex. Maybe someday? I remembered the discomfort of having just his fingertip up there, and...nope. Bottoming was definitely not my thing.

He ran his thumb over my lip. "I don't want to ever kiss another man or touch him the way I do you," he whispered, "but if we can have a meat sandwich with me in the middle..." A shudder moved him in my arms. "I—I can live with that kind of impersonal transaction. But, I'll be content with only you in my bed for all of eternity if that's what you prefer."

His declaration warmed my chest. "Okay, then."

"And Teach?"

"Hmm?"

"There's nothing wrong with not wanting to bottom, okay?" His blue eyes studied me with kindness rather than judgment. "I know you're new to this gay stuff, but please, for *love of my dick*, don't ever think you aren't enough, that you're less than—because you're everything."

My throat tightened, and I nodded, understanding why he'd used those precise words he'd often thought about himself. "Be a good boy, Sean, and give me your mouth."

Chapter 32

Sean

Three weeks left, I told myself while my man leaned against his desk in all his delicious virile manliness and lectured the class.

I didn't hear a damned word he said since I was too busy reliving our weekend together in my head. My ass still ached from the action back there, and I'd lost count of the number of climaxes I'd had in those three days. A few more than Matteo, but his old ass kept up with my needy one, offering me fingers the night before when his dick refused to rouse for our fourth or was it fifth go-round?

Poor baby. I'd given his pecker a few smooches, telling him it was okay and that I wasn't offended—I'd gotten off anyway. That bit of teasing had earned me a swift swat to my backside that had bloomed red and pretty alongside the purple splotches he'd sucked all over my ass.

I loved having his marks on me. His cum smeared over my body and deep inside my ass. I loved...

My chest tightened as he slid his gaze my way, lingering briefly on my mouth before moving on to Jazzie.

A sigh ripped through me, and had anyone looked at my

face in that moment, they would have seen how clearly I crushed on my professor. But he was just too goddamned delicious to not stare at.

Those shoulders. The scruff. The dark, piercing eyes that didn't miss a thing. Those strong hands and long fingers that knew how to stroke me just right.

Fuck me, I wanted him again.

We hadn't exactly put a label on what we were, but there was no question where we stood when it came to ownership and our commitment to one another. Insecurities plagued him as much as they did me, something I never would have guessed upon first meeting my stoic professor, but he'd allowed me in, shared his innermost secrets with me.

The bitch on my left cleared her throat again as though annoyed by my heart eyes, but I couldn't find a single fuck to give.

Class ended, and I tore my focus off Matteo to close my notebook I hadn't written a damn word on. My cell buzzed in my back pocket, and I pulled it free.

Micah: **I got the anchor his promotion along with a night with Jimmy since he's partial to blonds. We're in the clear.**

"Oh, thank fuck," I muttered, and the weight I hadn't paid notice to thanks to my weekend in Matteo's bed fled completely. Talk about a fucking relief. For the first time, I didn't even care Micah had been the one to save the day.

"You okay?" Jazzie asked, and grinning, I went to text Micah back, but another message popped up from him.

Micah: **Mind if I swing by your place tonight? There's something else I need to discuss with you.**

Well, that wasn't sobering at all.

Me: **Yeah**.

There was no point in asking him what he wanted to talk about. His planned meetings weren't ever on screen and usually ended up with me feeling like shit for fucking up again.

Guess my plans for sitting on Matteo's dick after dinner would have to take a back seat to work.

I hoofed it out of class behind Jazzie, and the second she waved and disappeared into the crowd, I sidled up a little too close to Teach where he lingered by his classroom door.

"Sean," he greeted me, his tone warm even though he stepped to the side to put some distance between us.

Oops.

It was just so goddamned hard to stay away from him when he was *right fucking there*.

We'd discussed acceptable behavior while on campus, and while it sucked ass I couldn't kiss his face off and claim him publicly, I would enjoy the hell out of breathing his scent deep into my lungs. And that boner from close proximity? Fuck yeah. He was so goddamned hot.

"Don't look at me like that," he muttered, glancing up and down the hallway with watchful eyes.

"Sorry, Teach." I grinned until his stoic facade broke the slightest bit, his brown orbs promising a yummy punishment if I didn't cut shit out. "So, tonight—"

He shook his head, lips pressed tight as if reminding me we couldn't talk about certain shit in the open while other students trickled past.

"Oh. Yeah." Why the fuck couldn't I listen or even remember the smallest requests he asked of me? Rubbing a hand through my hair, I nodded, deciding to blame him and his deliciousness. "Um...see you around, Professor D'Angelo."

Matteo dipped his head, and I sauntered off with an extra sway to my hips while pulling out my cell.

Not being allowed to even have a conversation aloud sucked even harder, but at least I had his heated gaze eating me up as I walked away.

Me: **Quit staring at my ass, Teach. Someone's gonna see how hungry you are.**

Snickering at myself, I shot off a second text to tell him our plans had changed like I'd been about to in person.

Me: **Gotta cancel tonight. Micah wants to talk shop with me.**

It was two agonizing classes before Matteo quit testing my patience and got back to me with a sad face emoji.

Sexy Teach: **Tuesday?**

Someone was needy—I loved that about him too.

Me: **Definitely. I'll come prepped so you can just slide your dick straight past my ring into the heaven of my hole you were praising all weekend long.**

Sexy Teach: **Jesus, Sean. Your mouth...**

Chuckling, my fingers flew over my screen.

Me: **You love it.**

Sexy Teach: **I do.**

I chewed on the inside of my lip, wondering exactly how much those feelings went beyond the physical for him.

For me?

There was such a thing as falling, then there was hitting the ground. But a healthy landing on two feet or my heart broken to pieces still remained to be seen.

Micah wasn't his usual no-nonsense, confident bastard self when I let him into my condo that night. He made straight for my living room and collapsed on the couch, head tipped back.

I stared a few seconds, baffled by his unusual behavior. "Uh...drink?" I asked before sitting down.

"Fuck yes."

Ooookay.

"Beer?"

"Vodka if you've got it," he mumbled under his breath.

My guts clenched, and I bit my tongue, holding off on conversation until I could sit down with him. We didn't do hard liquor too often thanks to Pop's drinking issues, so something was seriously wrong.

I pulled a bottle of Grey Goose from the freezer and splashed generous portions in two tumblers filled with ice. Fuck knew I was gonna need that shit if Micah's strangeness was any indication of what was to come.

"Thanks," he muttered, taking the cold glass and downing half of the drink in one go.

"Jesus, Micah." I perched on the edge of my recliner that was in a hell of a lot better shape than his piece of shit at his mansion and waited.

He eyed the ice, swirling the clear liquid around a few times before speaking. "I'm scared shitless."

"Ab-bout what?" I stammered, sudden nausea suggesting I run to the nearest can and empty the cold pizza I'd had for dinner from my stomach. Had more shit come of the pictures? Had the anchor spilled the story regardless of how Micah had managed to entice him to drop it?

Micah rubbed a hand over his face. "Jasmine."

A frown dented my forehead at the one-eighty. *Not what I had expected.* If he'd done anything to fuck shit up with my sister-in-law...

"What about her?"

"This pregnancy." He pursed his lips and shook his head. "It wasn't planned. I...I'm not sure I'm ready to be a dad, but Jasmine is so damn excited." He swallowed down the rest of his vodka.

My older brother had never been anything but confident. Sure of himself even when facing difficulties.

For the first time, I saw him as frail a human as me, and the fact he had fears and insecurities too set me back. Literally.

I sank into my chair and stared at the man I'd have bet my life's savings on had his shit together in every single fucking way imaginable.

Micah lifted weary eyes to me and huffed a laugh that held no hint of amusement. "I've never felt so incompetent in my life. Imagine what Pop would say if I said I'm scared out of my goddamned mind? Think of the bullshit he would spew if I told him what I really thought about becoming a father."

"If it was me in your shoes, he'd do exactly that," I said, "but this is *you*, Micah. You're the Fox son who can do no wrong. He'd probably sit you down for a nice heart-to-heart, encourage you, and remind you how strong and able you are. He'll give you a gold fucking star or trophy naming you father of the year before your kid is even born."

Micah's gaze roamed my face, and I shifted beneath his perusal. "You know, I've always been jealous of your easygoing, fly-by-the-seat-of-your-pants nature."

I blinked. "Huh?"

"You've been free to be yourself—never had to live up to Pop's expectations."

"Seriously?" A snorted laugh jerked my entire upper body. "I hate to break it to you, big bro, but I tried, I'm *still* trying, every *fucking* day to make Pop see me as something other than a waste of his sperm."

Micah frowned. "But you have such a fuck-all attitude that he can't wear down."

"That's the wall I've been hiding behind since I came off the soccer field in fourth grade, and Pop told me I should be a ballet dancer since I would never be the ball player you were. He then went back on his suggestion by reminding me I had two left feet and would probably fail at dance too."

My brother's eyes widened. "Fucking hell. He said that to you?"

"In front of the entire team."

"Shit." He rubbed a hand over his mouth. "That's why you never played another sport, isn't it?"

I nodded even though Micah sounded certain of his assumption.

"This whole time, I've been striving to be the perfect son, and you've been doing the same?" he asked.

"Guess so," I agreed, "but where you accomplished your goals, I've been one massive failure after another. You hear about a job well done while I get ignored. You earn his smiles with your accomplishments when a frown uglies his mug whenever he looks at me."

Micah toyed with the empty glass in his hands but didn't take his focus off my face. "That's why you're going for an MBA again, isn't it?"

"Yes."

"Fuck that, Sean." Micah scoffed and set his glass aside, stretching his arms across the back of the couch, owning the space with his usual take-charge presence. "Don't fucking do *shit* for that bastard. Live how you want. I might manage to get the old man to smile sometimes, but I've never been able to make others laugh like you do. Yeah, I'm jealous about that part of your personality too even though I give you shit for it. Your blunt honesty is damn refreshing. Wish I didn't naturally hold back so damn much."

I blinked.

"It takes all kinds of people, Sean, and while you're a pain in my ass sometimes, I wouldn't change shit about you. I fucking love you, man."

I chuckled, hating that my throat went tight, cutting my amusement off.

Micah had been my only cheerleader in life since Mom tended to bow beneath Pop's lordship over the Fox household we'd grown up in. My older brother had been my role model. Along with Grandpop, he was the one who built me up when Pop wasn't around. Until that moment, I hadn't realized I'd had the support I needed all along.

I'd been blinded by bitterness and had missed out.

But no more.

"Love you too, big bro—and thank you for always being there for me."

"Anytime, kid. Seriously. You're one amazing guy. Best thing Pop ever did for me. So, do me a favor—don't kill yourself for a degree just to prove something. I need you at top performance, and I'll be honest, you've been dragging ass. We make a great team, and nothing will break Elite down. Nothing, you hear me? We're going to grow old, hopefully not fat, and rich as shit working side by side."

"Fuck yeah, I want that." Peace I'd only ever felt at Matteo's feet slid through my body, and sudden longing for my man made me antsy as fuck.

My man.

"What's that look for?"

"Huh?" I focused on Micah rather than the picture in my head of heated dark eyes and luscious lips.

"That." Micah nodded his chin toward me. "It's like you...holy shit." A grin split his face. "What poor soul stole your fickle heart?"

"The Prince Charming of my childhood gay dreams," I said on a sigh.

Micah settled in for the story, and his eyes lit the fuck up. "Who is he, and where'd you meet him?"

"Matteo D'Angelo, and the first day of classes."

"Huh." Micah shook his head. "I thought for sure it would be someone older who tied you down. A daddy type, not some frat kid younger than you."

"I don't need a daddy, thank you very fucking much. Pop hasn't done that much of a number on me."

Micah chuckled. "Tell me about this kid I'm assuming you'll give up escorting for."

"Damn right, I will. Take my popular ass off the menu for good, big bro."

"Done. Now talk."

"He teaches my Financial Advising class."

One of Micah's eyebrows popped up.

"Not a *kid*," I reiterated.

"Tell me you're being smart about this, Sean," he stated quietly....slowly as though making sure I heard his every word.

"You know me better than that," I muttered, squirming on my chair.

"Shit. Isn't fraternizing with students against BC's code of conduct?"

"Yeah, but we're being super careful."

"Sean."

I gave Micah my full attention without trying to escape the sure reprimand since out of anyone, he had my best interests at heart.

"Quit before you get in trouble," he urged, his blue eyes insistent.

"I can't let him go, Micah. No fucking way. He's...everything to me. That'd be like me asking you to turn your back on your wife."

He shook his head, snickering at my adamant tone. "No —quit the nonsense of *school*. Drop out and protect both your asses."

"And offer up another reason for Pop to say I told you so?" I shot out, my stubbornness holding onto that drive to prove myself to have worth. Be enough.

"Who gives a flying fuck!" Micah barked. "Haven't you figured out yet that he'll never be satisfied? You know after you snuck out after Thanksgiving dinner, he told me I was destined to be the next shitty father in the Fox line?"

Holy. Fucking. Shit.

I stared, sure I'd heard wrong. Pop had put Micah—*and* himself down? "*What?*" I sputtered.

"You aren't the only one Pop goes all negative on, Sean. He said it in front of everyone before he and Mom left. Jasmine. Her parents. Fucking asshole. I was tempted to tell him to get the fuck out and never set foot in my house again."

"Shit, I'm sorry."

Micah shook his head. "Not your fault."

We sat in silence for a few seconds as the reality of what I'd always thought to be true crumbled around me. "I wasn't aware he treated you that way too."

My brother shrugged. "I'm just better at pleasing him, I

guess. Fuck, I wish I had more of your strength to stand up for myself."

I barked a laugh. "What?"

"You." Micah waved a hand at me. "How do you just not care? How can you laugh stuff off and walk away with a bounce in your step as though you don't give a shit what he thinks?"

"It's all fake."

"But your smiles aren't," Micah said, his stare penetrating. "You've got an inner joy that I've never had, some secret happiness I've always been envious of. But Jasmine—" His voice cut off abruptly, his eyes growing wet. "She's...yeah. She's that for me. Every single day."

Throat tight, I nodded, understanding what she'd gifted him. Fully. "Hey, Micah?"

"Yeah, little shit?" he said, brushing a forearm over his wet eyes.

"You're gonna be a great dad—and I'm gonna be the best uncle who ever lived. Know why?"

"Why?" He slumped again on my couch.

"Because we recognize what a crap role model is, and both of us make better choices than our sorry excuse for a father."

He blew out a breath. "You're right, Sean."

"Say that again," I teased, snagging hold of that warmth his words of praise always filled me with.

Micah grabbed one of my throw pillows and whipped it at my head before getting to his feet.

I followed him to my front door where he pulled on his coat.

"Shit...forgot about this." He pulled an envelope from the inside pocket, handing it to me. "Arrived at the office yesterday."

"What is it?"

He shrugged, zipping up his coat. "I don't open your mail, you little shit."

I stuck my tongue out at him and locked up behind his chuckling ass. He left a lot more confident a man than when he'd arrived.

Me. I'd done that. Sean mother-fucking Fox.

I sat back down on the couch and checked out the envelope—actual fucking stationery-type with vines and flowers on the backside.

The single sheet inside held a few lines of neat cursive... signed by that man of the cloth virgin I'd hooked Zack up with back in early September.

A slow read assured me he wasn't another Jackson Zerig. Quite the opposite.

He thanked me profusely for making discrete access to sexual gratification possible. For choosing a kind-hearted employee who'd gone above and beyond in showing him that having a sex drive can be a beautiful thing.

Some might see EEMM as "unholy," he'd written, but he went on to claim that I had taken part in saving him from the pit of hell he'd sunken into from living a lie his entire life. My throat tightened over his words of edification, his assurance of how I'd made an old man's wishes come true.

I'd been successful. I'd done a *good fucking job*—without a goddamned degree. My heart swelled to bursting in my chest, a sense of...pride and accomplishment damn near flooring me. I folded up the thank you note, planning to cherish it forever.

Between that letter and Micah's visit?

My teary eyes had been opened to a future where I could move forward in whatever way I wanted.

First, fuck Pop and all his expectations no one would

ever meet. He could go suck a goddamned egg and choke for all I cared.

Second?

I sat down at my desk, swiped my homework into the trash can, and wrote up a brief email that granted me the freedom to pursue Matteo.

Matteo

"Professor D'Angelo, this is Dean Sommerfeld."

My guts clenched up tight at the voice coming through my cell. There was only one reason he would be reaching out to me at eight on a Monday night. "Good evening, Dean. How can I help you?"

"Well." He sounded put out, which tripled my heart rate. "I received two emails in the last hour, both of which pertained to you."

"Oh?" I croaked, bracing myself for what I had feared from the beginning. Sean Fox had proven to be trouble time and again, and my poor choices had finally come to bite me in the ass.

"The first was from someone on campus. They stated some very disturbing accusations pertaining to you and Sean Fox."

Exactly as I'd expected.

I sank onto my couch, eyes closing as I ran a hand through my hair. "I can explain—"

"The second email," Dean Sommerfeld spoke over my mumble, "was from Mr. Fox himself. He's dropped out of school when there's only three weeks left before the semester ends."

He what?

"I don't know what happened between the two of you," the dean continued, unaware of the riotous emotions coursing through me, "and since he's no longer a student at our college, I'd prefer to keep it that way—unless there's some sort of legal fallout ahead of us?"

I swallowed hard. "Definitely not, sir. No. There's nothing to concern yourself with."

"Good. No harm, no foul, then."

All things holy...

"Correct, sir," I managed to croak.

"I have a nice glass of Chianti with my name on it and no time or energy to waste on gossip. I hope you have a good evening, Professor D'Angelo."

He hung up before I could bid him the same.

No curses spewed from my lips, and no thoughts raced through my befuddled brain. I sat and stared, unseeing and baffled.

Sean...

Blinking, I swiped my cell back to life to call him but hesitated. He'd texted about his plans with his brother, but I wanted answers, goddamnit.

Me: **Why did you quit?**

I shot off my text, realizing I hadn't included any context or explanation of how I knew.

Sean: **Because I'm perfect the way I am and don't need some goddamned piece of paper to prove otherwise.**

Laughter tore from me, my heart racing for a whole other reason.

Me: **That's my good boy.**

Sean: **I could be an even better boy if you'd like some company.**

Me: **Can I come to you this time?**

Sean: **You can COME to me, on me, or in me whenever the hell you want, Teach. Preferably sooner than later.**

The things he said...

Me: **Be there in twenty.**

Sean: **Don't you need my address?**

Snickering, I texted back that I might have done some perusing of his paperwork at college.

Sean: **Such a rule breaker, stalking me like that.**

Me: **I blame you.**

Sean: **I'll gladly take that. Now, get your ass over here so I can wrap my heels around it while you fill my hole with that delicious dick of yours. And bring a bag because I'm not letting you out of my bed until morning.**

"Jesus," I hissed, adjusting my cock in my sweats.

I hurried into my room to pack some clothes like he'd suggested, bumping into Katie's bureau in my haste.

The vase jostled, and I pulled up quickly, my hand shooting out to keep the glass from toppling over.

A relieved, rushed exhale left my lips that I'd caught it in time—but the slightest breeze I'd created with my mouth brushed over the brittle stem and its single petal. The dried piece detached and fluttered downward in silence, coming to rest atop the wooden surface.

The last petal had fallen.

I waited for pain to lance my chest, tears at the very least to well in my eyes and haze my vision.

But no curse, no promise of a lonely future settled over me.

I'd thought my chance for a happily ever after had been ripped away from me along with Katie's last breath, but perhaps the loss of that petal was the sign from beyond I'd been waiting for that she approved of my choice.

I want you to be happy.

Katie's final words to me whispered through my mind.

A small smile curved my lips, and I didn't mourn my loss—of her or the representation of that single flower I'd kept in her memory.

"I hope you find happiness. I hope you find peace," I quoted what I always did while reminiscing our time together beside her grave. "I hope you remember our love as I do, but I'm finally ready to move on. I'm going to grab hold of my second chance and live life to the fullest."

Quietness lingered in our bedroom after the words left me, but it was a peaceful silence rather than aching emptiness of grief from being alone. My heart felt light, excitement for a new beginning making my feet eager to move.

A few, quick minutes later, I started up my car, my mind returning to the phone call that had prompted my rush to pack.

Who had contacted the dean about me and Sean? Perhaps another student in our classroom who'd noticed how we looked at one another? We'd done well in keeping our distance from everyone except...

Hanson.

"No." I snipped the word aloud to myself while merging

onto Route 1. "No way he would do that—hey, Siri, call Hanson."

Calling Hanson, a feminine British voice replied.

"Matteo!" he answered. "Were your ears ringing? Albert and I were just talking about you."

"Did you email Dean Sommerfeld about me and Sean?" I cut right to the chase rather than chuckling like he did.

"No! Why would you even consider that?" He sounded surprised enough I believed him.

"The dean told me he got an anonymous email about us, and you're the only one who saw Sean and I in a compromising situation."

"I would never, Matteo. Your friendship means to much to me—and I'm not a petty, drama-loving old man."

I exhaled slowly, merging into the far left lane to pass some slowpoke taking a Sunday drive on a Monday night. "I know—I just can't think of anyone else who would have seen something—*anything*—worth reporting."

"How much trouble are you in?" Concern laced Hanson's voice.

"None. Sean dropped out."

"He what?"

"Quit."

"But...but he's been working so hard. He doesn't have the best grades, but he's a dedicated student."

I nodded even though my friend couldn't see me. "He was indeed."

"Do you believe he did it for you?" Hanson asked.

I smiled, remembering Sean's text where he'd built himself up enough I'd heard his sassy attitude through his words. "No. He did it for himself."

"What are you going to do?"

"Make that boy mine since I'm free to do so."

Hanson laughed loudly. "I'm glad for you, Matteo. Truly. And don't worry about the tattletale. Whatever power they thought they had over you no longer exists. Be happy, my friend."

Ten minutes later, I stood in front of Sean's condo door, my heart beating heavy. We'd discussed exclusivity, had spoken of a future, but I wanted more from him. I'd given myself the bisexual label a couple of weeks earlier, and I was ready for a second.

Boyfriend, partner...whichever he preferred.

I knocked, and the door ripped open before I inhaled a full breath.

Sean smirked, fisted my hoodie, and yanked me inside.

We collided with an oomph escaping both of us before he kicked his door closed.

"Missed you," he said right before claiming my mouth.

He tasted as sweet as caramel with that hint of masculine warmth I'd become addicted to. I could kiss Sean every day for the rest of my life, and I still wouldn't get my fill of him.

We ended up in a tangled mess of limbs and half-removed clothing atop his bed. I hadn't seen much of his condo on the way into his bedroom, nor did I care. I sank into his prepped hole with a slow thrust, my sweats hanging off one of my ankles.

"Fuck yes, baby," Sean groaned, wrapping his bare legs around my ass. "You're so deep inside me. Jesus." He yanked my head down and stole my breath yet filled my lungs at the same time.

Overwhelmed didn't describe me in that moment. His scent, his taste on my tongue, and his tight ass sucking on my cock...my head spun.

"Sean...fuck, you're so good. So perfect for me—" I cut myself off from declaring my undying love I'd felt sure of once that final petal had fallen. He was too young for talk about rings and forever. If I spilled how much I wanted with him—

"Don't stop now, Teach," he moaned.

I chuckled and thrust deep, losing my head over how we fit together. "I don't plan on it, sweet boy. You're the cutest thing I've ever seen," I murmured since he loved to be told that. "As blinding as the sun, as delicious as a Boston cream donut. You're the reason I smile every morning and the one I most look forward to seeing every day."

His grin lit his face, his twinkling eyes taking on the teasing glint that made my balls tingle. "*You love me, you think I'm sexy*," he sang with a purred voice while gyrating his hips beneath me.

Damned right I do. I nudged deeper into his hot, slick ass, biting my tongue.

Our smiles faded as deeper emotion crept into the energy rippling between us.

His gaze flitted over my face as though memorizing every laugh line he'd caused, every small imperfection from age he claimed to not care about. "Didn't think it was possible someone would come along and tame my wild ways."

"I tamed you, huh?" I asked, pulling out so only the swollen head of my cock remained in his tight clasp.

"Fuck yeah you did, Teach." He glided his hands down along my spine to my ass, slowly easing me back into the silken heaven of his body. "You're the only one I want, baby."

"So, are we...boyfriends?" I asked and stilled, seated as deep in his ass as I could go.

"Fuck yeah," he breathed, smirking and shooting off fireworks inside my chest. "Now kiss me and make me come, *boyfriend*. Fill me up with your cum so we can do it all over again."

Chapter 34

Sean

Matteo stayed at my condo more often than not. Being so close to BC as compared to his home farther north, it made sense. It had only been a couple of weeks since we'd very publicly started to date, but I was ready for him to sell his and Katie's house and move on—*in*—with me.

Like yesterday.

The two nights we hadn't shared a bed since officially becoming boyfriends, I'd been fucking miserable. A whiny brat whose manipulation skills didn't work on my man. No amount of pouting had gotten me my way, but he'd had tests to grade and a faculty Zoom meeting.

Our second official date had been with Professor Hanson and his husband Albert, and what a blast that was compared to the old man bore I'd expected. I was excited and antsy, my mouth uncontrollable even though I tried to be all mature and shit but failed as usual.

Albert got a kick out of me, and Hanson—no more "Professor", he'd demanded—had both hugged me at night's end and thanked me for making their friend smile again. Fuck knew I'd given them a bunch of laughs over dinner too. I was pretty sure they both liked me, thank fuck.

I'd gotten a red ass for my sassy, crass talk over the dinner table but then got an earful of praise about how warm and wet my hole was and how well I took my lover's cock. Win on both ends, in my book.

Literally.

Jasmine's morning sickness lingered, so I ended up hosting Micah's monthly Elite Sunday afternoon party for December.

Kellen and JJ had spent a few days in Jersey with JJ's adoptive family and swung by on their way home. Mason and Jasper agreed to hang with us, and Drake along with a few of the other guys from the gay branch of MM showed up with food and beer in hand. We were a smaller group compared to all the retiree friends Micah often invited to his place since my condo didn't have the space his did.

Something I had he didn't? A living room wall of windows overlooking the harbor rather than a back yard that needed to be mowed, fertilized, watered... No fucking thank you.

It was my first time hosting, and I'd been thrilled when Matteo agreed to help me prepare. I'd expected him to hang back from stepping fully into my life even though I'd quit classes, but he jumped in with both feet, proving to be the best boyfriend ever.

If anyone had questioned our age difference or teased about his ability to keep me satisfied after greeting him in my entryway, I'd have kicked their asses right back out the door.

Matteo stayed close by my side, his hand often on my lower back or brushing against mine while the guys made themselves comfortable. Constant awareness of his presence had me on the verge of a chub all day long even though he'd taken good care of me before we'd crawled out of bed.

"You're amazing." The whispered words and hot breath on my ear caused a shiver to slink through my body. Fuck, I loved when my sexy Teach snuggled up on me from behind. "And you look cute as hell in your reindeer sweater," he murmured, sliding his hands beneath the knitted top to caress over my stomach.

I pushed against Matteo's groin with my ass, ignoring the second dish of taco dip I'd been ready to pull from the oven. Mitt on my hand, I reached around and grabbed his nape. He slid his hands fully around me, grasping me tight against him in a possessive hold.

"Can't get enough of you, sweet boy."

Turning my face, I gave him my mouth, losing myself as I always did to the soft cushion of his lips and his taste on my tongue. So. Damn. Delicious.

Fuck, he made me hard.

And having access to him without the forbidden aspect *and* the stress of classes? My stomach had finally lay off from making my life a living hell. It seemed as though I'd avoided the threatening ulcer, and antacids were no longer acting as addictive candy. Coffee still burned on occasion, but I'd gotten back to my usual eating schedule and didn't feel sick twenty-four-seven, thank fuck.

A cough and chuckle sounded behind us, and I cursed, pulling my mouth from my boyfriend's.

"Go away," I grumbled at Kellen and Mason, who stood at the island grabbing seconds or thirds from the spread everyone had contributed to.

"Be nice." Matteo swatted my ass and stepped back.

My face heated as both of my friends snickered. I

waited for someone to tease about him taming me once he disappeared into the half bath.

"He's perfect for you," Kellen said, and I popped the taco dip out, shutting the oven door again with my hip. "The daddy side to keep you in line and a heart full of praise to rain down over you."

Well, damn.

I didn't call Matteo daddy, nor did that kink tick off any boxes for either of us, but yeah. I liked how he looked after me. Cared for and encouraged me. He was all the things I'd been missing thanks to my emotionally deadbeat father—but that was another story, one I'd decided to leave in my past unless chatting with my new therapist.

Pop could go fuck himself, but I would show up for the monthly family meals at Micah's—with my boyfriend in tow to keep my spirits up.

"You're the happiest I've ever see you, Sean," Mason said, his hazel eyes warm and peaceful, something I'd never noticed he'd lacked before Jasper had entered his life.

"It's all because of my man," I stated even though Matteo insisted time and again that my own recent choices lended to my smiling face.

Mason's grin widened. "*That* I can understand." He lifted his bottle of water toward me as though saying "cheers" and moved back toward the living room area.

Kellen grinned as our friend sauntered out of the room. "At the rate the Elites are finding their soul mates, the business might be in jeopardy."

I glanced around the group of friends and co-workers lounging around my space beyond the archway leading to my room framed by a wall of windows. "Nah. There's always another guy willing to lay pipe—I mean *lay* down their life for the betterment of EEMM in order to earn a living."

A chuckle rumbled from Kellen, but JJ walked up behind him and wrapped his arms around his waist in the same way Matteo had done to me. Fucking loved that for my friend.

"I want to thank you guys again for your help with the whole Zerig situation," I said.

"Micah called and told us it's all taken care of," JJ said, his dark eyes intense as always.

"Yep, and thank fuck, because I was about to lose my shit."

"He also said you dropped out of college."

I grinned, not one trace of shame or embarrassment smacking me like I'd expected. "Best decision I ever made—wait. No, that would be talking my hot professor into me—literally."

"He looks good on you," JJ said with a teasing note.

"You should see *me* on *him*," I shot back with a wink. I'd angled my full-length mirror toward our bed the night before so I could enjoy watching how I rode his dick. What a sight it had been.

A shiver licked over my spine remembering how he couldn't tear his focus off my face no matter how much I begged him to look at the mirror. He'd claimed there was nothing better than seeing the real thing right in front of him.

Drake came into the kitchen, an empty beer bottle in hand. He glanced at me, snickered, and shook his head.

"What?" I tossed his way as he pulled open my fridge for another drink. "Be a sweetie and grab me a beer while you're in there."

"Never thought I'd see the day when heart eyes took

over your face," Drake said with a chuckle.

"Yeah—" I caught the bottle he tossed me "—well, I can't wait until some ginger grabs hold of your heart and sticks a fork in it. You'll be just as done as me."

A grimace flitted over Drake's eyes as he twisted his cap off. "Not gonna happen."

I snorted. "Careful with statements like that. I never thought I'd be taken off the market either."

Matteo came back from the bathroom, and the heated look he gave me twitched my dick in my jeans. He got all up in my space, and fuck how I loved his lack of reserve, his freedom to simply be with me. "You're off the market, hmm?" he murmured, wrapping his arms around me again and nibbling on my ear.

My fucking knees wobbled.

"Knock that off, Teach, or I'm gonna pop a boner in front of all my friends," I said loud enough to hopefully embarrass him that he'd want to yank me over his lap after all the guys went home.

"Now why do I have a feeling it wouldn't be the first time?" he teased right back.

I pinched his ass, but he only chuckled and planted a loud, smacking kiss on my cheek. "Pats game is about to start," he said, "and since there's not much room, you better sit on my lap."

"With or without clothes?" I asked, grinding my semi against his.

"Behave, sweet boy."

"Or what?"

"He'll spank your ass red," JJ stated loudly, and a few snickers sounded from the living room.

But I didn't give a flying fuck. Not when Matteo gazed at me like I hung the sun in the sky.

Chapter 35

Matteo

The semester ended, leaving me free to head south for the holidays with my family. Since Sean had zero interest in spending that time around his father, he agreed to accompany me to South Carolina to meet my parents.

I shouldn't have worried about the fact I'd fallen for a man.

Mom snagged hold of Sean the second we walked into the house, yanked him into her arms, and cried happy tears for a full-on five minutes. Even Dad got choked up.

"Hey, little bro," Alessia said in way of a greeting to him, and Sean's face had split into a grin.

But it was Claire-bear who'd stabbed absolute joy through my heart when she'd walked right up to him and looked up at him with adoring eyes.

"You're cute, Uncle Sean," she declared.

My sweet boy's lower lip actually trembled, and he squatted down to her level. "And I've never seen such a beautiful little lady," he replied, his voice rasped. "The rainbow tutu? Slay, girl."

She didn't hesitate to throw her arms around him, and he had no choice but to pick her up and stand again. She snuggled into him, happy as a princess who'd found her prince.

I understood. Oh, how I did.

"Someone is smitten," Alessia whispered while hugging me after my boyfriend and his precious cargo followed Mom and Dad into the living room.

I hope you find happiness. I hope you find peace.

The words I always said over Katie's gravestone whispered through my mind like a gentle caress, tightening my throat. I would never forget the love I'd shared with her—and I would remember her always.

But I'd made a promise to her, and I looked forward to living the rest of my days with the man who'd brought me what she'd wished for.

I had to clamp my hand over Sean's mouth to keep him quiet on Christmas Eve. When I railed him from behind, he tended toward noisy, and while I usually got off on hearing him beg for me to thrust harder, deeper, my parents and Alessia down the hall wouldn't.

We collapsed onto the bed once finished, and I peeled off the condom I'd put on so we wouldn't have a mess to clean up.

"Hate those fucking things," he muttered, tossing aside the towel I'd laid down beneath him to keep our sheets free of cum.

"I promise when we get home, I'll flood your ass with cum so you can feel it leak out of your sore hole."

"Mmm, talk dirty to me, baby."

Snickering, I pulled him against my side even though we'd worked up a sweat and would need a quick shower before sleeping. While we caught our breath, I trailed my fingertips down his spine, my mind wandering as it often did to that fantasy I'd brought up a few weeks back.

"Not tired of me yet?" I asked, unable to help the insecurities that sometimes roused in my head. At least Sean appreciated my being candid about them.

"No fucking way," he didn't hesitate to answer, propping his chin on my chest so he could see my face with the help of the open blinds allowing the full moon to cast soft golden beams over us. "I love you as-is, Teach. What we have is more than enough."

"You...love me?"

"Fuck yeah." Sean's grin lit me up inside. "Have for a while. I quit college to protect your ass."

"Lies." I smacked his backside, making his eyes go dark with rekindled desire.

"Gave up other dicks and holes for you," he reminded me. "If that isn't love, I don't know what love is."

I ran my fingers through his silky hair, tugging him higher up my body. He scooted upward like a good boy.

"I love you too, Sean," I murmured inches from his mouth.

Wetness welled in his eyes. "Seriously?"

"I never thought I would have love to give again, but for you?" I cradled his face in my hands, soaking in how his heart thumped against mine. "It's alive and vibrating. I would do anything for you."

"Except bottom." Sean pouted with a teasing glint in his eyes.

I studied him, my mind once more going to that three-some I'd suggested.

"What?" Sean asked, his smile fading.

"If you do ever grow bored, I have an old membership at Chantelle's, an exclusive sex club, and maybe we could try something a little less vanilla."

"Get out." Sean barked a laugh. "My brother and another ex-Elite are members there."

"Small world," I murmured, trying not to grin.

Sean blinked. "Holy fuck. You...that's where you first met Micah!"

"Yes."

"Wait." He frowned, that possessiveness flaring in his eyes. "Why the fuck did you even *go* there that night?"

"It wasn't to hook up," I assured him. "I'd simply visited to see if perhaps what you roused inside me went beyond wanting to explore life again."

"And?"

"I realized I was ready to start living, that it was okay to move on."

Sean's eyes cleared of pissiness. "So, why visit in the first place if you aren't into pain? I mean, you pack one hell of a swat in your right hand."

I realized what he was really questioning.

"Katie and I didn't have that sort of relationship. She liked to kneel for me. Same as you, she suffered from anxiety, and she often found peace sitting at my feet."

"Does it bother you I'm doing what she did?"

"No." I ran my thumb over his lower lip before pressing mine to his for a brief, chaste kiss. "Your willingness to submit to me in that way fulfills a part of me I never expected to enjoy again in this lifetime."

"So it's my sassy side that's bringing out the Dom in you."

I snorted at Sean's lilted voice that bordered on singing his usual *you think I'm sexy* song. "I'm not a sadist, but if you want to explore other kinks, my membership at Chantelle's is easily renewed for a pretty penny. I'll learn to be whatever you need, Sean. I'll admit I'm a voyeur when it comes to sitting in the lounge, but I've had no interest in participating in sceneing with others. But if that's what you need..."

"Hmm." Sean pursed his lips, his eyes twinkling. "So if I said I wanted to tie you up to a cross and flog your ass before eating you out?"

I shuddered and not in the pleasant way. "Not sure I'd be up for the flogging."

"The ass eating?"

"Sweet boy, you can put that talented tongue of yours anywhere you want on my body."

"Next time I lick your hole I'm shoving it in, Matteo."

"As long as your hand is wet and stroking my cock, I think I'm okay with *that* tiny bit of penetration."

"Fuck, yes," Sean murmured, shifting to rub his thickening cock against my soft one.

I raised an eyebrow and grabbed hold of his firm backside. "Someone is needy tonight."

"When it comes to you, Teach," Sean breathed against my mouth, "I'll never get enough."

Chapter 36

Sean

a little over a month later...

"I'm sorry to bail on you like this." Drake sounded disappointed, and since he'd never cancelled on Elite, I couldn't be upset.

Even if Valentine's Day was less than a week away and our employees were booked solid thanks to the sad, lonely souls wanting to be spoiled by men who were paid big bucks to satisfy clients.

"Don't worry about it, Drake," I said over my cell. "We'll figure something out."

Even if I had still escorted for Elite, I would have been off the menu for Valentine's. Matteo hinted he had big plans for us that night but wouldn't tell me, no matter how much I'd tried to manipulate him into spilling.

Drake exhaled loudly in my ear. "My dad rarely asks me to visit, and this time, there's some big event or shit. Not really sure. He's being cryptic as fuck and said I had no choice—I have to go."

I got it. Totally. Unlike me and Pop, Drake and his dad were bosom buddies, and it had been a hot minute since Drake had last gone to New York to see his old man. I envied my best friend and the close relationship he had with his father.

Pop had gotten his negative two cents in over my quitting college when the family met for dinner in early January, but with Matteo by my side and holding my hand, along with my therapist's weekly help, I'd learned to look at his poor ass in a different light.

Mom had told me he was just like his father, and while Pop acting like an ass couldn't be blamed on my grandfather —men made their own damned choices—I knew where it stemmed from. The poor guy never had a father figure to build him up and offer him words of praise either.

It was no wonder he'd grown up bitter and angry all the time.

But not me. No fucking way. I'd broken that generational curse by snagging the hottest professor on the planet, a daddy type who treated me like a king.

Life. Was. Good.

"It's time you took a break anyway," I told Drake, getting back to the matter at hand. "You've been booking without one for going on two years."

"What can I say? I like my job," he said with a hint of lightness in his tone our entire conversation had lacked.

I used to enjoy the fuck out of escorting too until the sexiest man on the face of the earth tied me down.

Best decision I'd ever made.

"Give me a holler when you're back in town, and I'll

have BetsyAnne hook you up with some of our best tipping customers."

"Will do, Sean. Thanks again, man."

"No problem," I assured him but wasn't *really* sure. But, I would take care of shit, same as I'd been doing since quitting school. I'd stepped up to the plate for Micah, especially since Jasmine still had morning sickness plaguing the hell out of her. Poor big sis—I didn't know how she handled being nauseous twenty-four-seven for so damn long. Just... ugh. Two months of those damn stomach issues had about done me in.

But both she and Micah were madly in love with the baby girl growing in her belly, and I expected the second they finally got their hands on the little princess, they would say it had been worth every second of discomfort.

Thank fuck I had a dick and not a uterus.

I shuddered even thinking about pushing an eight pound—

Nope. Wouldn't go there.

"One hour!" Matteo hollered from the bathroom.

"Yeah, yeah," I muttered to myself and put through a call to Zack. He was the only Elite not booked for the upcoming weekend, same as the year before—because he'd begged off. He had something personal against the holiday, I guessed. "Sorry to bug you, but I need a favor," I said once he answered.

"Are you shitting me?"

"No, man. Drake has to take a last-minute trip to New York, and I've got clients for both Friday and Saturday in need of some lovin'."

"Fucking hell, Sean."

"I know, man—I'll owe you one, okay?"

"*Ten*, not one."

I didn't even bother trying to negotiate with Elite's hottest escort now that I'd retired. "You got it. I'll have BetsyAnne send the files over to you."

He grumbled something under his breath.

"Seriously, Zack, I appreciate you. You're doing one hell of a job." In my time of dating Matteo, I'd picked up on his way of making people feel good. Offering praise rather than teasing or nitpicking like I'd been fond of doing.

All a part of the change I'd gone through.

"You ready?"

I set aside my cell and turned to find my delicious boyfriend in nothing more than a towel wrapped around his waist. Water droplets clung to the dark hair on his chest and eyelashes. "Goddamn, Teach, you're so fucking hot. How about we skip our dinner date with Hanson and Albert, and I eat you instead?"

His eyes darkened, but he shook his head. "We blew them off last—"

I snickered at his word choice, and he stopped speaking, rolling his eyes at me. "Go on," I said, waving my hand.

"You're such a brat." He shook his head but smirked. "It's their tenth anniversary next weekend, and Hanson is going to ask Albert to marry him again."

"Huh?"

"You know—repeat their vows and have a party sort of thing."

"Gotcha." I stood and stretched, my T-shirt riding high, baring a flash of skin between it and my low-lying sweats.

Matteo's gaze dropped down, and I exaggerated my movements, shifting my hips around a bit.

"Tease."

"You love it when I tease."

"Damned right, I do." He beckoned me toward him. "Come here."

I couldn't resist his commands when spoke in that low, husky tone. Shivers pebbled my skin. "Where do you want me?" I asked with my sassiest voice.

"On your knees."

Oh, but not for the reason I often did whenever stress got the best of me. I dropped down in front of him, eyeing the twitching towel in line with my face.

"Get busy, sweet boy."

"Fuck yeah," I breathed and unwrapped my favorite dick like it was my birthday. I buried my face in his groin, sniffing his soap and underlying male musk I couldn't get enough of. Rubbing my face all the fuck over his soft balls, I hummed an approving noise in my throat. "Smell so good, baby."

"I taste even better." He pushed tapped his thickening cock against my lips. "Open up and make me happy."

Matteo didn't have to tell me twice. Being a good boy always earned me the best kinds of rewards. Maybe I could get him to tell me his plans for the following weekend once I sucked every drop of cum from his balls.

Intent on doing just that, I swallowed him down, pulling a grunt from his lungs.

"Shit—Jesus, Sean. Your mouth…"

Oh, how the words of praise rolled off his tongue as I used mine to drive him insane.

"Such a good boy, Sean." He ran his fingers through my hair, tugging whenever his thick head buried deep in my throat. "Fuck, yes." He held me tight, cutting off my air, but I waited patiently, peering up at his lust-darkened eyes, the love in them turning me on as much as having his dick lodged in my esophagus.

"You're such a good boy for me. So perfect."

He let me breathe, and I popped off, gasping and using my hand to stroke his spit-slickened length.

"Lay down, Teach. I want a taste of your hole."

"Jesus." He clenched his jaw and backed up the two steps to our bed. He sank down on the edge.

I crawled forward, my focus on the darkness between his cheeks. "Prop your feet on the edge of the mattress and make me the happiest boy ever."

He'd let me have him a time or two—only the tip of my tongue inside him—and I honestly didn't miss not having an ass to own with my dick. I'd yet to grow bored of bottoming for him; he was that fucking good in the sack. My hole couldn't get enough of his cock.

I grasped the backs of his knees and lifted, revealing his hairy pucker. "Fuck, I love this sight."

While he loved my waxed body, I got off on him being au naturel at his back door. He kept his pubes around the base of his dick trimmed for me, though. Fuck, was that hot.

I licked up his crack, and he cursed, his hole clenching at the feathered stroke. "Mmm, baby, so, *so* good." I took another slow taste from ass crack to weeping slit, lathing around his glans before sliding down to tongue his pucker.

The darker flavor of his ass made my dick leak, and I shoved my hand inside my sweats.

He propped onto his elbows and held his knees for me.

It took a few minutes of nonstop eye contact and my loving on his ass for his hole to loosen up a bit, but I didn't push for what he wasn't too thrilled about. One hand on his dick, the other on mine, I stroked us in time with my licking over his ass and taint.

We both leaked like goddamned faucets, and I was there for it. Made for easy hand jobs.

I sucked on his hole, groaning. "I love eating your ass, baby."

"Anything for you." His eyes promised as much as he watched me devour him.

"Hmm." I probed a bit with the tip of my tongue, causing both our dicks to buck in my hands. "Can I put it in?" I asked, all trace of teasing or flirting gone in my desire for him.

"Go ahead, greedy boy." His hole instantly clenched, and I chuckled, tickling him a bit with soft licks.

"Gotta relax for me, Teach. Don't wanna hurt you."

He blew out an exhale. "I trust you, Sean."

I lingered in licking, and the second he went pliant, I applied some pressure.

He grunted, dropping back onto the bed.

But he didn't tell me to stop.

I watched his chest rise and fall with heightened breaths as I continued to gently tongue in and out of his ass, probing a little deeper each time.

"Fuck, Sean."

"Too much?" I asked and kissed the inside of his thigh.

"No...it's okay."

But not engine cranking.

I finished with his ass crack and suckled my way up to his leaking slit.

"Jesus," he hissed, his hands fisting in my hair. "Just like that—yes."

Grinning around a thick cock wedged into one's throat didn't exactly work, so I set to edging the fuck out of him, swallowing down every droplet of pre-cum he gave me.

There was nothing sexier than Professor D'Angelo writhing on our bed, begging me to let him come.

But I wasn't looking for a mouthful.

I wanted a sore, plugged ass to remind me how much be loved me while we went out to dinner with his friends. Edging Matteo teased the fuck out of me to the point I couldn't wait any longer.

I stood and shoved off my sweats

Matteo eyed me as I retrieved a bottle of lube from his bedside table. He squeezed the base of his rigid length as I stood in front of him, snapping open the cap. "Get that fine ass over here and sit on my cock."

"Yes, sir," I agreed, climbing aboard, quickly stuffing some lube in my hole then dribbling some down his length. Rather than impaling myself, I teased us a bit more, rubbing my crack over his hard-as-fucking-nails length, getting us both nice and wet. "You're gonna feel so fucking perfect in my tight ass, Teach. Gonna stretch me just how I like it. Fill me up."

"Sean," he warned, his tone low as he grasped my hips. "Lift up onto your knees. Right fucking *now*."

"Yes, *Daddy*," I teased.

He growled and swatted my ass. Fucking *hard*.

Hissing, I shifted until the tip of his cock pressed on my hole. Holding his gaze, my heart beat pounding every beat for him, I sank onto his length, cursing as he stuffed me.

He swallowed audibly, his Adam's apple bobbing. "Sean—fuck, I love you."

I lay over his chest, spearing my fingers into his hair he'd grown a little longer at my insistence. He made one hell of a sexy pirate in my fantasies.

Now, if I could only get him to put on a little eyeliner...

"Love you too, Matteo. So goddamned much."

"Then twerk that ass on my cock and show me," he demanded.

I obeyed like a good little boy.

Epilogue

Sean

"So where are we going?" I asked, giving my man a side eye over his secretive smirk.

We'd already wished each other a happy Valentine's Day and all that shit—my first one with someone I could call my own. While he'd surprised me with dinner at some fancy place in the North End, he'd stated our night wasn't over yet once we'd finished.

But he refused to tell me jack shit about what else he'd planned.

Matteo pulled into a parking garage and gathered my hand in his to lead me toward an unassuming building that didn't give me a single hint as to where we went.

The entryway didn't reveal much else—but the buxom blonde who exited a door marked "Private" on our left sent a shockwave of a thrill through me.

I recognized her from that Christmas party three years earlier when Micah had announced EEMM's gay branch and made me the manager.

Mistress fucking Chantelle.

My boyfriend had brought me to a goddamned sex club.

Blood rushed straight to my dick as Mistress Chantelle greeted Matteo.

"And you must be Sean, Matteo's sweet boy," she purred. Her eyes glittered with happiness as she took me in from head to toes.

A shiver of excitement slid down my spine. Neither Matteo nor I were into exhibition, so I hoped whatever Matteo had in mind for us wouldn't include some sort of sexual act in the lounge.

"The room is ready as you requested," she told Matteo even though her welcoming gaze had returned to my face.

Room—so definitely something private.

But what sort of kink did he plan on exploring with me? We had sex toys galore at home, all used on me, of course. He hadn't changed his stance on bottoming, which I'd been perfectly content with. Sure, my dick wished for a hot, tight hole on occasion, but Matteo gladly got onto his knees for me. He was all I needed.

Oh, shit.

I swallowed audibly, glancing over at him.

His dark eyes met mine, full of love and a whole lot of lust. "Ready to fulfill that fantasy of yours?"

"Oh fuck," I whispered, having to press down on my suddenly aching dick. "Yes—Jesus fucking Christ, yes, *please.*"

Chuckling, Mistress Chantelle motioned for us to follow her. She led us through a set of double doors into the dim lounge. The scent of leather, sweat, and sex brewed in the air like an erotic feast for the senses.

The sounds of flesh slapping rose from a spanking and two couples having sex without a care about their live audience looking on. A woman stood tied to a Saint Andrew's cross atop a dais, her backside covered with red lashes from the flogger gripped in hand by the Viking standing beside her.

Over a dozen submissives knelt for their seated Doms as I often did with Matteo whenever I needed to clear my head. A Domme held a leash to a young man garbed in a puppy outfit.

Whatever floated their boat.

Me? I focused on that fantasy Matteo had hinted about months earlier, one that promised my dick something a little more than a warm mouth or tight fist.

I leaked pre-cum while following Chantelle through her lounge to a door. She paused after opening it for us.

"Third room on the left," she stated, still smiling. "Enjoy your evening, Sean. Matteo." She dipped her head and turned on her stiletto heels, leaving us alone.

Matteo motioned me forward, and I hurried down the hallway like an eager kid about to get their first blow job.

He snickered behind me, and I immediately slowed, suddenly unsure about revealing my excitement. I didn't want Matteo thinking he wasn't enough, that I couldn't wait to sink balls deep into an ass.

I stopped at the third door and spun, grabbing Matteo and yanking him against me. "Have I told you how much I love you?"

He smirked, his eyes darkening as our groins rubbed together. "A time or two."

"And you know you're everything I need, right? I don't —we don't have to do this."

Matteo cradled my face in his hands as I grabbed hold of his ass to keep him pressed along my front. "I'm confident in what we have, Sean. Promise."

My heart raced, and I nodded. "As long as you're sure."

"I am. Come." He planted a quick, chaste kiss on my

lips and reached behind me for the door handle. "Give me the pleasure of fulfilling one of your fantasies."

Releasing a slow exhale, I followed him into a large bedroom draped in shadow, stopping right inside the door. Four dimmed sconces allowed for some sight, enough for me to make out the young man standing across the room near the foot of the bed, hands clasped behind his back.

"Happy Valentine's Day, my sweet boy," Matteo murmured against my ear, sending a shudder through my bones.

"Fuck...he's so damned pretty," I whispered the same sentiment the younger Mr. Chesterfield had about me when I'd been a birthday present from his bear of a husband right before classes had started.

Matteo had questioned my tastes when it had come to my topping men in the past, and he'd paid attention.

My gift stood slightly shorter than me, a true twink with only a hint of muscle on his thin frame. Big, innocent eyes took me in as I did the same with him. From the top of his head with his mop of blond, wavy hair to the pale blue lace panties covering his hard cock, he hit all my dick's *I want to dive in and plunder* buttons.

I salivated to taste the wet spot where pre-cum darkened the lace covering his erection but needed to know how far Matteo was willing to share our night together. "Limits?" I kept my voice low, a private conversation from my gift.

"I have no wish to be physical with him, but you?" Matteo brushed his lips over my neck while wrapping his arms around me from behind. "Feel free to do as you want and tell me when you're ready to have your hole filled."

While Matteo's selfless declaration shot adrenaline through my blood, I had limits of my own. I entwined our fingers together atop my stomach, squeezing lightly. "I want you with me the whole time," I whispered for his ears alone. "Touching me. Petting me while I take my pleasure in him —but I'm not going to kiss his mouth."

"Thank you," Matteo murmured, and I realized he wasn't super comfortable with the arrangements he'd made.

I turned, studying his face in the dim light. "Matteo..."

He pressed his lips to mine. "You have my permission to satisfy the one part of you I can't."

"You're more than enough for me just the way you are," I reiterated what I'd told him before.

"And you're my perfect fit in every way," he offered in return. "Now be a good boy and unwrap your present."

I turned, once more taking stock of the submissive twink there for the sole purpose of pleasing me.

"Lose the panties and get on the bed," I said, my voice husky with lust as I moved closer to him. "Lay on your side facing the wall."

"Yes, sir," he murmured with a sweet voice and obeyed like a good little sub, but I didn't get off on his willingness to listen to my commands. It was Matteo's hands unbuttoning my shirt from behind me, his hands skimming over my torso before slipping the cotton off my shoulders that turned me on.

Matteo nuzzled my lower back while shoving my jeans to the floor, and his gentle removing of my shoes and socks made my skin pebble with anticipation.

He lathed up through my crack with his wet, warm tongue before giving me a harsh swat to my right cheek. "Go on," he murmured, his lips brushing the base of my spine.

Plan forming in my head, I moved to the edge of the bed and bent over, elbows on the mattress and ass in the air.

Matteo groaned at how I'd put myself on display, and I waited with heightened breaths as he stripped behind me.

"Jesus, what a sight you are," Matteo said, grabbing hold of my cheeks and dropping to his knees.

I shuddered as he licked over my taint, flicking my piercing with his tongue. "So good, Teach. God, I love having your mouth on me."

The twink shivered, so rather than touching him, I gave him all the dirty talk in the world, watching as he grew as restless as I did.

"You like my filthy mouth?" I asked, and he whined, wiggling his ass on the bed.

"It's so damn hot."

My dick ached to be sucked into tight heat. My hole slackened beneath first my lover's tongue then fingers.

"That's it," I told Matteo, "stretch me good—now a third."

I grunted as he worked another finger in my needy ass, eyeing my gift's hairless pucker a few feet in front of me. He glistened with lube...

"Are you prepped?" I asked as Matteo licked up through my crack, clear to my nape.

"Yes, sir. I'm all ready for you."

A quick glance at the bedside table revealed what I needed, and I made quick work of sheathing up my pre-cum soaked dick. I took Matteo's hand, pulling him onto the bed with me. Of the same mind, we settled into a three-spoon position, my lover's hands on my ass and hip as I finally touched my gift.

He was warm. Soft. His pale skin glowed in the lowlight.

"You're so beautiful."

The twink beamed at me over his shoulder.

I shifted his top leg forward even more, opening him up for me as Matteo shoved lube up my ass. "I'll go slow," I murmured, using my other hand to angle my dick toward his hole.

He sighed as I breached his ring without difficulty, and I groaned as his wet heat sucked me in deep.

"Jesus," I hissed, grabbing hold of his hips. "Matteo—fuck me, baby...please."

Matteo crowded in close, the warmth of him, the solidity of his body keeping me grounded. "I have you, sweet boy."

One slow thrust of his lubed cock sank him balls-deep into my ass, and I cursed, my dick bucking inside the young man in front of me.

Finally—fucking *finally*, I was the beef in the middle, and holy fucking hell, what a rush. My head spun and heart raced. Adrenaline crashed through me, my libido begging me to fucking *move* already.

I lingered, soaking in the warmth of being consumed from the front and back.

"Okay?" Matteo murmured against my ear, rubbing a hand over my pecs and tightened nipples.

"Fuck yeah. Just soaking this moment in."

"This doesn't have to be the only time," Matteo stated, his hot breath ghosting over my nape before he kissed me there. "You should know by now that I'll give you anything."

I was fully satisfied in our relationship, but I wasn't going to get into a deep conversation when my dick ached to thrust.

"Love you so goddamn much, Teach," I stated and rocked back and forth, fucking and being fucked with one stroke. "Oh Jesus." I gulped and repeated the motion, moaning hoarsely.

"Okay?" the twink asked.

"More than," I bit out from between clenched teeth.

We'd had a mere few minutes of foreplay while Matteo ate my ass, but I already neared my end.

"Not gonna last, goddamnit," I muttered.

My gift moved in time with my hips in their instinctual dance toward completion, his whimpered pants adding to the sounds of my lover and I enjoying each other's bodies.

"Jack yourself," I ordered.

He obeyed, his hole clenching around my dick.

I hissed, tightening my hold on his hip.

"Oh shit," he whispered and gulped.

"Gonna come on my sweet boy's dick?" Matteo asked him, thrusting deep inside me.

He whined. "Yeah—fuck yeah, I am."

"Wanna feel it—milk my dick," I whispered against his ear.

A low whine flooded from him, and his ring pulsed around me as he shot across the satin sheets.

"Ah, fuck." I groaned.

Matteo cursed against my ear, and we came as one, my cock emptying into the condom as my lover filled my ass with his cum.

Shortest fuck ever, but I didn't give a shit.

My gift sighed and stretched before pulling off my dick and rolling toward me. Pink flushed his cheeks, but he didn't meet my gaze while he focused on removing my condom and tying it off.

Matteo remained buried inside me, his arms still firmly wrapped around my middle as our third took care of cleaning my softened dick with tissues from the bedside table.

"Can I be of service in any other way, sir?" he murmured quietly before glancing up quickly.

The boy was shy as fuck, a beautiful little thing that would make a real daddy happy one day.

"You fulfilled my number one fantasy," I told him. "Sorry I didn't last longer."

"You were perfect," he murmured, his face flushing as he peeked at my dick.

Those words of praise...goddamn, did I preen. "Thanks, kid."

"I'm not a kid," he snipped with a heated glance before looking away.

Matteo chuckled against my nape.

I wanted to offer the kid a job in that moment, knowing he would make Elite a shit ton of money. But what would my boyfriend think of employing someone I'd fucked?

Yeah, better to let that one go.

I didn't even ask his name, simply offered another thanks before he pulled on a dark blue silk robe and slipped from the room.

Matteo reached between my thighs and gathered my limp dick in his hand, gently squeezing. "This is mine."

"So is my ass," I assured him, clenching around his softened girth.

"Brat," he muttered and laughed, slowly backing out.

I rolled and pressed against his chest. Our little sexcapade hadn't even lasted long enough for either of us to break a sweat, but I had no fucks to give. It was the dripping of his cum from my hole that fulfilled me.

"So?" he asked, his dark eyes dancing with happiness.

"Was being the meat in the middle everything you thought it would be?"

"It was hot as fuck for a few brief moments, but I'll be honest, Teach—you're all I need. But thank you for giving me this fantasy."

"Anything for you, my sweet boy."

"How about just a shit ton of praise next time you devour me?" I suggested. "Fill my ears with all those words that make me swoon and feel like a king. Tell me how cute I am. How delicious my ass feels around your cock. How well I take you—"

Matteo cut me off by shoving his tongue between my parted lips.

I sank into kissing the only man I wanted for the rest of my life.

THE END

About the Author

USA Today bestselling author Lynn Burke is a CrossFit and coffee addict. Her three spawn dictate how often she can be found hunched over her Mac, typing as fast as her fickle muse cooks up hot stories.

You can find more about Lynn at her website: www.authorlynnburke.com

Also By Lynn Burke

Abel's Obsession

Divulging Secrets

Healing Storms

In Between

Reluctant Lumberjack

Resisting his Mate

Billion Dollar Love Anthology

Blood Born Series

Bonds of Worship Series

Dark Leopards MC

Darkest Desires Series

Devil's Outlaws MC

Elite Escort Series

Elite Escorts MM Series

Fallen Gliders MC

Forbidden Obsession Duet

Found by Fate Series

Midnight Sun Series

Missing Link Series

Risso Family Series

Sandy Ridge Series

Sinful Nature Series

Vicious Vipers MC